Ghost Glasses

Rikki Goodwin

Cover Art Design by: Kelly Moran/Rowan Prose Publishing
Photo Credit: Adobe Images/Deposit Photos
First Edition
ISBN: 978-1-961967-74-8
Rowan Prose Publishing, LLC
www.RowanProsePublishing.com
Published in the United States of America

Praise for Rikki Goodwin:

"If you're a fan of light, cozy horror that's high on the creepy factor, then you won't want to miss Lovers' Leap.*"*
-E.M. Lund, author of *The Urbex Trip*
"Lovers' Leap *gets its hooks in you from word one and doesn't let up."*
-Jo Kaplan, author of *It Will Just Be Us*
"Lovers' Leap *hooked me from the very first page. I was more invested in these characters from the prologue than I have been after reading entire books. Goodwin's descriptions are vivid enough to make your insides clench, and I found it genuinely creepy throughout. I finished reading in the small hours, and I regretted it when I finally turned out the light."*
-Laura Livingstone, author of *The Boy With the Heart of Sea Glass*
"Creepy and engrossing in equal measure. Trust me, if you read this book and think you know where it's headed...think again."
-Tom Carter, author of *The House of Whispers*

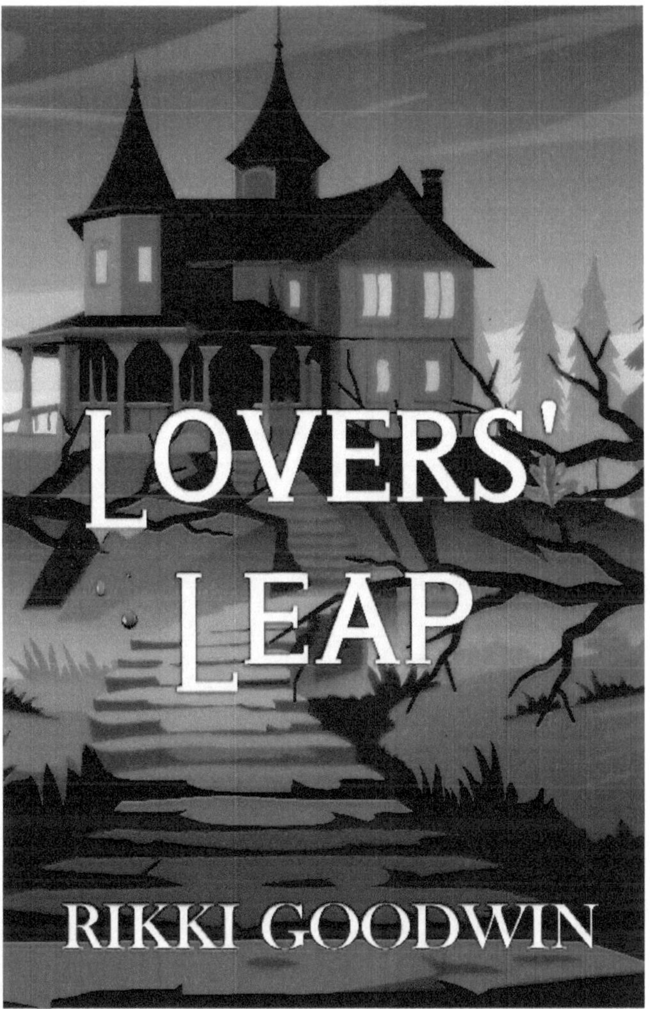
LOVERS'
LEAP
RIKKI GOODWIN

For you, on the days you feel invisible.

Chapter 1

T he sun has surrendered, drowning behind the stark sky-line far too early, and now the temperature plummets from chilly to fatal. The gritty puddles that dared to form during the brief attempt at daylight are transforming into treacherous little unmarked skating rinks. I can't decide if it's to my benefit or not that this means the train car is even more full than a regular evening.

"Excuse me." I step carefully around a woman's feet planted protectively over her hoard of dirty bags to claim the window seat beside her. I'll require the distraction of the view, however dark and bleak. As I fling myself down onto the wet plastic seat (I can only hope it's only melted snow), I realize why so many people have elected to stand as opposed to sitting here. An eye watering smell of ammonia surrounds my seat mate. "Thanks." I fix a bright smile on before letting my tone drop down to something meek, hardly audible. I whisper through my teeth like a terrible ventriloquist. "Can I just chat with you for a minute?"

She ignores me, like I assumed she would, tapping an intricate pattern with her fingers along the bag she clutches closest—the only one that zips closed to protect her belongings. *Tap-tap-tap.* I watch her mouth move with silent words. Maybe they'll be enough to make it seem as though we know each other and are here together, certainly not each vulnerable and alone. I'm good at pretending conversation, and if I can do it convincingly with my seat mate, things might just be okay.

There is another sound, another tapping, moving slowly down the center aisle. I sink low in my seat. I've never had one follow me onto the train before. The train has always been my safest place, neither here nor there, always full of people to immerse myself within. I was sloppy today, to allow it to follow. Too bold.

Tap-tap-tap. I can't turn my head. I can't scream. I have to pretend it isn't there at all. "Can you help me?" I ask my seat mate, trying to control my quaver. I don't know what will happen if I'm spotted, but I certainly don't want to find out. It's almost funny how strong my sense of self-preservation is, even now. Keeping my panic tamped down into a tight little manageable ball in my chest is taking up so much of my concentration.

My seat mate watches her fingers. I nod and emulate her, stare down at my own hands clutching my notebook, take a slow, even breath. We are calm, we are unbothered.

I can see it though, out of the corner of my eye. It's two rows up, and I can't *not* see it. The train hugs a curve, and it gives a startled squawk, scrabbling talons on the salt encrusted floor. A wave of guilt crashes over me like a gust of wind out on the sidewalk. I've led this thing away from the only place it knows with my carelessness. I've only ever seen it at Hazel Crest station, and now we're trundling away. I steal another glance as it's occupied with regaining its balance. Will it understand how to get back, or is this train car its new home, another place I'll have to avoid forever?

It has finally righted its huge, feathery body, and resumes its slow prowl down the aisle. It's most like an ostrich, I've decided. In my notebooks, I've always called it the "big bird," which is silly, I know. I like calling them silly things, to take away a little of the terror. The name does nothing to help with my panic bubble now, though. Sure, in recollection it may seem like a big bird, but in the moment, its human mouth takes center stage. All the parts of it that are certainly like *no* bird, like no creature that should exist. So much larger, too, within the confines of the car, so much more unnatural. Its impossibly long, impossibly thin neck curls and uncurls as it pushes that horrendous face right up to each passenger as it passes. Testing them. Every single traveler is passing the test, completely oblivious. They continue gazing out the window, or at their phones. One man, intent on replying to an email, actually puts his hand up and pushes that horrible face away when it blocks his line of sight, like it is nothing more than a fly! I stare, open mouthed and utterly jealous, taking mental notes.

I turn away as it approaches. I hope it can't hear how loud and fast my heart is attacking the inside of my chest, insisting I must run, I must fight, I must do *something*. I do nothing. The head appears slowly at the edge of my eye, creeping closer, closer, only inches away. I pray it doesn't recognize me. If it does, I'm well and truly doomed. As it slides between my face and the window, I try to see past it, to put my eyes in soft focus. It will know if I'm looking at it.

Its head is almost perfectly round, covered in dusty black feathers that stick up in odd ways like a duster used one too many times. Its eyes are tiny, sparkling black onyx chips. They don't have any intelligence, like a dog's or a cow's does or even one of those cute jumping spiders. They're dead eyes. I pretend that I'm looking at the street outside the window, but I can see its mouth. Where a beak would be if the monster were really anything like a bird at all, there is a shockingly red, almost feminine mouth. It is grinning at me now, I can see the glint of its perfect, toothpaste commercial white teeth.

Its head sways in front of me, taking in both sides of my face, and I hold perfectly still. Please just go, please, please, go. The head snakes back and away, and I exhale as softly as I can, not realizing I've been holding my breath. I've passed.

Tap, tap, tap. The big bird moves on down the aisle, bumping seats and nudging the oblivious passengers as it squeezes past. I wipe the sweat from my forehead, hoping I'll have room to creep out behind it at the next stop and leave the thing to whatever destiny I might have accidentally brought to it. But what will happen if other passengers attempt to leave and the bird is wedged in the only aisle, blocking their exit? Will they be forced to see something incomprehensible? Would it break them?

It was my notebook that caused the whole debacle. I'd been on the train, minding my own business, and when we pulled into the station I'd been daydreaming, gazing out the window, much as I'd been pretending to do just now. But as the train lurched to a stop, a free newspaper dispenser sat outside my window, and that little innocuous box had triggered some kind of feeling. A *memory*, even.

Memories are difficult to come by for me these days, so I knew I had to act. I *remembered* storing a full notebook in that yellow dispenser. I had to know what long forgotten things might be written inside.

I, of course, hadn't recalled that that particular platform belonged to one of my least favorite monsters until I had accidentally locked eyes with it. I should have turned around right then instead of doing what I'd done. I was cocky. I decided I could beat the beast across the platform, to the stand, and back to the train doors before they shut, but I knew I'd have to run. I knew what would happen if I ran from the big bird. If it realized I could see it, it would give chase. It always did.

I thought it would be fine as long as I could get back onto the train before it pulled away from the station. I never, *ever*, in a million years thought the bird would follow me into the car.

The thing must be getting frustrated. It makes some low burbling noises in its throat, and I know what's next. It howls, the scream of a woman, high and anguished and ungodly loud in this confined space. I forget myself and gasp, putting my hands reflexively to my face, dropping my notebook to my lap. I'm certain my reaction will betray me, that the big bird will be hovering directly over my head and grinning down at me with those perfect teeth and idiot eyes.

"Oh, God." A man's voice. There's a scuffle and all the other passengers turn their heads back, so I think maybe I can get away with it, too. "What stop is this?" the man asks loudly, almost screaming really.

I can't help but inhale sharply again. This man, he's behaving just like I am. Terrified, but doing his best to pretend everything is normal, doing his best to act as though there isn't a horrific monster shrieking and ruffling its feathers only steps away.

This man *sees* my monster, my big bird that no one else has ever even blinked twice at.

He's shaking and sweating, gathering his laptop bag from near his feet. The big bird is standing before him in the aisle, grinning broadly. It pierces the air with its awful shriek again, testing.

As is the unspoken rule on public transportation, the other passengers deign to ignore the man's question once they've decided there might be something wrong with him, and all start to turn away in their seats, embarrassed for looking back at all. I continue to watch, unable to turn away now that the bird's attention is elsewhere. The train rolls to a stop, and the man hurriedly stands.

He's blond, young, and maybe handsome in an "I'm going to sell you something you don't need" kind of way. His clothes are expensive and fashionable. He's sweating profusely, and his pale skin is beet red. He's not handsome right now, only terrified.

Others are standing, too, ready to either exit, or move to more coveted seats. I join them, scooping up my book, attempting to keep my expression as bland as oatmeal, but I feel like it's probably as pale as oatmeal, as well. The bird faces off with the man, blocking the aisle and the ten or so passengers trapped between it and the doors. The man realizes his way is barred belatedly, craning his neck, scanning for any other way around the beast. "Oh, God," he whispers again.

The bird utters a few clucks and gurgles, then raises its horrible, huge wings. It can't fly, I'm sure. It has to weigh a good three hundred pounds. But those wings are menacing enough. It turns its horrible head to an impossible angle, and the whole train car seems to freeze, suspended in the moment. It grins even wider, the red lips stretching twice the length a human mouth could, and then it abruptly lets its entire neck fall slack. The head dangles obscenely upside down, swinging back and forth like a pendulum, cackling a beautiful woman's most disdainful laugh.

The man opens his mouth in horror.

"Don't scream," I call. I know it's futile, just as I knew my seat mate with her bags and tapping fingers wouldn't respond, but I have to try. I have to try with everyone, I can't give up. "Don't scream. Just walk past. Walk slowly. Look away."

And then: a miracle. The man turns, mouth still open in a silent scream, and looks at me. His eyes meet my own, and he sees me. He *sees* me.

I place a hand to my throat, and my heart might stop beating for a moment. "Oh!" is all I manage to utter. Hardly a word at all. I could say so many things and be heard. I could say anything. Everything.

But the big bird lifts its wings higher and charges, dangling head flopping back and forth, banging along the seats, alternating between a laugh and a low pigeon coo the whole way. The man screams then—despite my advice—and swings his laptop bag wildly at the thing, which instead thunks heavily upon the arm of his seat mate who has been waiting impatiently to get by. "Hey, man, what the fuck!"

The blond man runs without a word of apology, runs as fast as he can towards the slowly opening train doors. He actually jumps *onto* a recently vacated seat, then hopscotches forward over the rows, past the beast in the aisle. The ungainly bird turns as quickly as it can and scrabbles after him, knocking people down with its outstretched wings as it goes.

"Wait!" I scream. I have to catch up with him. I *have to*. I look down beside me. "Excuse me." I try to extricate myself from my window seat and instead tangle my feet up in one of my seat mate's grocery bags. I go down hard onto the grooved floor of the aisle, my forgotten notebook flying from my arms. Nobody says anything, nobody tries to help me up. "Shit!"

I kick my feet loose from the bag and claw my way back up. There's a clog of people at the door, attempting to enter and exit at the same time. People are still dusting themselves off in the aisle from their inexplicable tumbles to the ground, which I know are already sliding from their memories, replaced with mundanity. Both the man and the bird are already off the train. The chime gongs, announcing the door closing. "Wait!" I cry again. I have to get my notebook first. It's all for nothing if I lose it. It's under the feet of a woman with her nose buried in a book.

"Excuse me," I beg her and she, of course, can't hear me. I growl in frustration and shove her legs, maybe harder than necessary, to reach my notebook. I snatch it up just as I feel the telltale lurch of the train beginning to pull away. "No!"

I run to the door and jam my fingers between the rubber edges, willing it to pry open. It doesn't budge. I peer desperately out the scratched plastic window, my forehead actually pressing against the greasy film like countless foreheads before mine. I can see the man sprinting down the steps away from the platform, sliding dangerously on the ice. The big bird hovers at the edge of the steps, pawing the ground with its huge feet. I hear its horrible shrieking even as the train gains speed and it's completely lost to sight. I let my head bounce off the door a few times without much feeling.

"He's gone," I tell everyone. No one cares.

I sigh, and trudge back down the train car. There's nothing I can do until the next stop, I suppose. I may as well attempt to settle my nerves. My seat next to the window is still open, and the bags I've left carelessly strewn down the aisle remain there as well. The woman is still sitting, still clutching her backpack, still tap-tap-tapping her fingers. "Look, I'm so sorry about this," I say to her, and start collecting her things, stuffing random items back into the grocery sacks. I set them down by her feet. "I'll just sneak past you again." I take my seat beside her.

My hands tremble around my old, waterlogged composition notebook's edges. I gather myself and turn, not to the front, but to the very last page. The very last entry.

May 16th, 1976

It's been so, so long. I snap the book shut again, and instead pull out my much nicer, pristine book, barely two pages used. I have to commemorate what happened here before I go losing myself in the past. I flip to a new page.

December (I flip back a page to see the date on it. Usually, I'll just sneak a glance at a fellow passenger's cell phone screen, but my seat mate doesn't seem to have one, or at least isn't as mindlessly drawn to its screen as the average person) *10th, 2023. 58 years, four months, and four days:*

A man saw me on the train today. This is no false alarm, he certainly looked straight at me, met my eyes. He was probably in his late twenties, blond, no facial hair. Slight build. Unfortunately, he also saw the big bird, who, as of this writing, is no longer at Hazel Crest station. It followed me onto the train and followed the blond man off again one stop(?) down. I think it was only one stop but might have been two.

I hesitate, trying to decide what to do with this information. Should I plan to go back? See if the man appears at the station or on the train again? I wish I was artistic, I would sketch his face so as not to lose it in my mind. I'd need to be able to pick him out of a crowd. It's so difficult to keep faces apart. There are too many of them, beating at my brain like moths against a window. I'll never remember, I know. I don't even remember my name.

"What do you think I should do?" I ask the woman next to me. I close the notebook and turn to face her and find she has fallen asleep. Her head rolls side to side and comes to rest against my shoulder as the train car rumbles. I pat her finally still hand and leave her there. It's nice to be close to someone.

My own restless hands wander back to my notebook from 1976. I'll just stay here until the end of the line—the woman seems like she needs the rest. We'll rest together, and I'll reminisce.

I'm thinking of leaving the city, my handwriting from the past whispers to me on the first page. I'm startled. I feel like the idea of leaving has never occurred to me before, even on the coldest and grimiest of winter days like today. Chicago is my home, where would I possibly go? And why? *There have to be other people like me,* I read. *I'm so tired of being alone in this, I have to go look for them.*

I snort softly. Oh, sweet past me, you have no idea what loneliness is. How long had it been since I'd written this? Eleven years? Basically, no time at all. But also, I am intrigued. It's true that I have never met another person like me. Or, at least, I don't *remember* ever meeting someone. Not until this man today, that is. He saw the big bird, there's no doubting that. Nobody besides me has ever taken any notice of it.

And he saw *me.* I haven't locked eyes with another human being in over fifty-eight years. Not since the night I died.

It's bizarre to think that I would be over eighty years old if I were still alive right now. I wonder what it would be like. I wonder what I would have been like. I try to envision myself as an old lady, fat and happy, feet up and knuckles sore from crocheting. I'd have a little dog and a silly husband. I'd crochet them matching sweaters and they'd both wear them happily because they'd love me. I don't know how to crochet or knit. I should learn, right? I've got the time, of course. I should learn.

Back to the mystery man. *He's* not dead (that impatient man yelled at him, nobody's *ever* yelled at me) and he maybe didn't realize that I am. He sees dead people. He might see them all the time and not even realize it, just casually walk past them on the street, not knowing he could be the only contact they have known in countless years if only he would say hello to them. *I* could be walking past people every day that see me and don't think twice about me, having no idea. On the flip side, I could be walking past *others like me* every day without even realizing. If ghosts aren't transparent or bloodied or otherwise visibly dead, how on earth can I expect to know the difference? Both me and them saying nothing, assuming the other wouldn't acknowledge them. What can I do?

I think about making a sign, standing on a street corner. "*Can you see me?*" And then I think about all the people I've seen holding similar signs, and how they are purposefully, determinedly ignored by everyone. I ignore them too, sometimes. When I'm in a rush, maybe I don't even say hello. One time (alright, many times), I stole a whole cash register from a department store and handed out cash to everyone I could find with a hat or a cup sitting in front of them. It's a delightful time. None of them saw me, of course, but I'm sure they must have noticed the money, later. If I learned to crochet, I could make scarves and hats and gloves for people and just slip them in their sleeping bags and shopping carts. I should do that. *Learn to crochet.* I write it down in a margin.

I'm thinking of leaving the city, I'd written. Would it be easier out there, maybe, to make a connection with people? Here, on this very train, I watched dozens of people ignore a very living man asking a simple question. I'm positive that I'm the only person who has spoken to the woman currently sleeping on my shoulder for the entirety of her train ride, and she can't even hear me. In the city, dismissiveness, callousness, minding your own business, it's the way things work.

Maybe out there, in one of those little towns I read about where everyone says, "Hello!" when you walk down the street, maybe it *would* be easier. The train is already hurtling down the line towards the last stop in fits and starts. I'm already on my way, and I didn't even realize it. I feel a pang of loss for the blond man who I'm sure I'll never see again, but he's a person of the past now.

I'm leaving home.

August Waters: *Alright, folks, welcome back to my channel. Y'all having a sinister Saturday? Tonight's the night you've all been waiting for. We're finally spending the night in Emerald House, supposedly the most haunted house this side of this Mississippi. We'll see about that! We've got Johnny boy here handling the cameras, Miss Amethyst on lighting, and as always, yours truly will be manning the "special" equipment: my eyeballs. Are we finally going to snag some actual proof tonight, or is it a bust? Stayed tuned to find out.*

I see CatofNineD1cks has commented asking if I've tried therapy...again. Yes, Cat. I've been to therapy, I go twice a month, and Dan the Therapy Man thinks my channel is a healthy outlet, so suck it. For anyone new to the channel or whatever, let me give you a little background:

When I was three years old, I was waving and talking to people at the supermarket checkout lane, you know, kid shit, when this man I waved at absolutely lost it on me. He ran over, started shaking me and screaming in my face, asking me over and over if I could see him. He was absolutely bonkers, man, crying and shit, like sobbing. Anyway, I'm a kid and I'm obviously terrified so I start screaming for my mom to help me. She comes over and picks me up and puts me in the cart, but the dude doesn't leave me alone. He's still right there and grabbing my hands and staring right into my eyes and asking me if I'm God. That would all be a wildly traumatic experience, but that's not the worst part: My mom didn't see him. Nobody saw this fucker except little toddler me.

The dude got right in the car with us and came back to our house with us and I'm like, ballistic, in the back seat because I'm so scared, right? My mom is pretty freaked out because I'm telling her there's a man in the car with us and she thinks her precious baby boy has lost his last marble. She calls my dad home from work, and they end up taking me to the emergency room, because what the fuck else are you supposed to do, right?

The man comes with and he's kind of calmed down too and he starts telling me all this crazy shit. He says he's dead, but he didn't leave, and everyone has just been ignoring him and I'm the first person who has ever seen him. He says he doesn't remember his name, but he died in that grocery store before I was born. He begs me to please just talk to him. So, I do. I name him Fat Man, because kids are horrible. At the hospital, I tell them what Fat Man tells me to say. I say I was just pretending but the lie got too big. My parents are ultra pissed.

Fat Man stuck around my house, even came to school with me when I started kindergarten. But the teachers caught me whispering to him and started to get worried, and the other kids thought I was weird, and I got embarrassed and told Fat Man to just leave me alone. He seemed really devastated, but he left, and I've never seen him again. Obviously, this sounds like some imaginary friend bullshit, but when I was like twelve or thirteen, I got to thinking about the Fat Man and did some digging. There had been a man who'd died of a heart attack in the grocery store we were at. I found his obituary. Charles (Charlie) O'Neal. Beloved husband. Here, I keep the obit in my wallet. There's my Fat Man.

So, basically, I'm out here at Emerald House because I know for a fact ghosts are real, even though I haven't really got the proof yet. We probably walk by them on the street all the time and don't even realize. I'm also out here on livestream because I'm looking for Charlie. Charlie, man, if you ever see this, come find me, okay? I'm sorry.

Chapter 2

I'm staring at my reflection in a truck stop bathroom. At least, my eyes are focused on the glass in front of me, but I'm not really comprehending any visual input, it's just the spot my eyes happened to be focused on when I flipped inside out. I'm deep inside my own mind right now, and things are not the way I left them. Why am I doing this? Why am I not in the city? Where was my train of thought leading me?

Train.

I should have stayed at the train station. Something happened at the train station that was monumental. Which stop was it? Not the one with my book. I finger the outline of my notebook through my coat. It was another one. I remember a woman tapping her fingers along a bag. She had crocheted scarves on, and I'm going to learn how to crochet to make her a new one that doesn't smell. I tap my fingers now, my eyes coming back to life and watching the pattern in the mirror. What was it, what was it?

Someone comes into the bathroom, and I jump at the intrusion. She's wearing comfortable clothes and smells like a long car ride. Body odor. Car exhaust. The vestiges of mascara fleck the bags under her eyes. I wonder where she's going. She gives herself the briefest uninterested glance at her own face (*spend longer, don't rush, love yourself,* I want to tell her) before proceeding to pick her nose, and I realize I'm actually the one doing the intruding. I step out.

I don't think I've ever been in a truck stop like this. It's gigantic, and at least half of it is the oddest assortment of knickknacks I'd ever imagine in one place, let alone a place meant to fulfill the needs of travelers. What is someone on a long car journey going to do with a twelve inch tall ceramic prancing unicorn sculpture covered in glitter? I wander the aisles in bemusement for a while, then take a suspicious looking doughnut—is it mold, or is it blueberry?—out of a brightly lit cabinet on an end cap.

I munch on it (blueberry) and wander over to the register. It's the middle of the night, but there's still a short queue. I sidle up to the man waiting to be served next. He's a young, Black man, maybe the age I was when I died, or a little older. He's short, heavy, and wearing a ball cap over hair that's growing out a little too long to be contained by a ball cap. I notice he's buying the same style doughnut I'm currently enjoying, and decide it's meant to be. I'll be going wherever he goes today.

"Hi there!" I say to him, and that finally triggers my god forsaken horrendous hole of memory. I should be looking for the man that heard me on the train. Damn it. I should have stayed up there and found him. Why didn't I stay? Right. Yes, the big bird.

This man doesn't respond like that blond man might have, but that's all right, he seems nice enough. He pays for his doughnut and coffee and what must be a lot of gas, based on his total, and we head outside.

He shivers and lets out a little, "Whew!" as the frigid air wraps us up and pulls us forward into the night. We hunch and waddle like penguins all the way across the parking lot, staring at our feet to keep from slipping and to keep the gusting salty air from pinging into our eyes, far enough that I start to wonder if he had just *walked* to the stop and I am accidentally following him home, before he takes a quick turn down the row of idling semi-trucks on our right.

He climbs into a sparkling purple cab with hardly any salty spray marring its paint, and I decide that this was an excellent choice. What better way to hitchhike, right? I scramble up awkwardly into the passenger side, the door catching the air like a kite and almost flinging me back to the concrete in its bid for freedom. I haul it shut, with much muttering and fumbling. The interior smells vaguely of onions from whatever fast food he'd stopped for last, but it's pleasantly tidy. I move a paperback book off the passenger seat and near a curtain hiding the sleeping area behind. The truck driver is getting situated in the driver's seat, eating his doughnut. He had no issues with the climb or the door, it must get easier with practice.

I can do almost everything I did when I was alive. I feel solid, and whole. I see my reflection in the mirror. I can hold things and open doors. I'm fairly certain that other people see me, they just don't really register me. No one is surprised when I walk into a building; no one thinks the door opened on its own. While I feel like I might get bumped into more often than the average (alive) person, no one tries to sit on me on the train. This truck driver doesn't notice me shuffling around in his passenger seat, or that his cab door opened and closed without him. I must be there, to him, in some way. I can read and retain information (although my retention pond must have a few leaks), can listen to music, and even sing (maybe not well).

"So, what's your name? Ever been haunted before?" I ask conversationally.

Resolutely ignoring me, he notates times on a clipboard and shifts into gear.

"Where are we going?" I take his coffee from the cupholder and steal a sip. I smile, cream and sugar. I love coffee, but I'm too dead to pretend I don't like it doctored up a little. This guy won't notice he's sharing with me. "South? Are we leaving the state? What are you hauling?"

He's checking his mirrors and slowly maneuvering out of the parking lot.

"Sorry. I'll let you work." I set his coffee back in the holder and pull my knees up to my chest on the seat, the only way to stop myself from pressing every button on the dash and opening every compartment. I'm honestly like a little kid in new environments. I'm not trying to be nosy, I just want to see how everything works at least one time.

Once we're on the highway, I turn the radio to a classic rock station, and we sing for a while. *He* has a nice voice, but I bet that he'd be caught dead before singing in front of other people. I wonder if he became a truck driver just so he could sing along to the radio shamelessly. "You have any family?" I ask, giving in to temptation and standing up to check out the sleeping area behind the seats. "Wow, it's a whole little apartment back here!" He has a small television, a tiny refrigerator, several well read books (most are good ones!), but no pictures that I can see. I snatch his clipboard from beside him instead and sit back down, buckle back in.

"So..." I flip the pages as if I'm grading an essay, maybe going over a resume. "Sean Frances, huh? You don't strike me as a Sean for some reason. Isn't that weird?" I look over at him. He's singing the chorus to 'Like a Rolling Stone' and humming the parts he doesn't know, which is most of it. Humming to Dylan is an awful lot like just mumbling incoherently and it makes me giggle. He scratches at the shadow on his neck that's beginning the journey to full beard. He must be on the road quite a bit. "I bet you have a nickname."

I check the route on his clipboard. Next stop: Louisville, Kentucky. I sip Sean's coffee and watch the cornfields flit by, all dowsed in fresh white snow.

When the music is cut off by a calm, repeating tone, Sean presses a button on the dash and the chime and is replaced by a woman's voice, even clearer and louder than Creedence had been just a moment ago. I marvel at the technology, everything progresses so quickly!

Sean clears his throat. "Hello?"

"Buddy! How are you? You're not talking and driving, are you?"

"No, Ma." He sounds a little exasperated, a little embarrassed. "I'm doing good. Working a lot. What's up?"

"I want you here for Christmas, Buddy. No excuses." The woman's voice is firm. This is not a request.

"Ma, I really can't. It's a busy time for work—"

"I don't care. You call in sick if you have to. Three years is long enough. You can't avoid coming home forever."

He closes his eyes for way longer than I consider appropriate while driving something that requires eighteen wheels before answering. "...Alright, Ma."

"Good. I'll see you Thursday, then. I'll make up your old room for you. I love you, Buddy. We all love you and miss you."

"Bye, Ma."

"Aha! You're a Buddy!" I clap once. "I *knew* it, not a Sean at all." I look over at him grinning, and am shocked to see that he has tears running down his face.

"Buddy?" I ask. The name feels so much easier on my tongue for him, natural and right. "Are you okay? Do you want to talk about it?"

He apparently does *not* want to talk about it, but the tears continue to fall unashamedly, and his breaths hitch with his sobs. He keeps both hands on the wheel and his swimming eyes remain fixed on the road before us. He might not want to talk about it, but it's obvious he needs some support. Any notions of moving on away from him and his route are gone. I'll need to stay, at least through Christmas. Maybe he'll feel my presence, at least a little bit.

August Waters: *Alright, lovely Amethyst, walk us through what we can expect to see and hear tonight here at Emerald House.*

Amethyst: *Well, the current owners have temporarily vacated the premises, not just for our hunt tonight, but because they've been having some pretty disturbing events happen pretty frequently.*

August: *Such as?*

Amethyst: *They often hear footsteps in the upper hallway, items moved around the house, cabinets and doors opening and closing of their own volition, and also lights being turned on or off. One night, the owner swears her cat was picked up and carried around the room by unseen hands.*

August: *Sounds pretty wild! Any background information on the house? Any ghostly suspects we might be able to call by name?*

Amethyst: *Well, the house was built in 1875 and had changed hands several times over the years, obviously. I have some names here of owners that we can try, but there isn't any actual proof of anyone actually dying in the house.*

August: *Hey, they don't have to die here for it to be home. I used to hang around hospitals looking for ghosts and never saw one, to my knowledge.*

Amethyst: *You're a creep sometimes. Also, a little bad news...*

August: *Mmm?*

Amethyst: *Well, I asked the lady of the house when the occurrences began, and she said she and her family members had a movie night and watched Poltergeist. It all started after that. They might just be a little creeped out by some good old fashioned Spielberg effects.*

August: *My own lighting specialist, a skeptic! May this night be the one that makes you believe, lady!*

Chapter 3

I gave Buddy some privacy at the hotel we stopped at on Christmas Eve. He left the trailer at his work after our last run to St. Louis. I'd never been and was thrilled to see the arch. Buddy didn't seem impressed, but then he's had a lot on his mind since the phone call. We stopped by a little dingy apartment in some little western Illinois town I'd never even heard of before, for appropriate "visiting family" clothes, and now we were on our way to his mother's house in Iowa. I didn't really understand why he didn't just stay home until tomorrow or arrive at his mother's a day early, why stop at a hotel at all? But at his little apartment, his quiet mood had soured into something like depression. It was obvious he hated it there. And his apprehension towards going to his mother's was absolutely palpable. He didn't sing with the radio anymore, and I'd caught a tear in his eye more than once.

I've been wondering endlessly why he's so distraught, frustrated with his lack of personal effects and as always, with my inability to communicate. I walk through the hotel parking lot, trying to decide how to spend my night. It's a small town, just a wide spot in the highway, really, and everything looks shuttered up tight against the cold and the dark.

I hope that Buddy is sleeping peacefully, that he has good dreams of better times and wakes up tomorrow ready to face the holiday at home, whatever that means to him. I wish I could talk him through it.

But I can't sleep.

I haven't lost consciousness at all since, I assume, my death. I cannot escape from the reality of my afterlife. I am here for every second of every hour. This, even more than the occasional horrific monster chase, is what makes me think I may be in some kind of purgatory, maybe even some kind of hell.

There have been times in my life where I can become so absorbed in a thought that I find I have sat motionless for long spaces of time—hours, maybe even days. But the hours aren't lost on me, every single agonizing moment of every single monotonous day. I've counted more sheep than have ever existed on earth, probably. I've tried sleep aids, but I'm pretty sure that drugs don't have an effect on me anymore. I spent a while really into meditation, thanks to my lingering crush on George Harrison. It could be relaxing, but...no sleep.

I come upon a little church, whose lights are on and parking lot is full. It looks like every car in town might be here. Voices raise in song and drift across the snowy air. I consider for a minute, and the draw of community it too strong for me to resist. I slip inside.

Midnight mass. I smile and sit in an empty place in the back and let the music and worship and happiness wash over me. I'm not a religious person anymore. I don't remember if I was while I was alive, but I do remember my mother was.

She'd outlived me, and I'd stayed in my childhood home with her, unseen and unheard, until lung cancer dragged her from the apartment and into a hospital bed. Her last bed.

I was, ashamedly, kind of excited for my mom to die. I realized it, even though I tried my best to push the feeling down then. Every morning, her cough would sound worse. She'd eat less and less, looking grayer and weaker and older every day. And I'd secretly think, *is today the day?* when I'd hear the rasp in her breath. I couldn't wait for the possibility of her seeing me again, talking to me. I wouldn't be alone anymore.

I waited with bated breath at her bedside at the hospital. I literally never left her side. It's funny, I can't remember Buddy's face now that I've been away from him for a few minutes, but I can see the chair I sat in in my mother's hospital room with vivid clarity.

My mother never did see me—not when she was delirious, not when she was dying, and not when she was dead. No portal opened, no angels or demons appeared, no bright lights to follow. She was just gone.

I've never been as devastated as I was in that moment. I'm sure I never will be again.

With no family left, I stayed at the hospital for a long time, waiting, and watching. It was a disgusting, morose, horrible pastime. I observed many, many deaths. I watched people like my mother slip slowly away to age or disease, surrounded by family or all alone. I watched people like me whose lives were cut short by accidents and violence. Some people had their whole lives ahead of them, so full of promise. Some people were full of unshared secrets. Many of them deserved more time. I never found another like me, unless we were all invisible to each other.

After my long, horrible weeks haunting the hospital, I franticly sought out every person of every faith I could find, looking for answers. I just wanted to be seen. I wasn't, and bitterness consumed me for a while.

But as the people around me light candles, passing their tiny flames from person to person and laughing over spilt wax, I think maybe I've softened over the years. Maybe my soul is just defective, or I earned this half existence. I can't really blame an unknown deity who may or may not be hanging around for my plight. Besides, the sweet amateur singing of the congregation is a balm on my heart. I find myself thinking of Buddy mumbling through Dylan lyrics and smile. No difference between the two from this side of the veil.

I'm still sitting in my pew as the last worshipper wishes the pastor goodnight and braces themselves against the cold as they walk out. The pastor begins moving about the room, blowing out candles, picking up left behind programs, muttering good-naturedly to himself.

I stretch out in my seat (these really are *not* comfortable), and hum the tune of the last song the congregation sang as I gather my coat from beside me.

The pastor drops the hymn pamphlet he was collecting, and it flutters through the air in my peripheral vision. "I'm sorry," he says, and I watch him replace his "alone" face with his "we have guests" face. "I thought everyone had left!" He scans the room again, looking through me. "Hello?"

I roll off the bench and thud to the floor. "Oh!" is all I can manage at first, my breath knocked away. Twice now, that little exclamation is all I can articulate when it matters. "Hello, hello! Wait just a second!" I rush to him, take his hands in mine. "Hello!" I search his face, my eyes crawling around, digging for any hint of recognition, any sign.

"Hello?" he says again softly, less sure of himself. "I could have sworn I heard..." He begins to walk toward where I had been sitting, easily slipping from my grip. "Hmm."

"No, no, no. Please! You *did* hear!" I'm instantly sobbing, pushing him, yelling in his face. "You heard me!" I desperately start humming again, hoping for him to hear, but I've completely forgotten the tune.

I flit around him helplessly as he finishes cleaning up the sanctuary, turns off the lights, puts on his coat and leaves, all without ever so much as glancing at me again despite my grasping hands and ungodly shrieks. I'm nothing to him. I'm nothing to anyone. I don't exist. I might be used to it by now if it weren't for these tantalizing moments where—for only a moment—I have the audacity to hope. I fling myself back onto the awful pew and stare at the ceiling morosely until morning. I try to be positive, I really do. I say, "That's twice now. Twice in just a few days. Maybe it's getting easier." I don't believe it. I feel further away than ever in this moment. I can't even be bothered to write down what's happened in my notebook.

I trudge back towards the hotel in the morning, still in a black mood. I stop at a little coffee shop and grumpily take a blueberry muffin for myself and a coffee and muffin for Buddy. The muffin has actually softened my mood considerably by the time Buddy climbs inside the cab, looking much younger and cleaner in a button up shirt, slacks, and freshly shaved face. Buddy never wears a winter coat—I assume it's too cumbersome in the truck.

He looks at the coffee and muffin and makes his puzzled expression: a raised eyebrow and bit lip that strike me as both charming and silly. He shrugs and takes the muffin. A grin creeps across my face, and my bad night is shoved away in my mind. I do adore the way people are so quick to accept and forget what should be impossible. If someone were to ask Buddy where that muffin came from, he'd probably swear up and down he grabbed it at the coffee shop.

"Alright, man. You can do this," he tells himself in his side mirror, and puts the cab in gear.

"That's right, Buddy! I'm here for ya." I pat his shoulder. He doesn't notice. "We can do this."

Since we were only a couple hours from his mother's house when he stopped last night, the drive should feel like a quick one, but it's been complete, apprehensive silence. Each minute feels like its own hour. I sip Buddy's coffee. He stares straight at the road, his face a determined mask, misery peeking through only in the eyeholes.

Buddy's mother lives in a cute split level home in a cute, tiny town. The yard looks magical under a thick layer of snow and topped with multicolored Christmas lights. Buddy parks across the street and starts psyching himself up to go inside, unknowingly cheered on by me.

There are already several cars in the driveway, covered in gross highway sludgy snow and salt. I get out and come around to Buddy's door. He climbs down slowly. I hook my arm through his. "Come on, Buddy. You're not alone." I smile at him, hoping that maybe he can feel my positive energy. It's working for me, anyway. My evening is already almost completely forgotten.

We walk inside without knocking. The foyer is already full of coats and boots. Buddy slips his own boots off, and I follow suit. There's laughter coming from upstairs, but as Buddy quietly tries to shut the door behind us, a voice calls down. "Who's skulking around in my doorway?"

A woman appears at the top of the stairs. She can't be more than five feet tall, and she wears a sweater that appears to be made out of silver tinsel and a huge skirt striped like a candy cane. She looks like a festive teddy bear. Her cheeks crinkle up and her eyes immediately sparkle with tears as she gazes down at what can only be her son. "Buddy! You came!"

My own eyes immediately sting. What I wouldn't give to go home, to have my mother waiting for me with open arms. The house is the warmth that only comes from the oven being on all day, from being full to bursting with family and laughter. Just standing in the foyer is like a hug.

Buddy forces a smile and heads up the stairs to her waiting arms to endure an actual hug. I follow more slowly, nosily inspecting the photos along the staircase. Buddy's family is a large one. Here's Buddy's mother and father, surrounded by a teenaged, thinner Buddy, and three girls, probably Buddy's sisters. Here are the sisters, older, in various photos with children and significant others. Ahh, here is one of adult Buddy, with his arms around a woman with a shy smile and button nose, and a toddler with all of the cutest features of both of her parents. I brush fine dust off the top of the photo frame. Maybe she left him and took the baby. It's hard to be with someone who's never home, I imagine.

I sigh and finish my climb. Buddy has been led into a packed sitting room, and is exchanging overly polite greetings with everyone. Everything feels forced and fake, except for the worried glances the women exchange while he isn't looking. He must have taken the breakup badly. He spins away from a sister's embrace to face where I'm standing by the couch, and I notice the little girl from the photo clinging to his leg.

She glares at me without letting go of her father. "Who are you?"

I sit down, hard, on the floor. Maybe it's more accurate to say that my legs suddenly just don't support me standing. "Oh," I say. And then quickly remember to say, "Hello!"

She jumps visibly and releases Buddy's pant leg to approach me. He didn't notice. He hasn't looked down at her once. "You can see me?" she asks, and her eyes are as big as moons.

Oh, God.

I nod, tears that were already so close to falling now streaming. "Yes. Does your family not see you anymore?"

"I thought they were maybe mad at me." She sits next to me. She's a little older than she was in the photo, maybe five or six. She still has Buddy's round face and dimples and her mother's nose and eyes, but she's covered in filth, and her clothes are torn and discolored. A bib of what I hope are old food stains covers most of the t-shirt. This poor kid. "Who are you?" she repeats. "Why can you see me?"

"I'm...I..." How much does she know? How much does she understand? I don't want to scare her, and I don't really know the first thing about kids. "Tell you what. Let's go get you washed up and changed for dinner. We'll talk more. Do you have any clothes here?"

"Hmm. I don't know. There's a box in Gramma's closet with my name on it! I didn't want to be a snoop, I thought there might be presents in it. There's not any under the tree for me..."

She fidgets, tugs on the edge of her shirt and her earlobe in quick turns.

My heart clenches again, and my mind is spinning like a tornado, with plenty of debris plunking down everywhere. This is horrific. *Plunk.* This changes everything. *Plunk.* I'm talking to another ghost. *Plunk.*

There's someone like me, and she definitely didn't do anything to deserve this so maybe I didn't either.

The tornado fizzles, leaves its destruction scattered around my head. I have *got* to figure this out. "Okay!" I clear my throat, adopt the cheeriest voice I can muster. "How about you go sit with your Daddy for a bit and I'll go look in the box, so we don't ruin any surprises."

She gives me a smile that shows the dimples of the lost girl in the photo, and goes to sit at Buddy's feet. I stand shakily and move down a hallway where I assume the bedrooms will be, letting my mask of a smile fall as soon as my face is turned away. The first one I choose seems a good guess, with a queen sized bed and country-chic decor. I open the closet and rummage. There's a red plastic tub in the back that reads "Addie" in black permanent marker across the top. I lug it out, and run my hands along the letters. God. Poor Buddy.

I finally manage to make myself remove the lid, and I breathe in the smells of the little girl's life. I feel bad letting that air escape. First order of business: clothes. There's a christening outfit (too small), a Pegasus Halloween costume (not very practical), a green velour Christmas dress and shiny black dress shoes (perfect), and a blue sundress. Thankfully, there are also a few toys so I can give the kid a present. Beneath those are three full photo albums that I can't bear to look through, and finally, framed, a newspaper clipping. Rebecca Dale-Frances, 26, and Adeline (Addie) Frances, 5, were both greeted by the Lord this December the 29th, leaving behind a loving husband and father, Sean (Buddy) Frances, 25...

I stare down at the faces on that clipping for far too long. I feel like I should be used to death in my condition, but a tragedy is always a tragedy. I touch Rebecca's beautiful face once before I replace the frame. Where did she go? Why is Addie still here?

I take a plastic horse with feathery wings and cotton candy painted on its rump, and the clothes, and put the box back. I head back out. "Addie?"

She jumps up at the sound of her name (*oh, how long has it been?*) and runs over to me. I hold up the dress. "Would you like to wear a Christmas dress?"

She nods enthusiastically. "I remember wearing that before!" She eyes the hand still behind my back. "Did you find me a present?"

"Well, it's probably an old present. Do you still like…" I whip my hand around dramatically. "Ponies?"

She squeals and grabs the toy. "Sugar was my favorite pony!" *Was.*

"So. I'm going to run you a bath. You remember taking baths, right? You get all squeaky clean, and when you're done, I'll try to comb your hair and put it in a pretty braid, and you can wear your Christmas dress. Sound fun?"

She looks concerned. "Won't Gramma be scared? I don't want to scare her accidentally."

I smile. "She won't even notice. She's busy with all this company! We don't want to be late for dinner, right?"

She considers for a moment before maybe deciding I probably know what I'm talking about, and skipping off to the bathroom.

I decide to ask her some questions as I'm trying my best with her hair. It would probably be way easier if I knew the first thing about textured hair, but luckily for me, Addie seems to remember things from life much better than I do, and has been guiding me through. "So, Addie. Do you stay here with your grandma?"

"Uh-huh." She fidgets a bit, like it seems she always does when she answers a question. "My mommy is gone. They had a big sad party for us." She turns back and looks at me seriously. "We were in a car accident."

"Do you remember the accident?" Before she can respond I quickly add, "You don't have to talk about it if you don't want to."

Laughter floats through from the other room in the pause before Addie answers.

"Kind of. No. I just remember after. I was standing on the road, and I was in the car, too. Everyone was worried about the me in the car, but they didn't see me standing right there!" She crosses her arms, still frustrated at the injustice of it all. Same, kid. "Hey, what's your name?"

I bite my lip. I'd forgotten again. Forgotten that I'd forgotten. "I actually don't remember."

Addie laughs. "That's silly. You can't forget your own name! Unless, did you get a bump on the head?"

"What?" I stammer. I touch my head, suddenly terrified that I look like a gruesome corpse to this child.

"You know, like on TV. You get a bump on your head and forget who you are. Neesha? One time on *Steven Universe...*"

I let my shoulders relax and her words wash over me. When she finishes telling me about a television character named Garnet getting amnesia, I smile. "No, it's not like that. It's just. I haven't had anyone to talk to for a very long time, you know?"

"Are we ghosts?"

My smile vanishes. Is this another thing she picked up on TV? But she's not stupid. It probably took her less time than me to figure our situation.

"I guess so."

"Why? Why isn't my Mommy a ghost? She's dead, too. I saw."

I'm speechless. The comb I was using lays forgotten in my lap. Addie is still turned around, staring at me seriously. "I...I don't know. You're the first other ghost I've ever met."

"How long have you been a ghost?"

"A very long time."

"Like ten years?"

"Longer."

"Like a zillion years?"

I laugh, pick up the comb. "Probably not that long." I resume combing her hair. "Why did you decide to stay with Grandma?"

"Well." She turns to sit facing forward again, starts pulling on her earlobe. "Daddy stayed here for a long time, after. He was real sad. I was going to go with him when he started driving his truck again, but I got scared. What if I got left someplace and couldn't find my way back?"

I nod. "That was very smart of you."

"Besides," She drops her voice to a whisper and nods toward the open bedroom door out into the hall. "I think Gramma knows I'm here, sometimes. It'll be all quiet in the house and I'll be playing or singing, and she'll look up like she heard me. One time, she even said my name. She gets real sad when no one's home. I like to keep her company."

I nod again. What a sweet kid. A memory of my early ghost days floods back, when my mother was still alive and I was trying every means to get her attention in the apartment we'd used to share.

Handwritten notes from me sat unread around the house. I tried this method of communication repeatedly because it just made *sense*—I could handle things, move them, alter them, and then my mother could handle and use those things after me. She must have seen them. But all of my letters, however large or small, were unnoticeable to her. She'd pick papers up and throw them out as if they were blank. One time, I wrote across the screen of our tiny television with permanent marker, and she just watched it like that for over a month, until it annoyed me enough to scrub the message away again.

However, she might read a book if I left it in a conspicuous place. She made certain dinners sometimes if I placed the ingredients on the counter. She'd listen to the radio and sing along if I turned it on. Once, I'd left a photo of us on her pillow. She'd gasped when she saw it. She said my name aloud to the empty apartment. She couldn't hear me, couldn't see me. But that one time, she called out, as if I might be there.

A thought forms slowly. My mind is still picking through the tornado wreckage, it's hard to walk through in straight lines. "Earlier, you said you didn't want to scare her. Have you scared her on accident before?"

"Yeah. I was looking for some candy in the kitchen, and I have to climb up on the counter to get in the cabinets. I left them open...I didn't think she'd notice, she usually doesn't! Hey, can you use the red hair tie? For Christmas?" She hands a red rubber band back to me, and I wrap it around the braid I've managed. Not too shabby.

Something in my brain is firing. Her grandma hears her sometimes. The pastor heard me last night. People can hear us. Why sometimes and not others? But for now, I just smile at Addie. She's just a little girl, after all. "It's okay, I'm sure she's not mad. Let's go get some dinner, yeah?"

She jumps up and looks in the mirror, grinning at her reflection. "Okay!"

We go down the hall, Addie pulling me by the hand. The family is about to move into the dining room, we're right on time. "Let's go get seats first!" I yell and run ahead. It's so fun to have someone to talk to. I'm grinning from ear to ear now.

"Can I sit with the grownups?"

"I don't see why not!"

We pick chairs next to each other along the long table. The family filters in, and Buddy, without hesitation, sits down next to his daughter. "Oh," says Buddy's mother, counting to herself. "I must have miscounted the places. Christopher, be a dear and get two more folding chairs from the hall closet." Christopher, about twelve years old, rolls his eyes, but does as he's told.

I use the distraction of dinner to think. Addie has dropped her serious manner from earlier in her excitement and is eagerly eating food and listening to the adults talk, interjecting every once in a while to me. "Auntie Patty won't let Sam and Chris have sugar," she tells me, obviously aghast. "I had to stay with them one weekend and we had to drink water all the time, they didn't even have juice!"

"That doesn't sound very fun," I answer dreamily. Addie accidentally frightens her grandmother. A hundred ghost stories are running through my head.

Host: *Hello there, everyone! Today, we're welcoming self-proclaimed ghost hunter August Waters to the show. August, you've officially gone viral for your footage filmed two weeks ago in a residence called "The Emerald House." Some people are saying that it has captured the first true glimpses of paranormal activity on film, while others, of course, are calling it a hoax. We've brought you here to tell your story.*

August Waters: *First of all, *Bleep* those *bleep*ers who say this is a hoax. What more can you possibly ask for? I—*

Host: *Mr. Waters, I'll have to ask you to refrain from using profanity. This is an all-ages show. A lot different than the wild west of the internet, right? Ha, ha...*

August: *Sorry about that. Anyway, I've been searching for a bona fide haunting to film for literal years, as all of my true fans know. I have never,* never, *in all my filming, faked a haunting.*

Host: *Of course, of course. But people are saying that it's all been to heighten your credibility for this performance. No one would blame you! The effects you produced are astounding—*

August: *All right, man, we're done here.*

Host: *Mr. Waters? Mr. Waters, hang on...*

Chapter 4

"I think I need to stay here with my gramma," Addie says. She's back to hanging on Buddy's leg, because he's leaving today.

I asked Addie if she'd like to come with us. I promised that I wouldn't let her get lost, and that we could get new clothes and ride in the semi and take care of each other. I'm a little sad to lose her company, but her answer doesn't surprise me.

When I returned to my mother's house after my death, I didn't take a single step outside the house again for four years. I thought that something kept me there, some *force*, but these days I don't know if that's true. I think that I was mostly just afraid, and alone, and filled with the most powerful homesickness you could imagine. Being home didn't put a dent in that longing, especially because my mother didn't see me or acknowledge me at all, and that hurt more than if I'd just never seen her again, *so* much more, but the idea of leaving the house, leaving her, accepting that something was irrevocably damaged and would never go back to the way things had been, it was too much to consider. So, I pretended. I pretended, just like Addie does with her grandma.

I'd make my mother breakfast and carry on entire conversations with her, more conversations and deeper ones than we'd ever had while I was alive, I'm sure. I got to know her infinitely better than I ever would have if I had lived to my thirtieth birthday. That has to count for something, right? Even if the things I learned about her slowly trickle out of me like condensation, sweating out with every day I'm still here, I knew her.

Addie might be feeling all of those huge, horrible feelings now, somehow contained in her tiny body. She needs time. She needs to stay somewhere safe and comforting and familiar.

I promise I'll bring her new things to play with and to wear, and in turn, she promises me she'll brush her teeth every morning and wash up every night. I promise that I'll return.

"I won't forget," Addie says. "Promise you won't forget, too."

Can I promise that? What if I leave and forget to come back? What if I forget all about little Addie, just like I forgot my name? I look up at Buddy, who is sitting on the sofa, staring into space.

His mother sits across from him, occasionally attempting small conversation. The rest of the family has gone out for lunch, but neither of these two feel hungry, supposedly. The visit has not been easy on Buddy. No wonder he stays away. Addie looks so much like him, it's like a little miniature version of himself clinging to him. I hate witnessing this.

"I swear, I hear her sometimes," Buddy's mom says to the quiet room.

Buddy doesn't respond, but Addie jumps up and points dramatically. "*See?* I *told* you!"

I smile at her. "That's amazing, Addie. She must love you very much."

Addie deflates like a popped ballon. "Then why doesn't Daddy hear me?"

Oh, geez. I bite my lip.

"Well..." I pat the sofa between Buddy and I. She climbs back up with some trembling reluctance, tears threatening through the movement of her limbs, in how she keeps her face slightly averted. "Some people must just be a little more sensitive."

"Sensitive? What do you mean?" Addie's face scrunches up in confusion, her understanding of the word (if she has any) not making sense in this new context.

"I mean," I correct, searching for a better phrase. I can't expect a kid to know about psychic sensitivities. She hasn't spent countless hours researching our condition like I have. "I think it's easier for some people to notice us. You know how some people have really good eyesight, but some people need glasses? Your daddy just might be needing glasses is all."

"Ghost glasses?"

I laugh. "Maybe! I'll try to find him some."

I'm making promises I have no way of keeping to the only person I've talked to in over fifty years.

"It's like—" Buddy's mother begins again.

"Ma, can you not?" Buddy shifts, planting both feet in front of him. He's threatening to walk out without saying so. "This is why I don't visit."

"Buddy, please. I just need you to open your mind a little. I'm telling you what I feel in my heart." She tries to save her mascara through her own tears, they're blooming over her lower lashes and hovering there.

I reconsider my plans in the moment before the woman's tears spill to her cheeks. I could forgo the hastily devised plan I came up with over Christmas dinner. I could instead just stay here. I could stay in this house with Addie and her grandma for as long as I like. Addie and I don't have to be apart, and maybe, together, we could work with this crying woman until she finally can't ignore the open kitchen cabinets anymore. Maybe, with time, she would know we're here.

As I consider, Buddy lets out the most frustrated and pain-laden sigh I've ever had the misfortune to have heard, and rubs his face with his hands. My heart shivers and cracks like melting ice in my chest, and I'd do anything to take even a sliver of that pain away from him. The thought of letting him walk out that door alone and continue his shambling half-life without even a glimmer of hope is almost unbearable.

I'll have to stay with Buddy and go whenever he goes. Staying here would be nothing but sedentary comfort. On the road, I have a chance of actually finding a path forward for Addie, and that's what's most important. I hope that Addie understands that and isn't too upset when we leave. If I just keep Buddy around, there's no way I could possibly forget Addie. Another thought occurs, and I glance at Addie. "I'm going to grab something of yours from that box really quick before I go, okay?"

She nods but doesn't move to follow me. She just wants to stay with her father, and she's watching this sad argument like a tennis match.

I open one of the photo albums and turn straight to the back, hoping for a recent picture. I'm not disappointed. Here is one of Addie and her mother at an art museum, standing in front of a sculpture made out of chewed bubblegum. They are both captured mid laugh, and it's the most beautiful picture I've ever seen. I pocket it.

"Hey," Addie says as I slink back into the living room. Mother and son have thankfully decided to let the arguing pass and again sit in awkward silence. "You've got to have a name. How am I going to remember you if I don't know what to call you in my head?"

I frown. "That's true. Well, what name do I look like I should have? Am I...a Gertrude? A Myrtle?"

She giggles. "Definitely *not*." She hops up from her post at Buddy's side and stares at me appraisingly. I feel very self-conscious. "Hmm."

I do a little twirl, and she laughs again. "Constance? *Gretel?*"

She squeals with laughter for a minute before she can collect herself enough to form words. "Ms. Ethel has a cat that's got blue eyes like yours."

"Oh, yeah? Who's Ms. Ethel?"

"My sitter. She still comes and visits Gramma sometimes, they're church friends. Anyway, her cat is called Poppy. I think we should call you Poppy. 'Cause if I start to forget, I might always think about Poppy the cat and remember!"

So, she's forgetting things, too. I try to hide my concern. "Poppy is a beautiful name," I manage.

Buddy's cab is a somber, silent place after we've left his mother's house. He doesn't turn on the radio, and I feel like if did, he would turn it off again. I don't know what to say to him. There aren't any words to fix his pain, and even if I had them, I couldn't really give them.

Instead of watching his tortured face, I turn away from him my seat, curled up and facing directly out the passenger side window. The sameness of the landscape lulls me into a stupor. White snow, gray sky, only separated by the dark, bare trees and fence posts gliding languidly past as Buddy carefully maneuvers down the snow packed road. I imagine it's like a wraparound background in an old cartoon, just the same few trees and fences revolving across the screen of my window over and over. It's believable for a long hour, to the point where I find myself trying to find differences. That tree is a little closer to the road than last time, isn't it? This fence has chicken wire, when the last one was all wood, right? Or am I mistaken? Has it been the same all along?

It's a fun little game to play by myself, and I used to play it on the train, as well. But...I squint ahead, breath quickening a little. What *is* that? That's definitely something different. I lean forward and push my palms against the cold glass to get a better look at a fence post we're approaching. I thought at first that the post was somehow on fire, and there was thick, black smoke curling above it, but as we near the post, I realize it's a dark, solid shape, perched upon the post. I shiver, immediately thinking of the big bird, but it's no bird. It stands up as the truck rumbles past, and is out of my line of sight.

I lean down to stare hard in the rearview mirror. A tall, thin silhouette of darkness in the gloomy gray day, fast approaching the semi. My heart stutters in my chest. It's walking along the fence posts, its steps managing the eight foot gaps easily. I chance a glance as the speedometer, leaning back towards Buddy even though I hate the idea of the thing out of my sight. We're traveling at forty two miles per hour. How is it gaining on us? I stay leaned back away from the window, but here are its long, shapeless legs bounding from post to post right outside my window. I creep closer to the glass and lift my chin, trying to see the thing's face, high above me.

I can't see it from this angle, but it must notice me looking up. It must notice me because it bends its shadow arm into what is unmistakably a wave. *A monster.* I stare in dumb disbelief until the fence line inevitably curves away from the road. The thing follows the fence rather than the truck, and I see its full, bounding, unrealized body. I press my cheek against the window as it leaves the fence and hops amongst the bare trees, further and further from the road. After a while, the trees give way to barren snowy fields again, the cycle of background looping around to the beginning, and the thing sinks down into its crouch into the highest boughs of the last tree.

I sink back into the seat. Did that just happen? Was it only my imagination? "Buddy," I say slowly. "You ever see anything weird out here?"

I turn and look at him expectantly, even though I'm not *really* expecting a response. Not really. Just hoping. How nice would it be for me to be say, "Holy crap, do you see that?" and have someone there to say, "Yes, that's crazy!" or even, "No, you're crazy!" But, I just have Buddy.

"It's alright. You're still good company," I say, in case he somehow thought I was ungrateful. But, Addie's absence is like a dull headache. I can't believe how good it was to have someone to talk to. Someone smiling at me. I can't let myself forget her.

I find myself gazing stupidly at Buddy for too long to be appropriate, and drop my eyes to the dashboard. They happen to fall on Buddy's cell phone. I've never used one, though I understand the concept. It's a library, a telephone, a camera. It's everything. I wish that I could have one, but the whole not having a credit card or even a name makes it pretty much impossible. The portable digital world has been completely unobtainable, but I've spent many, *many* long nights hunched over a library computer.

I thought at first that I could perhaps email, or join a chat room, maybe instant message. I try each new method of internet communication whenever it becomes available, but the results are always the same. My emails send, my comments post, no one ever reacts or replies. I'm not there. It doesn't stop me from enjoying the content of the world, though. I'm only a forever spectator, just like any other aspect of my existence.

I've got a plan now, though. I borrow Buddy's clipboard. It hasn't been updated, yet. His schedule might be on the phone, but I don't want to pry. I just want to browse the internet to start formulating this plan for Addie for real. I finally scoop the device off the dash. *Dang.*

"Hey, Buddy, what's your password?" I ask.

Buddy drives. Silently.

"Cool, cool. Thanks."

I set the phone back. I'll just have to watch next time he opens it. Instead, I pull out my notebook. I need to outline my plans before they trickle out of my ears. Maybe I should mention the Post Hopper too, but first:

ADDIE

ADELINE

ADDIE ADDIE ADDIE

5 YEARS OLD

Grandma's house (Buddy's mom) 208 May St Garden Grove Iowa

ADDIE IS WAITING FOR YOU

I stare down at the words, try to soak them in. As an afterthought, I scribble "*Poppy*" at the bottom of the page. Can't forget *my* name again.

We stop for lunch at a cheesy little silver diner before Buddy picks up a new trailer. I sit next to him in the booth long enough to decipher his phone's passcode over his shoulder, then slide around to the other side. He spends his time notating his new schedule from his phone onto his trusty clipboard, and I spend my time jotting down notes (his passcode first) in my own notebook.

I wish I could tell him to order the chili cheese fries when the waiter comes. I can smell them from here, and they are probably amazing. "Buddy," I whine. "The cheese fries. I *need* the cheese fries." I wonder how much ominous ghost wailing is actually just whining.

He asks for an omelet and a cherry cola, and I try not to be disappointed. "And, maybe I'll do some of those chili cheese fries on the side?" he asks sheepishly, and the waiter nods and takes the sticky menu away.

"Yes, Buddy, you are awesome." I clap in excitement, grin at the waiter's retreating form.

Buddy says nothing.

As he finishes his work stuff and starts mindlessly scrolling that magic little computer, I steal his clipboard and copy the destinations and dates. I leave big gaps between each destination. I'll fill those in when he's driving and it's my turn to scroll.

The food comes. Buddy's omelet is thicker than my forearm and almost as long. I immediately dig into the fries. They are greasy, salty and an absolute mess. I'm in love. Buddy pulls the plate back towards himself to try some, and for a moment, we're both tugging on it. He looks up at me. Not really *at* me, our eyes don't meet, but for a second there, I get the impression that he thought someone might be across the table from him.

I hold the plate for another heartbeat while my own seems to pause. Buddy's eyes narrow, then his brows droop into something that looks almost like fear. I could push this moment. I could hold these fries hostage long enough that he'll realize something is amiss. My palms slick with anticipation.

But I don't want to mess this up. I don't want to scare him. Not now, when he's my ride, my companion, my link to Addie.

I release the plate, and the moment passes.

I take my opportunity with the cell phone as soon as the GPS voice tells us it'll be ninety seven miles until Buddy's next turn off. Plenty of time to relax. I take a chance and turn on the music, and while Buddy doesn't immediately start singing along, his index fingers bop in time to "California Dreamin'," and I'm reassured he's going to be all right.

Our next overnight stop is in Des Moines. I pull up the phone's search engine and clumsily tap on the glass: *most haunted lovations del moined*

Google helpfully corrects my spelling and shows me a list. I start copying addresses down in my notebook. It's time to find my own community. For me, yes, but especially for Addie.

Streaming Service Looking to Adapt Haunting Footage into New Series:

Reports are coming in that the television and streaming giant, Netflix, has approached August Waters in hopes of collaborating for a new series. While details are scant, fans are rife with speculations.

Some believe the network is hoping to produce a recreation of the stunning footage Waters streamed of his "Emerald House" encounter, while others argue that there are hopes of putting together a crew to film Waters at new supposedly haunted locations, hoping to recreate the magic with a higher production quality.

The "Emerald House" footage has recently taken the internet by storm, creating a heated argument that hasn't been seen since the blue dress/white dress debate. Did Waters truly interact and film supernatural entities, or is he a budding technical filmmaker talent? Either way, we're excited to see where these talks with Netflix lead.

Mr. Waters has been reached out to for comment, and he is recorded as saying, "You want to hear from me? Watch the stream."

Chapter 5

I have a whole night ahead of me to explore the city of Des Moines while Buddy sleeps. I have three potentially "haunted" locations to hopefully visit, as long as I have time. I've written down explicit walking directions to each one, hoping to keep myself on track.

"All right, Buddy," I say softly. He's perusing his phone, quiet and relaxed. Contemplative. "Don't wait up, and don't leave without me. I'll be back soon." I reach into my pocket and procure the photo of Addie and Rebecca laughing at the bubblegum statue. I tuck it into the visor of the driver's seat before I slip out of the cab. I took it for me, but maybe Buddy needs it more.

It's windy tonight, and the gusts of frigid air seem to have swept the entire city indoors. I'm all alone on the streets. I sing "California Dreamin'" to myself as I walk. It seems appropriate.

My first stop is, funnily enough, a mall. Supposedly built on a monastery or something, people say they see ghosts of nuns wandering the corridors. Do monasteries even *have* nuns? I don't have super high hopes about finding and befriending a nun, but I would love to get Addie some new clothes, so I figure it won't be a waste either way.

I guess, to many people, a mall can be pretty spooky at night. These places that are meant to be filled with laughing and shouting people seem even more empty than any other quiet place. The silence in an empty mall is like a roar, a vacuum in space, an eternity. A mind insists that, surely, if there are no people in such a large place, there aren't any people anywhere. There's been an apocalypse, a virus, a culling, and no one is left besides you, and these shadowy, echoing, eerie closed storefronts. It doesn't bother me anymore, having spent *so* much time in malls after hours. But the feeling will always persist, and for me, existing as I do, so apart from and outside of the rest, the feeling hurts in its inescapable truth. I'm alone. *Except for Addie,* a helpful voice reminds me. Except for Addie. And if except for Addie, then why not except for a hundred more, a thousand more, a whole community more? An empty mall is only sleeping, after all. Tomorrow, it will open its arms and be full again. I'm only sleeping.

I creep around the huge building, looking for one of those weird little side entrances that cleaning staff and security guards often use. A white pickup truck with lights on the roof is parked next to what appears to be a tiny alley off the food court parking lot. *Bingo.* I follow the walkway past rows of air conditioning units and some hastily planted shrubbery, and find an unmarked door, propped slightly open by a brick.

I slip inside. As they usually are, this surveillance room is tiny and boiling hot from all of the electronics running, and the nighttime security guard has his chair leaned back to catch gusts of the winter air through the crack in the door. He's keeping an eye on the cameras and chatting on a cell phone.

He ignores my greeting, so I slip through the tiny space into the far door. It opens onto a hallway almost identical to the walkway outside, except instead of shrubbery, there are doors along one wall, each leading into the back room of a store.

A mall is an enjoyable place for me, especially early in the mornings or late at night when everything smells freshly mopped and vaguely electrical, like I've just missed some kind of chemical rainstorm. The only other patrons I'm usually in company of are elderly people getting in some exercise on the climate controlled, level ground. They power walk laps around the giant structure. Maybe if I had lived, I would be among them.

I can't help but reminisce over when malls were new, and all the teens and young adults flocked to them and hung out and put on fashion shows for each other. It was a whirlwind of life and color and smoke. I used to love going on Friday nights, dipping myself into the crowd like a warm bath.

I'm a coward. I'm afraid to cut my hair or dye it, afraid to add more piercing holes to my ears. I don't know how this "body" reacts to that kind of thing. What if my hair doesn't grow back? My Bardot bangs that I thought were cute at twenty-four years old certainly never grew out (and also never really looked like hers), so I assume it won't grow back. What if a pierced ear just bleeds and bleeds forever? I've never tried to hurt myself, and I've been very cautious not to do so accidentally. There's this whisper in the back of my head that tells me there's a way out of this half-life, if I only had the courage. But my stronger voice says that's not true, *can't* be true. I can't risk it.

So, I didn't join in on all of the beautiful hairstyles and wild colors. I didn't get a ring in my nose or in my eyebrow. But I *loved* the fashion. I wore a new, outrageous outfit every day in those first years of the mall. I practically lived (well, stayed) in there, trying on clothes and doing my makeup all night long.

As the world changed and people moved on to shopping online, the young people must have found different places to haunt. And so, I guess, did I. But I never lost my love of fashion. Even now, all these years later, I choose my clothing with the utmost care.

According to my notes, the ghostly nun is usually seen around the Panda Express. Weird, but I guess technically *I* can be seen haunting a Panda Express occasionally, so who am I to judge? That firecracker chicken is pretty good. I'm out in the main thoroughfare now, and I check the giant lit up map and head towards the Paranormal Panda Express.

I call out as I saunter through the mall, just in case. "Hello? Anyone here? I'm dead, are you dead, too?" I don't really know what to say to get a ghost to talk to me. I should probably work on that.

The restaurant in question is locked up tight with a pull down chain-linked screen. I rattle it. "Hello?" I wait a few minutes, wandering the immediate area quietly, just listening. I don't hear anything except my own breathing, and the far away echo of one of those scales that sit outside vitamin stores that you can feed a quarter, and it tells you your weight and BMI. "Have you checked your weight today?" it calls.

A bizarre imagining strikes me of the voice belonging to a ghostly nun, sauntering up next to me in her old timey habit and then yelling in the machine's cheery voice, *"have you checked your weight today?!"*

I shiver and then laugh at myself. I honestly don't think there's anyone here besides me and a couple of security guards. I pull out my trusty notebook and cross off the name of the mall from my list. Next stop, Limited, Too.

I spend way too much time shopping for Addie, but it's so fun to shop for someone besides myself. I don't know what kinds of things she might like, so I tried to bring a wide range of styles, textures, and colors with me. I'm just hoping the stuffed full shopping bags will all fit on my side of the cab, and I also hope it doesn't take Buddy another three years to visit his mother. Maybe I can leave some suggestive hints, like I did for *my* mother all those years ago.

I find myself not very upset about the lack of a fellow ghost in the mall. I'm mostly just so overjoyed that I've managed to stay on task for this long. I've only looked at my notebook a couple times to nudge me in the right direction, and thoughts of Buddy and Addie have remained clear in the forefront of my brain. It seems a significant improvement from the desperate attempts

I was making to get through a day back in Chicago. I couldn't make it from one train stop to the next without forgetting what I was doing.

The realization of how bad I'd gotten sends a shiver through me. How many things have I forgotten permanently? What if I've known plenty of other ghosts in the past, and their existence somehow slipped from my mind one day? Someone could be waiting for me, just like Addie is now, and I'll never return to them.

I shake the thoughts away before useless panic overruns me. I'd never forget another ghost. I won't forget Addie. Her name is in my notebook, after all. Her name...and my new name. I grin to myself. I have my very own new name. *Poppy*. Poppy and Addie and Buddy.

"Have a good night!" I call to the security guard manning the cameras. He's no longer on the phone, he's just staring into space in the direction of the monitors. I hope his shift is almost over. I leave the door propped open behind me as I step back out into the cold, clear night.

Next up, a haunted house, apparently currently occupied by the governor. I wrap my shopping bags around my wrist to free my hands and stare at my notes on how to get there. It's a two hour walk. I squint at the sky. I think I can probably make it there and back to Buddy, but I definitely won't make it to my third stop. I'm actually kind of glad about that, too. That one is an abandoned elementary school, and I'm not sure I have the mental fortitude for any more ghost children. Maybe next time.

I'm only a block or so into my walk when a building appears beside me like a magic oasis in the night. The windows are all lit, showing off the glistening wares, even though the store is obviously closed. "Bike World". A *bicycle*. Now, that would be useful if I'm going to continue taking these little detours from Buddy's route. I'm terrified that I'm going to find myself too far away to make it back to him before he leaves, and I'll never find him again. I've taken steps to prevent that from happening, but the fear persists. It's that same feeling of anxious homesickness that I used to get when I thought about leaving my mother's house, and later my own house. Maybe it's true that I'm now haunting Buddy.

I'll have to commit a little more crime than I really prefer to enter the bicycle shop, as it's locked up tight. No guard enjoying a night breeze here. Should I forgo a bike? Maybe pick one up outside somewhere? My time is short, and my morals aren't what they used to be. I break the glass on the front door.

The alarm that immediately sounds reminds me of the first time I stole. I was genuinely hoping to be caught. I sauntered into a jeweler's, right behind the counter, opened the case and extracted a huge, sparkling, ridiculous necklace. The store was busy and there were three employees close enough to touch as I slammed the glass door open almost hard enough to shatter, and declared, "I'm taking this, and I'm not paying for it." It was the show piece of the case, and I thought for sure, someone would at least notice it was missing.

I sat on the floor of the store for hours, listening to the employees, watching them rearrange the case so there was no big necklace shaped emptiness in its center. I watched, clutched the stupid necklace, and cried for a very long time. I'd completely forgotten that day, until just now. I reach up and run my fingers along my collarbone. I never wore the necklace, in fact, I don't think I actually even left the store with it. I must have just left it lying there, worthless to me, once my experiment concluded.

I feel bad now, but not bad enough to not look around. I finally realize a problem that I should have considered before breaking in: Where will I store a bicycle in Buddy's cab? I frown. I'm not going to steal a whole bike just to use for tonight, where is my head even at sometimes?

But then, I see it. Right there in the front window, where I could have noticed it from the street. An orange bicycle, and next to it, an identical one folded up small enough to fit in one of my shopping bags. A folding bicycle. Ingenious. I pick up the folded one, practice folding and unfolding it a few times, and then call "Hello!" to each of the responding police officers as they arrive. They ignore me, and I ride my new bike straight out through the broken door, Addie's shopping bags dangling from the handlebars, mindful of the pellets of glass around my new tires.

My ride is only forty minutes long, even with my frequent stops to check directions. I absolutely love flying along on the bike, tears whipping from the corners of my eyes in the cold wind. I can't believe I've never once (that I recall) thought to pedal around town on a bike. I suppose the busses and trains were convenient enough to not have to consider an alternate method while I was in Chicago. I used to love riding a bike when my mother didn't allow me to use public transport without a chaperone, but goodness, I must have been eleven or twelve the last time I rode. I guess you really never forget how, even if you forget everything else.

The governor's house is a magnificent old mansion. I can immediately see why people think it's haunted, with its sprawling grounds and Addams Family roofline. I fold up my bike and start wandering around the exterior. Everything is kept in immaculate shape, I feel like I've wandered onto a movie set or into a fairy tale. Fountains play somewhere in the distance even in the cold.

"Helloooo?" I cup my hands around my mouth as I call as loud as I can. "Any ghouls around?"

Nobody answers. There's a patio with several sets of doors leading inside. I try each one, and surprisingly find the last one pushes smoothly inward. No breaking and entering this time. I don't know if I've ever been in such a gorgeous building. Everything is staged with antiques and low, warm lights throw each room into a comfortable semidarkness, only jarred slightly by bright Exit signs. I run my hands along intricately carved wainscoting and find myself at the bottom of an elegant set of stairs. Patterned glass windows at the top let in a little moonlight, stained red and green and blue.

"Wow," I murmur.

I wander up the stairs slowly, and find myself gazing at the windows for what's maybe a long time. I love this house. I could stay here. Maybe I could be happy here, at least for a while. I take my shoes off and leave them by the window. There are so many beautiful rugs in here, I don't want to leave dirty snow prints.

I leave the things I'm carrying behind, too, maybe by my shoes, or maybe on a bench or in an armchair, I don't remember. I'm much too focused on taking in the architecture, the details, the warmth and life. I find a piano beside a large window and sit at it, gazing down into the gardens. The sun is starting to rise, and the bleak morning light is turning the powdery snow along the edges of the tree branches into glimmering diamonds. I open the piano, and plunk a few discordant keys. I should learn how to play. I have nothing but time, why haven't I bothered to learn any instruments? I imagine myself, sitting here for as long as it takes to learn everything there is to know about playing. I could master it. Maybe one day I could write my own music, and leave it for someone to find. A composer from beyond the grave, how neat would that be? I try a few more keys and eventually work out "Hot Cross Buns." It'll take some time.

I've never stayed anywhere with a piano before, at least I don't think. My time in my original brownstone is definitely fuzzy, even with the recent trip down memory lane, I have grown a cloudy mold over the little details. I remember mostly feeling at peace, until my mother got sick. I think I might have spent whole days or even weeks in a single spot, just breathing the familiar air and taking in the familiar sights, just existing. I wasn't writing anything down yet, then.

I've stayed in other places, though. This nomadic lifestyle is a fairly recent change. When I left the hospital after my mother's death, I decided I couldn't go back to the home we had shared for so long. I didn't want to smell her hairspray anymore.

I walked west, and found an abandoned old farmhouse surrounded by newer homes on every side. I decided it was perfect for me, fixed up the inside, and collected a lot of things I enjoyed. Books, mostly, and antiques. I even had a fish. I fed him every day, but I could tell he was a little confused by his situation. I was actually quite handy, after researching at length at the library. It's amazing what you can do with endless free time, endless supplies, and endless information.

By the end of my stay, the house was comfortable, and I really enjoyed my time there. I rarely left the premises unless I needed new clothes or new books. I didn't think I would ever leave again, and I did spend a few years in that Barbie dream house with barely a thought in my head until the day a realtor walked in, thoroughly surprised by the pristine condition of the property. My possessions were sold off at auction, and my house was purchased by a young couple.

I considered trying to haunt the couple and get my house back, but their presence reminded me what it was like to have a family, and I grew very fond of them. I ate their leftovers, watched television with them. Jim thought that Steven had brought home a fish, Steven thought Jim had done it. They painted my burgundy foyer a sage green I was sure would look horrible, but it didn't. When Steven's job forced them to move away, I didn't follow them. They took the fish, but I decided to stay with the house and see what the next family was like, what color they might paint the foyer.

I didn't connect as strongly with them. I think it was more to do with me, and less about the family. They felt more and more distant every day. I can't even remember their names, now, or whether they ever repainted any room. The divide frightened me, and I moved on. Well, I left the house. I'm obviously still here.

Thinking wistfully of my long lost collection, I wonder vaguely if there's a library in this house. I bet there is, and I bet there will be some interesting things to look through. I float away from the piano as if in a dream and start slowly wandering through doorways, looking for books.

I find an interesting one on the history of the house. I'm not usually one for non-fiction, but for some reason, this particular topic seems like something I need to know more about, if I'm to stay. I settle in a chair that was old before I was born and open the book.

The house comes to life just as I'm finishing the book and perusing the glossy black and white photos in the center pages. Suddenly, people are wandering around, opening window curtains and dragging velvet ropes around to block off certain areas. I stand and put the book back on the shelf.

"Hello," I say to a man with a wide broom. He's running it over the spotless corners of the room.

He doesn't notice me. I shrug and decide to find a kitchen. Some coffee sounds lovely. On my way, I pass two shopping bags, one pink and one lime green. I frown. They're ruining the perfect atmosphere with their obnoxious colors. I go over to remove them, to maybe tuck them away in a closet somewhere or even throw them in the kitchen trash. I peek inside one.

"Oh." I reach into a bag and pull out a small orange and red t-shirt with a daisy embroidered on the front. "Oh, no." Addie's clothes. Addie. Buddy. I'm suddenly frantic, woke up late with no alarm on a workday frantic. Realized I was supposed to pick up the kids from soccer practice frantic. My heart thuds. I have to go. Where are my shoes? I sprint up the stairs to retrieve them. My little bicycle is there, too, thank goodness. I have no idea what time it is. I should have grabbed a watch. I should have set an alarm. I should have been more careful.

I unfold the bicycle quickly as I'm running down the front steps and hop on, shopping bags swinging.

I'll save a lot of time being able to ride back instead of walk, but I know in my heart that Buddy is probably already long gone by now. The idea of being alone makes my eyes sting with tears. I pedal as hard as I can.

"Buddy!" I sob.

He's still here. He should have been on the road over an hour ago, but he's just now climbing into the driver's seat. I've never seen him start late before.

"I'm so glad you didn't leave." I fold up my bike and place it at my feet. I store Addie's new things behind my seat. "I was so worried!"

He's fiddling with his cell phone, and puts it up to his ear. After a moment he says, "Hey Rick, just checking in. I'm having a little bit of a late start this morning, but I'll be in Carbondale on schedule. Ah, just not a good night of sleep, I guess. No worries. Tell Marcia I say hi. You, too." He hangs up.

Thank goodness for small coincidences.

August Waters Deep Dive

With the frenzy that has come about over August Waters capturing what is allegedly an actual haunting at the infamous "Emerald House," we decided it's time to take a closer look at some of Waters' previous ghost hunting streams. Here are his top three fan favorite moments!

3. August and his crew, consisting of (maybe?) girlfriend, Amethyst Horton, and best friend Johnny Quint spent a spooky night in a forest preserve in southern Illinois, where August regales them (and his viewers) with a tale of a camping trip August took in the woods in the past. While not much happens on camera besides some bump-in-the-night noises, Waters' storytelling abilities cannot be denied. Watch the archived stream <u>here</u>.

2. Waters brings his crew to an abandoned coal mine shaft in Pennsylvania (location not disclosed, potentially due to trespassing). This stream was done in the middle of the day, which makes it even eerier. August is vague on what happened in the particular mine (again, trespassing), but insists he notices some activity only minutes into the stream. Again, not much caught on camera here, but August apparently sees (or hears) something so frightening that he demands the crew immediately leave, abandoning some equipment in the process. This video is a fan favorite at a scant nine minutes in length, where the last words recorded are August saying, "Our lives are worth at least $400 in equipment." Buy a shirt with the quote in his shop <u>here</u>. Watch for yourself <u>here</u>. Do you see what August sees?

1. This is the video that August insists is responsible for his core fanbase he says have been with him "since the beginning." It is also one of his earliest videos, posted to YouTube instead of his current streaming service, so was not live at the time it aired. Waters says that this fact is the only thing stopping this video from being his first "proof." "It's too easy to doctor a video before you put it on the internet," he claims. "You've gotta be right there with me to know in your heart its true." Taken in an apartment building in

Indianapolis, Waters spend several minutes apparently talking to himself while Quint films. Waters asks the empty room questions, and received long, awkward pauses as replies. Finally, Waters says, "Wait, please don't go." And the apartment door opens and shuts. Careful viewing of the video shows the deadbolt spin once to unlock the door before it is opened, but the video is not high quality. Watch <u>here</u>.

What do you think of August Waters' long career of ghost hunting? Is he a ghost whisperer, or is it all our imaginations paired with his impeccable stage presence?

Chapter 6

It's taken me almost two weeks to get up the courage to leave the truck again. I've planned out an evening many times, but when it comes time to leave, I only make it a few steps away before anxiety cripples me, and I bring my bicycle and my shame as I crawl back up into the cab. I've read through all of Buddy's science fiction books, and even watched a couple movies with him, snuggled into a spot on the floor near his cot and watching his phone screen at a severely tilted angle. But, earlier today he spoke briefly to his mother on speaker, and the guilt at having done so little to help Addie overshadowed my fear. I won't get sidetracked again.

My next investigation is a house in the country in southern Illinois. I'm taking a chance coming out here while Buddy makes his stop in a town eleven miles away. According to his clipboard, his next load won't be prepared until six in the evening tomorrow, so hopefully nothing changes and he's still there when I make it back to him. I now have his schedule for the next two weeks, so worst case scenario I figure I can meet up with him at a later stop. I also picked myself up a watch, complete with an alarm. I'm not losing Buddy. I'm not losing myself.

There are four miles of empty farmland between the property I'm biking to and the nearest tiny town. According to the articles I've notated, several acres of the surrounding farmland are even supposedly "haunted", with crops here struggling while crops everywhere else thrived. I wonder vaguely as I walk how I would possibly go about tainting acres of farmland, as a ghost. Sounds more like bad luck or silty soil to me, but I don't want to be a skeptic.

As the long driveway finally comes into view, I dismount and fold my bicycle to review my notes. Seven different owners in twenty years, each paying less than the last. There are accounts of hair being pulled, misty handprints on glass, banging noises coming from the attic and, the most repeated account, being woken in the night by a woman screaming and crying in the upstairs hallway.

I look from my notebook up to the house, carefully checking the windows for anyone watching me approach. There's no one. The house is still handsome, but beginning to fall into disrepair. The paint is peeling, and a few spindles on the wrap around porch are missing. The yard is tidy, though, and the sidewalks salted and shoveled. There's an older model minivan parked in the drive, and a haphazard pile of three bicycles blocking the walk between the drive and front door. I add mine to the pile, a little off to one side. I don't bother folding it.

The front door is locked (no one responds to my knock), but from the porch, the television inside is audible. I walk around the side, and find the back door leading into the kitchen. It's unlocked, and gives a cheery little creak as I swing it wide.

The kitchen smells of the bacon sizzling merrily on the stove, and there's a middle aged woman wearing a nightgown was humming to herself as she tends to it. She's making bacon, lettuce, and tomato sandwiches for an easy Sunday lunch, by the look of the ingredients on the counter. It smells excellent, and I'll probably nibble a corner of someone's when they sit down to eat. She doesn't notice me enter besides giving a little shiver as the gust of frosty air enters the kitchen with me. I quickly shut the door. "Sorry about that," I say to her and smile. "Lunch looks delicious."

She gives the pan a little shake and resumes her humming.

I wander into a casual sitting room, where a boy in his early teens is watching cartoons and ignoring some schoolwork sitting in front of him. "Hello there," I test.

He yawns, but other than that, has no reaction. Another live one.

"Hmm." There's a hall leading to the front door and also upstairs. I eye the stairs, a little warily. "Hello?" I called up. "Anyone home?"

I climb the steps, avoiding a pile of dirty laundry at the foot. At the top, I pause and look down the supposedly haunted hallway. I'm torn between apprehension and disappointment. I don't really know how many more false reports I can handle before I give up. The initial planning, the excitement, the letdown. It's a lot for me to go through those feelings, and the longer I'm away from Buddy, the more confused I feel. There's a fog that creeps in, and I find myself flipping through my pages almost constantly. I have to right now, in fact. *My mother had a parakeet named Bertie. Addie has dimples like Buddy's. Buddy semi cab is sparkly purple.* I nod to myself, mouthing the words on the pages, and after a moment, feel ready to call again. "Is anyone up here?"

I walk forward and the old floorboards creak beneath me. Sunlight is streaming in from a window at the end of the hall, and it's decidedly not frightening. I let out a little anxiety in a small sigh, and consider turning to leave right then, but the boards groan again, without me.

"Hey. Hey! Who's up here?" I run down the hall and throw open the first door. No one, just a bathroom, wet towels and discarded bits of clothes littering the white tiles. I bite my lip and try the next door, but with less enthusiasm. There's a boy, about ten years old, stretched out along the floor on his stomach, about a thousand plastic toy building blocks spread out in front of him. He takes no notice of my entrance, completely focused on his building.

"Oh. Hello there," I say, but I'm not the least bit surprised that he doesn't answer me. He probably won't even respond to his mother calling him down for lunch.

I decide to stay in the house overnight. I have time, I tell myself. I have to be sure, right? But really, I stay because the mother and her two sons are comforting to me. They had a huge argument over the television that ended with the youngest stomping back upstairs and slamming his door, and the mother having a glass of wine with her bacon lettuce and tomato. I miss people. I spend the evening reading one of the mother's romance novels and chatting with her about the ridiculous plot while she reads her own magazine in fits and bursts, occasionally getting up to do some small task, help with homework, or break up an argument. I feel like we could have been friends.

After the mother and youngest child have gone to sleep and the oldest boy has snuck out of the house and peddled away at top speed on one of the bicycles, I settle myself against the window at the end of the "haunted" hallway. I'm going over my notes again with a heavy duty flashlight borrowed from the kitchen junk drawer, romance abandoned, when I hear a faint scraping sound directly above my head.

I immediately assume a squirrel or raccoon family is living up there, but I might as well find the attic entrance anyway and take a look. I close my eyes and lean my head back, thinking. Will I have time? Maybe I should head back, I'm worried about being away for so long. Nothingness is nibbling at me. Another little shuffling noise makes me open my eyes. The attic access panel is directly above my head.

It's open, and there is a pale, horrible human face looming at me out of the darkness, lit from below by my flashlight's too bright beam.

I shriek in spite of myself, and actually fall backwards, back flat on the floor. The flashlight lays next to my uselessly startled hand, but the beam is bright enough that I can still make out the face, the hole. There's a sudden hiss like an angry cat, and the face above me retreats back into the darkness. Human hands appear, each finger worn down into bloody stumps, the nails gone. They are holding the tile that covers the attic opening, and they fit it back into place with a tiny clunk. All that my flashlight illuminates now is a square of slightly off colored ceiling with bloody handprints around its edges.

"W-Wait!" I cry, clutching my chest. I glance hurriedly around the hall for something to stand on and swear loudly, finding nothing. "I'm coming up there!" I hear a confidence in my voice that I don't at all feel.

Maybe I should just wait until morning, I think, as I pound down the stairs. There's a pantry in the kitchen, and I'm hoping there will be a step ladder in there. Or maybe, I'm hoping there won't be, so I don't have to go up and get a better look at the person hiding in the attic, talk to them. They saw me, *hissed* at me, sure, but definitely saw me. My heart is pounding, I don't want to do this, but it's the whole reason I'm here. Maybe they're just as afraid as I am.

Unfortunately, a six-foot stepladder is leaning against the back wall of the pantry. Plenty tall enough for me to be able to haul myself up into the attic with a little scrambling. I grab it and awkwardly waddle back across the house with it under one arm. I knock a lamp off an end table with it accidentally, and the lamp falls to the floor with a dull thud, but luckily doesn't break.

I park the thing under that ominous discolored square in the ceiling and gather my courage. I ask myself, for probably the eight hundredth time in my afterlife, *what's the worst that can happen?*

I climb up and push away the square before I lose the little nerve I have.

I'm instantly blasted with cold, stale air. It's an average attic smell, I guess, but concentrated and dead. A husk of attic.

There's also a tiny noise I didn't hear in my rush to get up the ladder steps, or maybe the tile just deadened the noise. Someone is crying up there.

My nerves deflate in the exact same rate my empathy ramps up. Sad is better than angry. Maybe I can help? Maybe we can help each other. "Hello?" I call up.

The crying stops. I breech the darkness of the attic with my head and shoulders. The flashlight is tucked into my jacket pocket, but I'll need both my arms free to heave myself in, so I'm going to have to do that part blind. "I think you and I might have some things in common," I say to the silent air. "I'd love to talk with you for a while, if you wouldn't mind."

I do a very ungraceful heave and flop myself onto the attic floor. It's dusty, and disturbed particles work their way through my lungs. There's been no sign of the other ghost since the crying stopped. "I'm going to turn on a light, if that's okay," I say. I try to keep my words light and friendly. I'm still afraid, but also nervous like I'm on a first date, or at a job interview. This is potentially someone to talk to. I want to make a good first impression. They don't answer me.

I point the flashlight towards the floor before clicking the button on the handle, I don't want to accidentally shine it right in my potential new friend's eyes. Who knows how long they've been hiding out up here? There's a slight rustling noise from further on down the room, and I slowly pan the flashlight in that direction, keeping it pointed low.

There is the regular attic detritus up here, cardboard boxes with random names or holidays scrawled on the sides chewed into by mice or squirrels, some broken furniture and toys, bicycles made for children younger and smaller than the one sleeping downstairs. There's another small shifting noise from behind a stack of plastic lawn chairs, and I catch a glance of a pale profile and dark, wild hair. "Hi there," I say quietly, and shift into a hunched standing position. I leave the flashlight trained towards the floor in front of them. "Can I come over there?"

The figure is low to the ground, and keeps their face turned slightly away. A pale hand appears in front of the face, palm toward me, as if to tell me the light is too strong. The fingers are certainly the same one that closed the attic hatch earlier—all gnawed away, dark blood oozing slowly over the knuckles. The stolen bites of BLT roil in my stomach.

"Sorry." I pull the light toward me, leaving them in heavier shadow. I make my way towards the figure. I hear scuttling along the room on either side of me, though the face has barely moved. *Mice. Have mice been chewing on their fingers?*

I'm close, now. Close enough to see the face clearly, even with the light pointed away. It's a woman's face. She turns toward me, and she is a mask of torment. Her eyes are sunken caverns, her cheeks are glistening with wetness. The white of her pupils show almost all the way around. Her eyebrows knit together high in the middle with long deep lines of worry and strife. Her mouth is a sad clown frown, all exaggerated creases, the corners pointing towards the floor. My heart flips uncomfortably in my chest.

I've made a terrible mistake. This is not a ghost.

Her jaw drops open like a loose hinge, and the mouth is too big, too wide, too long. It's a never-ending tunnel of night. The skittering noises on both sides of me grow loud and frantic. I take a step back, and then another. She screams. It's an unearthly, banshee wail. I drop the flashlight and cover my ears, sink back into a crouch. I can't help it, the sound is *unbearable* torment. It's the most heartbreaking, earth shattering shriek. Endless. Her hanging mouth is like a megaphone.

Suddenly, there are hands on me. Both my wrists are grasped and by the dim light of my flashlight on the floor, I see those nubbed fingers clutching. But then, I feel them also in my hair, on my ankles. The light swings around as another hand picks up the flashlight and points it back at me. I squint in the suddenly harsh light and see the looming, still screaming face just a foot from my own. She is only a head, attached to countless arms, countless grasping hands. They chitter around her like snakes. *No, like spiders.* The face I'm looking at is like the hourglass on a black widow. Just an evolutionary design to scare predators or ensnare prey on a spider's abdomen. A ruse.

I'm screaming back, begging, crying, apologizing, whatever. I don't think any monster has ever gotten me in its clutches before, through my dozens of close calls back in the city. I don't know what happens next. Will this thing drag me finally down into an afterlife I've somehow avoided? Will it hurt? The many hands have picked me up now, I'm dangling a few feet above the attic floor. I thrash and squirm. I'm being moved further away from the screaming face. "I don't want to die!" I cry, and the irony barely even reaches my own ears.

I'm unceremoniously dropped out of the attic access. I hit the ladder and clatter to the floor, tangled in it. I'm clutching my side, all the wind knocked out of me by the impact. I look back up into that little square hole from the floor, and my flashlight comes flipping down through the darkness and hits me square in the nose.

"Fuck!"

I'm holding my nose, it's gushing blood. The shrieking above finally stops and there's that tiny thump as the attic door is moved securely into place.

I look down at my hands, shocked to see my blood on them. I stand up shakily and wander down to the hall bathroom. The brightness of the overhead light is so strong I can almost hear it. I squint into the bathroom mirror.

I'm a wreck. My nose looks broken, and I'm completely covered in bloody handprints. It hurts to breathe in. I don't remember the last time something really *hurt*. I haven't missed it. I wash my hands and face in the sink, and I'm considering raiding the mom's closet for something not covered in blood, when a loud rattling noise sends me out of my skin.

It's the bathroom door, shaking in its frame. I force myself to relax. It's one of the people who live here, probably the older boy sneaking back home, trying to get in the bathroom and finding it locked. But...*no.*

Along the bottom edge of the door, four fingers, each missing the top knuckle, are holding on, rattling the door back and forth.

I feel a burst of rage and sweep across the room, throwing the door wide. I feel sick. The hand retreats back down the hall on the end of an outrageously long pale arm, covered with long dark hairs. There are hands all over the hallway, feeling around in drawers and sneaking under doors, touching the window panes and sifting through toys. They are everywhere, touching and soiling everything, their weirdly jointed arms or legs or whatever draping down like vines, all growing from that attic hole.

I'm done here. I don't need new clothes bad enough to stay another moment. The only thing I do on my way out is give one of the reaching hands a hard stamp. A cry echoes through the house from the attic. *Good.*

As I pass through the threshold of the side door (mindful to leave it unlocked for the teenager), I feel instantly better. My nose stops throbbing and I gulp in a full lungful of cold air. I feel reset, somehow. I check my face in the side mirror of the minivan, and though it's hard to tell in the dark, I'm pretty sure my nose is normal.

I whip out my notebook and flop down in the driveway. I can barely see by the light of the moon, but I scrawl something to the effect of my discovery on what I hope is a blank page. I'll have to test it out again later, but it's not something I'm looking forward to. Pain sucks.

Under where I've scrawled, "*leave building after injury?*" I write: "*Farmhouse- No ghosts, only another monster. Attic spider.*" I hope that's enough to jog my memory in the morning. I put the book back in my now blood-soaked jacket and start the long bike ride back to Buddy.

August: Hey all, hope you're having a...thrilling? Yeah, thrilling Thursday! I know, I know, corny. I also know I haven't announced our next hunt yet. You're all dying to see more ghosts, and I'm absolutely going to give them to you, but I want this next hunt to be something really special. I feel like the pressure is really on after Emerald House. I don't want to disappoint you guys.

Which brings me to my question for you. Do you *have* any places you think are definitely haunted and you think I should check out? Let me know in the GotGhosts email below. I'll be checking into researching any places you all offer up, so please give me your very best. I'm counting on you all!

Chapter 7

I can't keep on like this. After a dozen more nighttime investigations, I'm starting to think alive people just assume any place where people have died must certainly be haunted. Or even any place that has that certain abandoned house chic. Hell, maybe any place that happens to be dark at night. People jump at their own shadows and here I am, literally chasing those shadows. Maybe this was a terrible plan.

I look at Buddy's phone sitting in its holder on the dash and sigh. I look at Buddy, his face lit up green by the gauge lights in the dark. "What should we do, Bud?"

He sighs back. He's feeling pretty despondent, too, I think.

I grab his phone. "Ugh." I type in: *most haunted place in America.*

I blink at the results. Instead of the usual list of tourist attractions and real estate blogs, there are news articles. Link after link, all discussing the same place: Emerald House.

I click the top link.

Proof of ghosts? August Waters, a video blogger from Indianapolis, shook the internet this week with his newest video: a two hour walk through of "Emerald House," supposedly the most haunted building in America.

The video captures what many people are claiming to be the first real proof of ghosts. Mr. Waters (seen below with his filming crew)...

Interested, I scroll down to the photo.

"Oh. My. God." I actually stand, forgetting I'm in a semi cab and there's not really standing room. My head collides with the ceiling, and I flop back down to my seat. "Oh, my God! Buddy! Oh, my God." I hold his phone up to the side of his face. I squeal like I've just won the lottery.

The man from the platform. The man who saw the big bird, who saw *me*. He's smirking at me from the tiny bright screen.

I've found him.

I stare at the screen in wonder. I have to find this man and talk to him. How? Would he receive an email I've sent? I'll have to try. I'll send one from Buddy's email, maybe coming from an actual alive person will help. None of the emails I've created post-death seem to work.

It doesn't take long to find August Waters' vlog. I scroll down past the videos (I'll watch those later) to find his contact info.

Got a ghost? Email me, the page says. Oh, I've got a ghost.

I open Buddy's email and start a new outgoing message. I stare down at the blankness, the little line where a word will appear if only I could move my fingers. What am I supposed to say?

My fingers are trembling. I close the window. Maybe I should watch the videos first, get to know a little bit more about this guy before I contact him.

"Big things are happening, Buddy," I murmur. I set his phone down and reach for my notebook. I need to see when we'll be in Indianapolis next. I open it but get a weird little shiver down my spine. There's tension in the air. I glance over.

Buddy is gripping the wheel way too tightly, and I see sweat beading on the backs of his hands. His eyes keep flicking from the road to his cell phone.

"Everything okay?" I ask him.

He lets out a long exhale. "Get a hold of yourself, Bud," he whispers.

My eyebrows knit in concern. I look at the phone when he looks at it. It looks normal to me. I pick it up and examine it.

"Shit," he says. He's got his eyes trained on the highway now. Deliberately not looking over at me, or where his cell phone belongs. "I've gotta get some sleep." He immediately puts on the hazards and guides the semi slowly to the shoulder.

He noticed me, I realize. He doesn't see me, maybe, and he doesn't hear me. But he notices something is different. Should I push it? He looks so scared. What is different? I slowly set his phone back down on the dash, hoping not to frighten him further. I've been in this cab for days and days now with him none the wiser.

I remember both of us tugging on the fries at the diner. He felt me there, then. I know he did. Years of desperate attempts for my own mother to notice me had no results. Years of mingling with strangers, staying in their homes with them, nothing. What's different about Buddy?

I sit quietly while he notates the time, does all of the things he needs to do before sleeping for a while. He crawls into the back of the cab and draws the curtain. I'm suddenly afraid to leave the cab. What if he gets scared and leaves without me? I'm afraid to even shift in my seat.

An eternity passes, or maybe just a few minutes. I hear a tiny whisper, barely more than a breath, from behind the curtain. "...Addie?"

Oh, shit.

I bite my lip. I need to say something. He's listening for me. Maybe he'll hear me. But all I can really offer him is disappointment. "No, Buddy," I say. "I'm not Addie."

He doesn't respond. I don't think he heard me. After a while longer, his gentle snores fill the cabin. I sneak his phone into my lap as soon as I'm sure his snores are genuine. I might as well learn all about this August Waters.

I watch the most recent video first. It's him discussing the events of his breakthrough moment, "Emerald House." Apparently, the house is in a farming town in Indiana, near the Illinois border. He said that his previous "hunt" had been in downtown Chicago, and it had been a disappointment. Of course, he doesn't realize he ran into me.

I let my mind snap back into focus as he talks through the experience at the house. He tells us that the entity he encountered was an old man who did not die in the house, but in an accident in a nearby barn. The man hadn't been sure of the date of his death but had been hanging around the house to see his children grow and his children's children, before the house was sold off to a new family.

August said the ghost had not changed his routine and had been bumping shoulders with the current family for years, until quite recently when the family began to notice his moving and using things. August was very interested in this new development of course and pressed the ghost at length for any changes he might have recently made. The man assured August that he had been a man of routine in life and remained one after his death. He did, however, admit to having a fondness for the family's recently acquired cat. He would often pet it and it would follow him around sometimes.

None of this, it transpires, was actually on the so-called spectacular footage August and his team take at the house. According to August, the whole conversation with the ghost man seems like one sided nonsense. But, August apparently asked the man to move objects, to turn the lights on and off, etcetera, and those moments are the things that have the Internet in an uproar.

August closes the video by thanking the fans that have been with him since the beginning of his filming journey, (when he was just looking for "Charlie," whoever that might be) and welcomes new watchers. He says, "I've been getting tons of emails every day since the footage went up, but I still plan on responding to every single one. Just know that it might be a lot longer than it was when it was just my four friends and mom checking in."

That settles it. I'll watch some more of his videos, but I'll definitely email him before morning. I'll let him know the whole situation, tell him to maybe talk to Buddy for me. Maybe he'd even be willing to set up some kind of meeting with Buddy and Addie. That would be so wonderful! I tell myself everything is going to work out and press the tiny *Play* button for the Emerald House video.

By the time the sky has that purple, gray tinge of morning, I know everything I can about August Waters, and Buddy will probably think his phone isn't charging properly since I've nearly drained the battery. I have an email ready to send from Buddy's email account.

Dear Mr. Waters,

I don't know if you'll receive this message, as usually any letters I write go unnoticed. I died in 1965 and find myself in the position that your friend Charlie was in, and also the unnamed man in the Emerald House.

We have actually met once, about a month ago. You were on a train headed south in Chicago and had a run in with a monstrosity. She wasn't me, but I'm sure you remember her, big feathery body and creepy red smile. You don't forget a face like that, am I right? Anyway, a woman called out to you, telling you to ignore the big bird, and tried to catch you as you left the train, but couldn't get to you in time. She is me. You are the first person who has looked at me in over fifty years.

I'm writing to you now from the email address of a man that I suppose you could say I'm "haunting." He has a sad story of his own. He lost his wife and little girl a few years ago in a car accident. His daughter is still around, as I am, and I have spoken with her. I would love to help you maybe facilitate a reunion between them, if you'd be interested.

I can't drive, and I think the best way to go about meeting would perhaps be to speak with Buddy, the man who I am staying with. He's a long haul truck driver. Perhaps we could meet you somewhere along his route.

I don't remember my name, but Buddy's daughter has rechristened me as,

Poppy

I read the letter over several times, looking for grammatical errors, hoping the words make sense. I press the *Send* button and let out a long, slow breath. I can only hope he'll see the message. For now, it's onwards and upwards.

Our next stop is, coincidentally, Indianapolis, the place where August Waters last saw his childhood friend and first ghost, Charlie. I sincerely doubt that August will have read and responded to my email while we are in the city this time, but it's one of Buddy's regular stops. We'll be back in just a couple of weeks. I have a few locations I was planning on checking while we were in the area, but my discoveries tonight have put all of them securely on back burners.

When we get to the city, I'll be searching for a man named Charlie.

I'm still being cautious around Buddy. I find myself trying to decipher even his tiniest changes in expression. I'm in limbo, torn between wanting him to notice me and not wanting to frighten him.

He takes one more break before our stop in Indianapolis, at one of those giant trucker havens like the one where I originally found him. In fact, it might be the very same one, I confess I have almost no memory of the place from a few weeks ago, besides the doughnut I stole. I decide to go hunt for another one of those, and get one for Buddy, too. He hasn't been eating much since we left his mom's house, and I'm worried about him.

I wander into the conglomerate, sure that I've got at least a few minutes before Buddy will be back on the road. A trashy looking space opera's cover art catches my eye, and I snag it. I'm immediately positive I'll love it, and assume Buddy will, too. We like pretty much all the same things.

I'm halfway back to the cab before I remember: Addie. I didn't grab her anything! I need to be picking her up toys and games and books and clothes. She should be priority every time I find myself somewhere new. I try to picture her little face but can't quite do it. I remember she has dimples like Buddy's, and that'll have to be good enough for now.

I run back and snatch up a foot tall ceramic unicorn covered in pink and blue glitter.

"Buddy, you need to eat something!" I sing as I hop back into the passenger side of the cab. I stow the unicorn under the seat and set his paper wrapped doughnut in his cup holder. "It's blueberry!" I turn.

Buddy is here, ignoring me, of course, but I gasp. He has my notebook in his hands.

"Buddy..." My ears ring, my blood pressure rising. He can't be looking at my notebook. He can't see my words. Can he?

He's turning the pages as if they're blank. He doesn't seem to be taking in any of my musings. I let out a sigh and move to take the notebook out of his hands, but as I reach out, he turns the page again and stops.

"What...what is this?" he whispers. His voice is cracking.

I look down at the page and see Addie's name leap out at me over and over and over. *I can't forget her.* "Here, let me take that." I reach again. The same feeling of possibility is whipping through me like it did so long ago at the diner over cheese fries. How could I seize this moment, make Buddy stop wondering, start really *seeing*?

Buddy interrupts my frantic thoughts by letting out a wail, then flings the book toward me and buries his face in his hands. "What's happening?" He sounds like he's underwater.

I instinctively bat the book down to the floor to keep it from hitting me in the face, but now I pick it up and put it back in my jacket pocket where it belongs. I can't believe I left it laying around like that. Buddy is crying into his hands, and I have no idea what to do about it. Should I just leave him alone? I'm obviously upsetting him with my presence. I had no idea he would notice my book. Nobody ever notices my things. I wait, as quietly as I can.

Eventually, Buddy rakes his fingers down his face to wipe away the worst of the tears, and takes a long, slow breath. I hold mine. Will he remember what upset him? Will he look for the book?

He looks, but instead he notices the doughnut in the cup holder. *Really* notices it. Notices that it doesn't belong, and that he didn't put it there. He *notices*. "All right. What in the *fuck* is going on here?" He asks no one in particular, or maybe me, whatever. He picks up the doughnut and glares at it.

"It's blueberry," I say again, meekly. Now that I'm looking at him, at his kind face and dimples and his shadow again on its journey to beard, I can remember Addie's face like she's sitting in the cab with us, too. Buddy is my link. He's keeping me grounded. I can't lose him.

Buddy takes a suspicious bite, and then sighs. "I love blueberry."

August Waters: *Hi all, welcome back to my stream. Hope you're having a creepy Friday night. So, I know you've all been messaging me and talking amongst yourselves throughout all this madness and wondering, "What's next for August? How can he top Emerald House?"*

I've gotta be honest, I've been asking myself the same thing. The hype has been cool, but I've been worried. This whole finding ghosts thing isn't something I can just make happen whenever, right? I mean, I've been trying for years! Now all these big names are reaching out to me, wanting to make deals, and I'm like, I don't know what all I can really offer without the ghosts.

Well, lucky for me, my fans have got the ghosts. I opened my email for the first time after my last video, and I've got messages from all over the world from people telling me their stories, begging me to come out and see their haunting. I can't wait to do so. I'm proud to say I've accepted an offer from a very prominent streaming service that would like to create an original series based on my hunts.

Now, here comes the part where I ask for your help...again. One of the emails I've received is very interesting to me. I believe it might have been sent not by someone being haunted, but by a ghost itself!

Now, the email has been somehow altered or scrambled and can't be replied to. It's completely gone now, so I'm relying on memory of my read through. Basically, the sender claims to be ghost who doesn't remember her own identity, but told me she is currently traveling with a man called "Buddy," who is a truck driver. Buddy lost his wife and daughter in a car accident, and the ghost has told me that Buddy's daughter is also a ghost. Could this emailer possibly be Buddy's wife? We've gotta find out, right?

Now, this ghost gave me reasons to believe in this email that she is legit. The trouble is, I can't for the life of me find this "Buddy" she says she is traveling with. So, I'm reaching out to you, my newly huge watching audience: Do you know a Buddy the truck driver who has a dead wife and daughter? If so, information that leads me to his contact info with get you five hundred bucks.

I've set up a tip email: findbuddy@gotghosts.com

I know you can help!

Chapter 8

It doesn't take me long to find the inevitable hole in the chain link fence surrounding the supermarket, long abandoned since a toddler August Waters came shopping here with his mother. It's brazen, right next to the ancient sun bleached signs promising that this location will be open with a brand new remodel in the long past spring of 2018.

My stolen flashlight pans over the deteriorating store front. Most of the windows are gone, and only a couple have had an attempt made on them at being boarded up. Graffiti covers every inch of the brick, and most of the sidewalk on this side of the chain link. A couple of possibly occupied sleeping bags are under the overhand of the roof to one side, but I sincerely doubt I'll be bothering anyone with my non presence.

I haven't been really afraid of the dark in many years, in fact I don't even remember if I was afraid of the dark while I was alive. I doubt it, since I'd spent so many early mornings walking to work in the dark alone. But I have to admit, now, I'm a little uneasy.

The store's broken windows are black pits where my flash-light's beam doesn't want to penetrate. Slightly warmer air pushes out from them like half a dozen open, sleeping mouths. Their breath carries the faint stink of rotting food and cardboard. I suddenly wish that I had someone, *anyone*, to step with me into one of those mouths.

But no, not anyone. Who would I bring, Buddy? Buddy that doesn't even know I exist? And what if it *is* dangerous inside? I couldn't bring someone living into potential danger. And of course I could never bring little Addie here. The thought of her being exposed to anything that might upset her actually makes my stomach turn. I realize that I actually should have brought the ghost hunter. I'm doing things all out of order. I should have approached him first and then suggested accompanying him to this place.

But I have a feeling I won't find anyone inside, living or dead. It's the saddest looking storefront I've ever seen. It's just a hole left over in the world. Even the graffiti feels more like ancient writings, like the people who put it here are long, long gone.

So, I choose what looks like the opening with the least amount of glass along the bottom, and step forward. I sit on the sill looking out at the street for a moment before swinging my legs around, and I feel it. The tickling sensation of being watched from behind. Maybe even of being stalked. For decades, eyes on my back have only belonged to monsters. I can't shake the hunted sensation now, even if these eyes belong to a friendly face. I'm certain, though: there's somebody inside the dark hole behind me, and they *see* me.

I close my eyes and inhale the rank, stale air. I'm being stupid. I have nothing left to be afraid of. I hop down from the sill and into the cavernous pitch black. My flashlight catches the checkout lanes sprawled out in front of me. Most of the equipment has been knocked to the floor and smashed beyond recognition, but there are still the dirty imprints and vestiges of particle board where the conveyer belts once stood. The cheap tiles have been worn down from years and years of shopping carts getting pushed through the exact same tracks.

A shifting sound whispers deep inside the wide room. Too big to be called a "scuttle," more like the sound of a burlap sack being dragged. It lasts for only a moment, but my heart is in my throat (or, it *would* be, no time for semantics) and I whip the light towards the back. It doesn't illuminate more than the closest aisles.

It's early in my journey, but my courage is failing. I need to know what I'm dealing with in here. More importantly, I need to know if it really can see me. "Hello?" I make myself sing out, as loud as I can. "Is anyone home?"

The shuffling, scraping noise comes again. There's also an ominous metal creak, and I train my flashlight all the way towards the back wall that I think reads, "Dairy" just in time to catch the shadow of faint movement. There's a metal crash. Something large has been knocked over. Something is back there. Did it hear me call? Or is it only coincidence? Does it notice my flashlight? An animal, maybe?

"All right," I call. "I'm coming back there."

My flashlight stays trained in front of me so I don't trip over the detritus of years of destruction and rot. The graffiti and signs of looting and squatting end pretty quickly as I make my way towards the dairy department. Nobody has been staying back here. As I approach the metal shelving I assumed was just randomly disassembled and thrown around, I realize it actually seems to have been placed with some semblance of a plan. The dairy section has been effectively walled off by towering piles of sharp heavy shelf pieces, wire racks, and milk crates.

I frown and start following the haphazard obstacle to one side. There must be a way back there somewhere. I freeze. On the other side of the metal mountain, the heavy sliding noise comes again. I take a step. I hear the slide. Step. Slide. Step. A slide, a bang, and then the shelves beside me start to rattle and shift, disturbed. I scream, I can't help it.

A low, wet, choked scream fills the air before my own has even stopped. There's someone in here, and they know I'm here.

I step back and try to collect myself. This is fine, everything is fine. I *want* someone to see me, right? Plus, I'm already dead, what's the worst that can happen? But that's the thing. I don't know what the worst that can happen is. The attic spider's mangled fingers in my hair forces itself to the forefront of my brain, complete with my own terrified, ludicrous sobbing echoing, "I don't want to die!"

I shiver. I'm sure if it wasn't pitch black and smelling of rot and death in here, this would all be a laugh.

The gurgling howl comes again, and I consider just running for the door.

The shelves are being torn away on the other side of the wall, things are falling haphazardly towards me, and the metal on metal sound, accompanied by that awful wet screaming makes me feel like I've finally found my way into hell. I run back away from the opening being made and turn off my flashlight. I immediately knock into a lone shopping cart on its side and have to turn the light back on, just for a second. I just need a vantage point, to see but maybe not immediately be seen. I have to know what I'm dealing with.

There.

A rack of what might have once been greeting cards is still standing mostly upright a dozen feet ahead of me. I could stand behind it and it's short enough for me to peer over. The crashes and wails from behind me seem to be getting more angry and desperate. I train my light on the floor. Mostly clear, just avoid that jutting piece of particle board on the right a few steps in. I turn my light off and creep forward, my hands held out in front of me. Step, step, step, slight left, step. My hands touch the top of the display, and I skitter around it, duck down and place my back against it. I breathe for the first time in several seconds.

Whatever is making those horrible screams has made it through the wall of shelving and is now hovering nearby. Who made the wall? Someone trying to keep the thing contained and out of sight? Its raspy breathing shudders all around me, its weight takes up so much space. I'm going to have to look.

I stand and turn, train my flashlight on where I think it might be standing, and turn it on.

What stands before me is not human. I have to keep bringing the light up, up, up, to find its face. The eyes are huge gobs of jelly, the size of softballs, distended out from the sockets they belong in. They're sightless, milky, with no sign of pupils or irises. They droop above a gaping maw where a mouth should go. An entire pumpkin could easily fit inside that massive cavity without the thing's jaw even stretching. Giant, glistening teeth, all grinding molars, fill the hole on all sides, at all angles. They grind against each other chaotically as the creature starts to turn towards my light.

The body is translucently pale, layer upon layer upon layer of flesh, with no definition at all below that giant, gaping hole of a face. A huge, upright slug of mottled, pink, rubbery skin. As I stare, completely transfixed, it lets out another wet gurgle. I watch as dark fluid runs out of that hole and trickles down its front. For a moment, I think stupidly that it has wings, as two delicate bone white structures start to come forward from behind the creature. Then I realize they're arms. Arms, as thin as my own, but at least eight feet long each. There are delicate hands attached to them—long, slender fingers.

I gape as they reach forward towards me and cover half the distance between me and the creature in one grasp. They plant themselves flat on the filthy tiles and each finger, almost luminescent in the dark, strains with effort. Then that awful, heavy slide again. It's dragging itself across the floor toward me.

It's time to stop staring and start thinking. Obviously, I need to leave, but first...I have to be sure. "Charlie?" I make myself ask the thing. It's barely a whisper.

It could not be Charlie. This is not a man a child would wave to in a supermarket. This is not a man that could hitch a ride in a car. This is not a man that could be mistaken for an imaginary friend. This is not a man.

The thing gurgles again, but I decide that noise might actually be its breathing. It's only a few feet away from me now, and I have to crane my neck to gaze into those sightless eyes. It reaches a delicate hand out again and tries to grab me with surprising speed. My scream echoes through the cavernous space and I barely manage to dive to the side in time. Instead of me, the hand curls around the top of the greeting card display and shears it away with a clean snap. The hand pulls back and shoves the entire piece of rotted wood into that waiting, endless maw, then delicately wipes at the corner where lips would meet, if the thing had lips.

Something about the mindless motion stops my heart in my chest. There's an undeniable humanity to the action, even blown up to these monstrous proportions. "No," I whisper. "Oh...oh, no."

Realization crashes down on me, louder than any of the falling debris in this place, and just as devastating. This isn't Charlie, no. But maybe he used to be. Maybe, when he remembered his name. Maybe, when he had someone to talk to. But he's been all alone in this place for so long.

All that's left is the Fat Man. A monster.

I run out of that supermarket as fast as my legs can carry me. I'm hyperventilating, sobbing. I haven't felt this *much* since those first few days in the house with my mother. The heartbreak, the frustration. I remember it so clearly right now.

All those monsters. Those demons, plaguing me at every turn in the city. More and more all the time. I felt like they were hunting me. I was the only one who could see them. I thought they were only there to torment me, like that was their only purpose. How could I have been so self-centered? So stupid?

These supposedly haunted houses that I visit, only to be greeted by yet another horror. Why didn't I realize?

They're just *people*. They're just like me, just like Addie, except the slow seepage of their memories is complete. They've forgotten everything. They're feral, empty shells, only clinging on to a tiny leftover vestige of the person they used to be.

It will happen to me when I've forgotten everything. It'll happen to Addie. What will we become? What truck stop bathroom or brownstone apartment will I creep back to and become the barest version of myself? What horrors will Addie unwittingly unleash on the home she loved so much? Why is this happening to us?

"Buddy?" I sob, yanking open the door or the cab. "Buddy, please wake up."

I try to quieten my breathing enough to hear his snores from the back. There they are. Low and even. I flop into my seat. "Buddy...I really need to talk to somebody. Can we go see Addie?"

He gives a snort. "What? Huh?" He still sounds mostly asleep.

My heart is in my throat. Did he hear me? "I said, Addie," I say, cautiously.

There's quiet from behind the curtain for a moment. "Addie?"

I squeal. "Yes! Buddy! You can hear me! Oh, my God." I stand and fling the curtain open.

I'm greeted by a loud snore. He's gone back to sleep.

I start to cry again.

"Where's August?" Forum:

Fr3akshow24- *GUYS GUYS GUYS. I've got him! Buddy's real name is SEAN FRANCES. Works for Heartland Express, owns his own rig. Mother, Sharleen Frances. She lives in Garden Grove, Iowa.*

    FrogsPlayingHopscotch- *Look! I found pictures from the accident. So gross.*

    xXWinterRoseXx- *Addie came to me in a dream last night and said we should go visit her. She's so sad.*

    Fr3akshow24- *The address is 208 May St. Field Trip? FIELD TRIP.*

    FrogsPlayingHopscotch- *Addie didn't even live there. Sean's address is listed in Illinois. Here's a link to Google maps.*

    DeathByDefeat101- *The grandma says she's in her house. I can see ghosts, too. I'll go check it out, but I need a ride (I'm 14 but my mom says it's cool).*

Chapter 9

The morning starts off like any other. We're at a truck stop to fuel up and get breakfast, and I decide to get a coffee that's described as "cinnamon swirl." It's okay. I sip it. I didn't get Buddy one because he's still decidedly on edge about me and I really don't want to push it, and he returns to the cab with his own coffee and beef jerky. A weird combo, but whatever. He opens the bag, and the entire cab immediately smells like jerky. Cinnamon swirl jerky.

Before he's maneuvered out of the parking lot, his cell phone chimes. It's a text message. I don't recall him receiving any other text messages the entire time I've been hitching with him, so I curiously inspect the screen.

Travis: *Hey, bud, can u call real quick?*

Buddy glances at it and then does a double take. His face crumples up in mild confusion. He doesn't move to make a phone call, just turns his focus back to the parking lot.

By the time we reach the interstate, he's received two more texts. One from a "Jess," one from a "Steve- Realtor." Both messages are the same cryptic request for a call.

A half hour into his route, he pulls into a rest area. His phone has been chiming an alarming amount, and there have even been two phone calls. "What the *fuck* is going on here," he mutters.

Once parked, he finally retrieves the phone from its holder and stares at it as though it might explode in his hands. I'm guessing he's deciding which of these people he'd like to hear bad news from. Instead of deciding, he places the phone back on the dash and stares at it. It's ringing.

His hand hovers over the little green button to answer for long enough that I'm sure he'll miss the call, but then finally, he taps the screen. "Hello?"

"Hi, sweetie," Buddy's mother says. "Have you heard?"

"No, what's going on? Is the world ending or something? I've got like a hundred people calling me in the last few minutes."

"Ethel called me a few minutes ago. She said that Todd said—you remember Todd? You two used to go fishing together when you were little."

"I remember Todd, Ma. Go on."

"Anyway, Ethel said that Todd said his students—you remember Todd teaches at Washington Elementary now? Fifth grade."

Buddy closes his eyes and tilts his chin towards the ceiling in a silent, desperate prayer for patience.

"Anyway, Todd's students came to school this morning all a flutter about some program all the kids are watching these days. There's a man that tells spooky stories or something and all the kids are just *loving* him. And they come to school in the morning talking about what they watched, and they say this man is looking for someone."

Buddy doesn't open his eyes, just shakes his head a little. "Who's he looking for?"

"Well, according to Ethel, who heard it from Todd, who heard it from his students, it sounds like he's looking for *you*, Buddy."

"What? Why?"

"Now," Buddy's mothers voice shifts slightly, trying to make it sound a little sterner, remind him who he's talking to. "Now don't fly off the handle about this. I want you to just have an open mind."

I'm sitting, mouth hanging open, staring at him, hairs raising all along my arms. It *worked*. August Waters must have received—and been able to read—my email! If Buddy takes this seriously, we could be on the way to speak with a real live mediator between the living and the dead. This could change his life. My death. Addie's whole world. I'm watching the sweat beads form on his forehead as he remains silent for a few beats. Finally, he leans forward and his eyes open slowly. He's ready to hear it. I'm so nervous. What if he's mad?

"Apparently—"

"Yeah, yeah, according to Ethel according to Todd, etcetera. Spit it out, Ma."

She clears her throat. "The man says he was contacted by a spirit, and that the spirit is currently...following you. He says the spirit told him that you've lost some loved ones, and he'd like to act as a medium for you, so you can talk to...talk to them."

Buddy lets out a short bark of a laugh. "What? A spirit contacted him? Like what, in a dream?"

"No, I think Ethel said it was an email."

Buddy is quiet for a second and then starts laughing, and the laughs are almost hysterical. I laugh too at how ridiculous it sounds, but the wildness of his laughs are a little unnerving, and I quickly stop.

"Now, Buddy..." his mother calls loudly over him.

"Ma," he says, still chortling a little, wiping tears out of his eyes. "Do you hear yourself? Alright, humor me, why does everyone and their God damned brother and their students think this guy is talking about me?"

"Don't use that language," his mother snaps. "The man said he is looking for a long haul truck driver named 'Buddy' who lost both his wife and daughter in a car accident."

This proclamation sobers Buddy immediately. His mouth clamps shut. His eyes are wide, the tears from the laughter still leaking from the corners look dangerous.

His mother continues, slowly, evenly. "He says that Addie is around, and that he might be able to speak with her. I want you to meet him. I have his contact information for you."

"Ma." Buddy's voice is a whisper. "She's gone."

"That's not what the ghost sitting with you told this man. He said the ghost doesn't remember who she is. What if it's Rebecca, Buddy? She might be there with you right now!"

Buddy whips his face around and stares at the empty chair I'm currently in.

"Oh, no. No, no, Buddy. I'm not her," I say. It's obvious he doesn't see me or hear me, but the fact that he's actively looking for me right now is disconcerting. I feel exposed.

After the longest two seconds of my afterlife, he flings himself back against the headrest of his seat and jams the palms of his hands into his eyes. "Ma. This isn't right. This is *sick*. I'm not doing this."

"I'm going to invite him to the house."

"Ma, do *not*—"

"I'm inviting him, and I'd like you to be here when he comes. I'll let you know." She disconnects the call.

Buddy lets out a horrible groan. He punches the steering wheel twice, without too much feeling. He picks his phone up and raises it over his head, like he might crush it in his fingers or throw it out the window, but then he just powers it down and sets it back into its holder.

"Alright," he says.

I wait for him to say more.

"Who are you?" he asks. He asks *me?*

I'm suddenly speechless. Shy, even. I'm so used to being invisible that this sudden light shed on my existence is paralyzing me. "I..."

"What do you *want* from me? Why are you doing this to me? To my family? I never asked for this." He's crying now, and the tears aren't from laughter.

I reach out, tentatively, and put a hand on his arm. "I just wanted to help," I say weakly. This is all wrong. I didn't mean to upset him more, I just wanted to help! Isn't this helping? Why do I feel so awful?

He doesn't hear me. He doesn't feel me. I do the only thing that I know he might notice now and turn the radio on. The Village People are telling us where to go.

He stares at the radio, dumbfounded. "I want you to leave me and my family alone." he says, calmly. He turns off the radio. "You're not Rebecca."

I'm not Rebecca.

"You don't know me, you don't know my mother, and you didn't know Addie. You're hurting us. Look at me. I'm sitting here talking to myself."

"I can hear you," I say.

He doesn't answer. But he does say, "If there's someone here, I want you out."

I should get out, but I don't. I can't miss my chance to meet the ghost hunter, if there's even the slightest chance Buddy will go home. Besides that, I've grown so fond of Buddy, of his company and his cab. He's almost like a friend, even if he's pretty upset with me right now. So instead, I curl up on the passenger seat and try my best—for the first time—to stay invisible.

The tension in the cab is like a physical presence between Buddy and I. A huge, snarling monster breathing down my neck and keeping me from moving too quickly or breathing too loudly. I've been completely still and silent for almost two hours, and Buddy has been resignedly not even looking in my direction the whole time. His phone screen is a dark mirror reflecting both of us as it sits in its holder on the dash. I wonder if he even knows where he's going without the GPS.

I gather my courage and slowly, quietly reach out and touch the radio dial. I think I might hear Elton John's voice for a split second before Buddy reaches up and presses the knob back off. The movement is like a slap.

I scowl and turn it back on.

He grits his teeth, turns it off.

I reach forward one more time, but he says, "Don't even think about it. My cab, my controls. If I want music, *I'll* turn on music. You're not even supposed to be here."

I sit back, stunned with the weight of the fact that I'm being spoken to, even if it's to be reprimanded. I *exist*. I am not alone.

The quiet resumes, the beast between us regaining control...for about thirty seconds. Then, Buddy sighs and turns on the radio. "Alright. It's a good song."

August Rivers: Hey there, August here with an update on the big project. No, not the Netflix show, I mean the BIG project: Buddy the truck driver. By the time I woke up this morning, I had several emails in the Buddy inbox with all sorts of helpful hints.

Now, I haven't spoken to the man himself, yet, but I'm thrilled to say that his mother, Sharleen, has been in contact with me. She believes in what we're doing here on the channel, and says that she has felt the presence of her granddaughter in her home. She's graciously invited me and the team to visit.

Hopefully, Buddy decides that he'd like in on the action as well, but if not, we'll take the show on the road without him.

Make sure to tune in on Friday night for a very special livestream from sunny Iowa. Is Iowa sunny? Doubt it!

Chapter 10

E ventually, Buddy has to turn his phone back on. We're in the city to unload this trailer, but he doesn't know the last few miles of directions by heart. He reaches over and taps it, then turns on the voice controls to ask for the directions.

"You have, thirty-nine missed calls," the smooth fake woman's voice says when she's woken. "And fifty text messages. Would you like me to play them?"

"Christ, no," Buddy says.

"I'm sorry, can you repeat that?"

"No!" He asks for the directions and then groans.

I feel pretty awful. I didn't mean for *all* this attention to fall on him. I shouldn't have given that ghost hunter so much information, or maybe should have been more tactful in my email. I wonder if maybe I'd asked August to be more clandestine reaching out, if Buddy would have been more receptive. Hopefully, I haven't destroyed this huge chance.

When we reach the dock, Buddy wades through the nightmare on his phone. "Shit," he says and immediately puts the phone to his ear. Whoever he's calling answers on the first ring. "Hey, man. Yeah, I don't know what's going on. Jesus. I'm sorry, man. Just tell them I'm fired or something. Yeah. Oh, no, it's not necessary. I appreciate it, man, but I'd really rather just..." He pauses, listening. "Alright. Okay. Look, I'm really sorry." He pauses again. "I hear you. Alright. I'll check in next week. I'll try to get this sorted." He hangs up and tosses his phone into my lap.

I hold it. "Are you taking some time off?" I ask cautiously.

"Look," Buddy says.

I wait for him to say more, but he doesn't. His phone starts ringing in my hands and I yelp and drop it to the floor. We both look down at it. It's his mother.

"Shit," he says, and scrambles to reach it before it stops ringing.

I helpfully nudge it toward him with my foot, and he grabs it. He doesn't notice me.

"Ma?" He puts the phone up to his ear. I wish he'd use the speaker so I could hear what's going on, but he must not like it unless he's driving. "Ma, did you talk to that guy? Listen. Listen!" He pinches the bridge of his nose. "People are calling dispatch looking for me. I'm going to end up getting fired if this doesn't stop. Tell that man..." He pauses, listening. "No. No, I'm not going to take part in this, and you shouldn't be either! You tell him to put out a statement or something. He needs to leave us alone." He goes quiet again, and I can hear his mother's tone from my seat, though not her words. She's upset. I wrap my hands around my elbows, shrinking back into my seat. Everyone's upset now. This is all my fault. "Don't let him in the house, Ma. I've got a bad feeling. Just listen to me, alright? Ma? Ma." He pulls the phone away from his ear and stares at it. She's hung up on him.

"Buddy," I say. I wish I could just *talk* to him, but instead turn on the radio. It's a commercial.

Buddy turns it off. "Are you still here?" he yells at the ceiling as though I might be flitting around his head like a mosquito. "Haven't you done enough?"

Frustrated, I pull out my notebook. I hastily scribble, "*Addie wants to talk to you,*" rip the page out, and shove it directly in his face. "Look at me," I say.

I watch the dismissal on Buddy's face and am so forcefully reminded of my mother, of my house, that I want to scream. How can this writing be centimeters from his nose and he doesn't see it? How did he notice my notebook the other day? Why aren't there any *rules* for this shit?

"I'm hungry," Buddy says. "You hungry? Want to get some food? Since I can't seem to get rid of you?"

"I'm not hungry, I'm dead. But I could eat," I answer. I feel the tension in my shoulders break, and I see it mirrored in Buddy.

"I'm not gonna talk to you in a restaurant," he says.

I frown. "Wait, can you hear me, or not?"

He doesn't answer. He gets out of the cab, and I follow. He lets the people unloading the trailer know that he'll be back in an hour, and they tell him he's got two before they'll need the dock cleared. We start walking.

"You know," Buddy begins casually. The wind is fierce today, and I worry about him not having a jacket. "I guess if I'm going to accept there's a ghost following me around, I should also consider believing this shit about Addie. Why not?"

I bob my head so fast my earlobes flap in the wind. Maybe it'll be okay, after all! Maybe he'll talk to the ghost hunter, just for fun at first. This could all work out.

"I know it's hard to wrap your head around," I say excitedly. "And it probably hurts, but she'd love for you to know she's there, Buddy. I want to go see her again."

"And why not believe in Santa Claus? The tooth fairy? Aliens!" He cackles at this last one. "Are there aliens? You should know, right?"

I sigh. "I don't know that. I've only seen monsters." I shiver, thinking about the Fat Man. I need to talk to the ghost hunter about that. I wonder if there's anything to be done, or if Charlie is forever lost.

We walk through the wide parking lot and onto a sidewalk. "You like Denny's?" he asks. "Does anybody like Denny's?"

"I like Denny's," I answer. I hook my arm through his as we cross an intersection. "This is nice. You should talk to me more."

Buddy doesn't respond as we make our way inside.

"Hi there," the server greets us apathetically. They're all big hair and black eyeliner, incongruous with their uniform. "Booth or bar?"

"Bar's fine," Buddy says. "Oh, wait, no. Can I actually get a booth?"

"Whatever," says the server.

I slide into the booth across from Buddy, my skirt sticking to the vinyl upholstery. He chose a booth for *me*. He's thinking about me. This is really, finally happening. I actually have jitters, my hands shaking as I fold them in my lap. I feel like I'm on a first date.

"Know what you want?" the server asks.

"Uh..." Buddy does a quick menu flip. "How about this burger." He points. "With an extra side of fries?"

"It comes with fries."

"Yeah, I'd like an extra plate of fries on the side, too. And a water and a sweet tea."

"Sure." The waiter leaves.

Buddy looks across the table, a little to my left. "I feel stupid," he mutters. "I'm going to leave the extra fries. Can you just eat them or something, so I know I'm not crazy?"

I grin. "I'd love to eat some fries, Buddy. If that's all it takes, consider me a solved mystery."

When the food arrives, Buddy cautiously pushes the extra plate towards me. He's watching intently. I'm worried that he might not actually notice if I just sit here and eat them, regardless of his focus, so I pick up the plate and dump the fries onto the table, then slide the plate back to his side, empty.

I don't know how much of that actually registered with him, but something definitely did. "Holy shit. Holy shit," he whispers. He picks up the plate, inspects it.

I eat a fry off the table, pleased with myself.

"Holy...okay. Okay, okay. This is really happening."

"It's really happening, Bud." I eat another fry.

"Alright, we've gotta talk somehow, right? Like communicate?"

"That's what I've been saying!" I laugh. This is the best day of my afterlife.

"Everything okay?" the server asks.

Buddy lets out a little scream and jumps about a foot in the air. He clears his throat like that scream was maybe a cough or something. The server raises their severely drawn on eyebrow. "Um, yeah. Yeah. Sorry. Everything is excellent." Buddy wipes his face with a napkin, but it's not enough to hide his deep embarrassment.

"Ooookay, then." The server takes two steps backward and then promptly walks away. I wonder if they saw my pile of fries on the table.

"Actually!" Buddy calls.

I see the server's shoulders visibly slump as they halt their escape and turn back toward the table. "Yes?"

"Do you have a pen I can borrow?"

The server laughs. "I can't give up my pen! It's my good one. But hang on." They step away and return with a four pack of mini crayons. "There you go."

"Perfect," Buddy says. "Thanks."

We watch the server scoot back to the other side of the room before Buddy leans his head close. "All right, no more talking. But let's try something. I'm going to put my hand down." He shoves his burger aside, flips the paper placemat to the blank side, and rests his hand on it. "You come over here and move my hand. Write me something." He selects a blue crayon from the pack, scoots to the far side of his booth, and waits.

Could this work? I scramble over to the other side of the table and kneel next to him on the booth so I can see where the crayon touches the paper. I put my hands over his and try to move his hand.

I've tried to move people in the past. I can't do it. I don't exert any pressure on them. I can grab a person by their ears and literally hang from them, feet off the ground. I can't pull on them and get them to follow me. Occasionally, I can successfully shove someone hard enough that they might feel a little pressure, take an awkward step. Sometimes, people will turn their heads if I put a hand on their cheek, but they never notice that I'm the force behind those actions. On the flip side, people knock into me all the time with enough force that I go sprawling. I'm just not enough of a presence, I guess.

I pull hard on his hand with both of mine, and accidentally drag it clear off the table, leaving a blue streak of wax on the laminated wood. "Okay, okay," Buddy says, trying to hide the quaver in his voice. "Let's try again?"

His hand is trembling now as I take it in both of mine again. He knows I'm here. He's expecting to be moved. That's the difference. Comprehension dawns on me *That's the difference.* That's why I need to find a ghost hunter. He's actively looking for me. That's why Addie's grandmother hears her sometimes, she's *listening* for her. She *believes* Addie might be there, and she passed that belief onto Buddy at Christmas, however much he didn't want to receive it, the idea has been festering, and so? He's been noticing me. The family staying in Emerald House didn't notice their ghost for years...until they watched a movie about a haunted house. Holy shit.

I draw a careful line, lift his hand, draw another. I can't believe this is happening. "We're doing this, Buddy!" I laugh. The horizontal lines are more difficult, I keep accidentally moving the whole placemat with his arm.

"Here." He lifts his elbow.

"Thanks," I mutter, concentrating hard. Finally, after a long minute of careful marks, my masterpiece: *Hi!*

Buddy stares down at it like it's the Mona Lisa. He drops the crayon, flexes his fingers, stares at them. Then he slowly looks up. He stares right into my shoulder (I'm still kneeling instead of sitting), and smiles. "Hi."

I laugh and clap my hands and hug him and kiss the top of his hat. "I can't believe it worked!"

"Would you...like a to-go box?" The server has rematerialized.

Buddy laughs. "Yeah, yeah. That would be great. Hey, can you tell me something?"

"Uh. Sure?"

Buddy points to his placemat. "Do you see this?"

The server bites their lip. "Um. Yes, I do. It says, 'hi'."

Buddy laughs again. "I can't fucking believe it. This is wild. *Wild*."

"Yep." I'm starting to feel really bad for this person. "So. I'll just, go get you a check and a box, then?"

"Hey, can I take these?" Buddy asks, holding up the crayons and placemat.

"Yes."

"Great, thanks." Buddy beams down at the paper, then looks at my shoulder again. "Hey, we should get a white board or something, that would be way easier, right?"

The server is still within hearing range, but obviously chooses to believe that last remark isn't for them. I hope Buddy leaves a good tip, but this probably isn't even the weirdest table they'll have today.

We leave the restaurant and walk along the busy, un-walkable intersections, Buddy waddling awkwardly across the four lane roads at breaks in the traffic to reach a home goods store on the other side of the expanse of parking lots. This whole area seems to be nothing but parking lots, rows of big box stores lining the horizon. It's so much different than the city I know so well. I wonder if I had died out here, if I would have thrown caution to the wind and taught myself how to drive. But then, If I had died down here, I probably would have already known how to drive. In fact, I probably wouldn't have been walking to work in the early hours of the morning and wouldn't have died at all.

I remember the night of the accident pretty clearly now that I'm thinking about it. I had lived in what used to be the suburbs of Chicago, but over the years the area has pretty much become the city proper. My mother and I shared the upper floor of a brownstone duplex. I worked in a doughnut shop, and she worked at a newspaper. I longed to also work for the newspaper, but we couldn't afford the unpaid internship the paper offered me, so I was up and making doughnut batter at four every morning.

It was a summer night, and I was dreading going to the bakery. The night had sapped away some of the summer heat, but none of the humidity. My polo shirt stuck to my back as I walked, and rivers of sweat ran down each temple. It was going to be so much hotter once I was frying dough, and I already felt disgusting.

It was a six block walk to the shop, and I was the only person on the street at that time of night. I remember that my mother had started to worry about my walks, because the neighborhood was "changing." I remember adamantly telling her that I was perfectly safe.

My low heeled shoes clacking on the sidewalk and a steady cicada scream are the last things I remember hearing...besides the truck.

It was a stupid way to die, really. Not at all relevant to my life in any meaningful way. Not fitting. Not even really uncommon. A garbage truck was backing down the alley between rows of houses, and I assumed it would stop before it reached the sidewalk. It didn't, the driver assuming that the walk would be clear at that time of night. It wasn't.

The truck had run me over with both right side tires before the operator realized, and I think I was probably dead before the second tire. An unlucky accident.

I haven't thought about that night in many years, even if I haven't truly forgotten it, mostly because the whole thing had been so tragically and frustratingly avoidable. And after...well. *After* had been the most disheartening few days of my life. My afterlife.

There hadn't been any bright lights or choices to be made, no doorway to enter or whatever. I'd crawled out from under the truck, and immediately said, "Hey, man! Watch where you're going!" to the driver.

But the driver, and both of the men who hauled the cans, all got out and immediately started screaming. Praying. One threw up. "I was a mess under there. I threw up, too, when I looked, not going to lie," I admit to Buddy as we walk. I'm telling him the story out loud. It helps me remember, I think. I've told him a lot of stories while I've been passenger in the cab, my hand cramping up as I comment them all to paper as I speak. He's been a wonderful listener.

One of the men from the garbage truck finally had the presence of mind to run to the closest house and bang on the door, begging to use the telephone. None of them paid any attention to me standing there. It was like I wasn't there at all.

It took a long time before I got the courage to look under that truck. I honestly wish I hadn't. Seeing a dead body is one thing. Seeing your own sightless eyes gazing up at a filthy undercarriage, your mouth hanging open and teeth scattered on the cement, your sweat drying into a shiny line down your cheek, a reflection of the matte, dark blood drying in its track from your ear canal, is a whole other experience. I remember reaching out and touching my own hand. I don't know why I did that. "It was as awful as you'd expect," I say. "Zero stars, do not recommend."

I let the what ifs and could-have-beens buzz around inside my head as we trek across the wasteland. Buddy isn't talking much. Like a mirage, the store appeared much closer than it actually is, and he's worried about getting his truck back out of the dock before his allotted two hours are up. The wind howls around us and icy patches are hidden everywhere, causing us to randomly jerk forward or back, arms waving, when our footing is not as solid as we assumed. I find myself worrying about Buddy. Does he have his phone in case he falls? Are his hands warm enough? Is this too much exercise so soon after dinner?

But, here we are, warm air blasting our faces from inside the store. We've made it.

Buddy puts his hands on his knees. "Man. I've *gotta* get some more exercise. Brutal."

He ends up purchasing two dry erase boards. One he says he intends to hang in the cab of the truck, and one that's much smaller to keep with him. While he waits in line, I dash to the toy aisle and return with a blue plastic pony. I gently set it on the conveyor belt on top of the whiteboards. Buddy doesn't notice at first, which is disappointing to me. I hoped with him being aware of my presence he might be more attuned to the things I manipulate.

The cashier, however, scans the toy. "Oh, hang on," Buddy says. "That's not mine."

I nudge him with my shoulder. He doesn't notice. I shove him with my open hands, try to push him backward. Nothing.

"It's for Addie!" I say.

He blinks. "Oh, actually, I will take that after all," he says. "My mistake."

The cashier shrugs and puts it in a bag, and I squeal and hop up and down like we've just won a championship game. Buddy's taking this seriously. He realizes that there's a real chance there's a little girl at his mother's house who might like a toy.

The return trip feels different. I think Buddy is deep in thought. He hasn't spoken to me at all. I'm getting anxious. I'm so worried that my existence will slip his mind, or already has, and I won't be able to cope if it happens. I don't want to start over. I'm tired of being alone.

He gets into the cab, tosses his shopping into the back without a second glance, and fills out some things on his clipboard.

"Buddy?" I ask cautiously.

He sets his notes down and looks at his phone for the first time since his disastrous call with his mother. His mouth is a tightly drawn line as he scrolls through the endless texts and missed calls. He sets it on the dash with a sigh and starts the process of leaving the dock.

I consider turning on the radio just to remind him I'm present, but I don't want to come off as needy. Instead, I snatch the phone. I want to hear for myself what August Waters said to get everyone so intent on finding Buddy.

"Basically, the sender claims to be a ghost who doesn't remember her own identity, but told me she is currently traveling with a man called "Buddy," who is a truck driver. Buddy lost his wife and daughter in a car accident, and the ghost has told me that Buddy's daughter is also a ghost. Could this emailer possibly be Buddy's wife? We've gotta find out, right?" My eyes narrow as August Waters pauses to give a movie star smirk.

I frown at the little screen in my hands. He really just made that last part up. I know I need to talk to this man if I can. I know he can see me. He might be able to help me. He could at least help Addie talk to her dad. I know she would love that. But...

Maybe I don't like August Waters.

"Can you turn this shit off?" Buddy asks, and his voice is faint, quaking.

I gasp and spin to look at him. I didn't realize he would notice I was watching. He's sweating, biting onto his lower lip.

I immediately lock the phone screen, cutting off the smarmy sound of August's plea. "I'm sorry, Buddy."

He hasn't taken his eye from the road, but he removes a trembling hand from the wheel and pushes it at me, palm up "Give me that."

I gulp and place the phone into his hand. If I want this company, I'm going to have to be a little more considerate of my actions. He's shaking all over now, absolutely frazzled from interacting with me. He places the locked phone back into its holder.

"Now. I need to return this trailer, since you've gotten me a little leave of absence with your nonsense. Once I do that, we'll go ahead and try out the whiteboard, try to figure some things out. Until then..."

He leaves the phrase nebulous. I understand. Until then, please don't scare him to death. I smile at him. "Sure thing, Buddy." I turn the radio on, and I sing our way down the road. If he hears me, he doesn't comment.

August Waters: All right, I'm jumping straight into the nitty gritty here, no fanfare. We're standing in the kitchen of this lovely young lady, Ms. Sharleen. Say hello to the viewers, Sharleen, they've been dying to meet you!

Sharleen: Oh, um. Hello?

August: See that screen there? That's everyone's comments that are watching us. See everyone saying hello?

Sharleen: Goodness.

August: Don't be nervous, they're all friends. They love you. So, Ms. Sharleen, you've been telling me about the things you've experienced in the home since your granddaughter and daughter-in-law's tragic demises. Would you like to share those things with our viewers?

Sharleen: Well...there have been a few times when I'll come into the kitchen late at night for a glass of water, and my cabinets are all standing open.

August: Wow, that must be scary!

Sharleen: No, no. I've raised a lot of babies in this house. I know what kids do when they're looking for snacks. Buddy did it, his sisters did it, and little Addie does it, too.

August: Little Addie? Is that your granddaughter?

Sharleen: Yes, sir. I also hear her playing sometimes in the house during the day. Like whispering to herself, singing, you know how kids do.

August: Ooh, I've got shivers.

Sharleen: It's not scary, Mr. Waters. She's only a child. She's lonely.

August: So, you firmly believe that she's still present in the house?

Sharleen: I do.

August: Your son, Buddy, though. I notice he's not present here this evening. Is he not as confident? Not a fan of ghost stories?

Sharleen: You have to understand, Mr. Waters. This isn't a game. This is our family.

August: Of course, ma'am, of course. I apologize. I guess it's safe to assume Buddy and his spectral companion won't be joining us tonight. Hopefully another time!

Sharleen: I hope so. I guess it depends on how things go here.

August: Well, let me walk you through what we're planning on doing here this evening. You're welcome to stay with us, or, if you think it might be difficult for you, you're welcome to leave for the night. We promise to be respectful with your belongings. We've got thousands of viewers keeping an eye on us for you. Basically, Amethyst, here, will...

Hang on, hang on. Who's this? Hi there!

Don't be shy. I'm August. You must be Addie? It's okay.

Yes, I know Poppy! Poppy actually sent me here to speak with you. Isn't that nice?

Sharleen: M...Mr. Waters?

August: Ghost glasses? Yes, I guess I must have ghost glasses. I can certainly see you just fine. I like your green dress!

Sharleen: Mr. Waters.

August: All right, Addie. I'm going to talk to your grandma for a minute. We don't want to scare her, right?

Amethyst, baby, can you grab me a chair? I'm a little shaky, haha...

Sharleen: Is she here?

August: Oh, yes. She's right here, Ms. Sharleen. She's been here the whole time. Let's sit down.

August: Thank you for the water, Ms. Sharleen. I assure you, an experience like this is not something that happens every day.

Sharleen: What did she say? Is she okay? What does she want?

August: It's alright. It's alright. No rush. We've got plenty of time. Addie, what do you want to say to your grandma?

She asked if you can get your box of hair ribbons down in the linen closet. She can't reach them, and she's been wanting to put ribbons in her hair.

Sharleen: Oh, my God, my little baby...

August: She doesn't want you to cry, Ms. Sharleen.

Sharleen: *Why is she here?*

August: *You can talk to her. She's sitting right...here!*

Amethyst: *Hey, I think we caught a giggle.*

Johnny: *Giggle on camera confirmed. Right as you were rocking the chair around.*

August: *You hear that, Addie? Everyone heard you! It's all right, Ms. Sharleen. Addie, I bet we can maybe get people to see you do some other things. Would you like to? Do you have a favorite toy you'd like to show me? You can go get it. We'll be here.*

This is some serious shit, guys. I mean, full blown, true apparition. I think we might be able to figure out a way to get her on camera. Everyone is going to want to study this. She's a true miracle.

Sharleen: *Language.*

August: *My apologies, Ms. Sharleen. Oh! Johnny, living room, living room, don't miss the shot. What've you got there, Addie?*

Amethyst: *We've got a moving object, here.*

August: *Sugar? Well, that's an awesome pony name. This one is your favorite?*

Sharleen: *Sugar* is *her favorite pony.*

August: *Addie says that Poppy and her father came for Christmas, and Poppy found this in a box with Addie's name on it. Hold Sugar up high so the camera can see, Addie!*

Chapter 11

B uddy actually drives all the way back to his apartment before stopping for the night. I've spent the day making as many notes for myself as I can, planning out all the things I want to tell him on the white board, and the quickest and easiest ways to word each. I find myself going back in my notes to jog my memory on certain events from my past, but Addie remains perfectly clear in my brain, and I know that's who he's going to want to talk about most.

He doesn't have a dining room table, so we just stand at the tiny square of counter space in the galley kitchen. He cracks his knuckles. "All right, are you still here, ghost? I hope so. I don't want to keep calling you 'ghost,' so I guess first, I'll ask your name."

I pause. Short version? Long version? We'll start small and move up. I move to grab the back of his hand. I'm right-handed and he's left-handed, so everything is even more awkward. I end up standing with our shoulders touching, and my arm twined around his. Thankfully, I'm a little bit taller than him so I can crane my neck and see what I'm writing, or having him write.

Poppy

Start simple. My name is Poppy now, I guess.

"Wow. This is, this is really happening, huh? Poppy? Well, that's a nice name. My ma said you didn't know your name."

I purse my lips, and drag his hand across the board, erasing it.

"Ope, okay. We're going again." he says, with a touch of bravado.

This one takes a little longer.

Addie named me

Buddy drops the marker to the counter and takes his hand out of mine, unknowingly. He covers his face and sinks into a squat, sliding down the cabinet until he's sitting on the kitchen floor.

I sit down next to him. "I'm sorry."

"I just don't know if I can do this, Poppy, you know? I was just finally. Well. I wasn't *over* it, of course. But I was, you know, I thought I was kind of getting used to it." His words are all muffled being his hands, and his shoulders shake. "How am I supposed to move on if they haven't?" he whispers.

I think about how my mother never moved on, not really, even though as far as she knew I really *was* gone. I think about all the time I spent with her in the house, watching her grieve, starting with the very first moment she walked into our empty apartment for the first time.

When I opened the apartment door after my accident, I was overwhelmed by the smell of the house. It was like I had been away for weeks and just stepped inside for the first time. That smell you don't notice, the one that is just "home" in your head—it was overpowering. It was my mother's hairspray and the cigarette smell of my friends that always clung to me and our laundry detergent and her parakeet's cage and wet newspaper and fried dough. Our whole lives in a single smell. My whole life. Once I recovered from the enormity of it, I entered my bedroom and was greeted by a new shock.

I was sweaty and bloody. I traced my hand along the dried blood smear that ran from my ear and down my jaw, back into my hair. I was not injured that I could see or feel, my teeth (besides the bad one I'd had pulled in eighth grade), were all where they were supposed to be in my mouth, and yet, here were all the vestiges of recent damage. I showered and put new clothes on. My clothes had apparently not died and could be removed, but I swear they also remained with my corpse. I wadded up the ruined clothes and shoved them to the bottom of the kitchen trash because they were beyond saving, but I knew if my mother saw them, she would insist they could be scrubbed clean, mended, made good as new. I thought she'd make me scrub them when she got home. I don't think I really considered for even a moment that she wouldn't see me, like the trash collectors didn't see me, like the paramedics didn't see me. Of course, *she* would see me. I waited for my mother to return.

She took a long time. For two days I sat in a kitchen chair by the door. I was so worried, so overwhelmed, so desperately afraid, that I couldn't sleep. I didn't realize until much later that I'd slept for the last time, and would never sleep again.

I paced. I made phone calls, but no one could ever hear me even if they answered. We had a television, but I didn't turn it on. I was afraid to see news of my accident. It was two days of just my recently dead self in an empty house. I kept running back to the bathroom mirror. Was I rotting? Was I fading away? No and no. I looked fine. Normal. So normal that I started to question if what happened had *actually* happened. What if I had a weird nightmare, overslept and missed work? My mother would have still been at work if no police officer had shown up at her job with "the face." The face they all keep in a back pocket for when they have to show up at a family member's work. What if everything was fine except that I didn't show up to make the donuts and people had a grumpier, no sugary bread morning? I considered going to work, just to check, just to make sure I wasn't fired, but the mirror held me, trapped in the headlights of my own eyes. *You know better,* the eyes whispered. I checked the kitchen trash can that first night, when my mother wasn't home by the time she should have been. Bloody, sweaty, ruined clothes.

When the door finally opened and my mother came inside, she wasn't alone. My aunt, her sister, who had married a rich man and lived in the northern suburbs by a beautiful lake, was with her. My mother and her sister had not been particularly close during my life, but sometimes grief can bring people together. I guess that's nice. It was strange to see them standing next to each other, because they looked the same in every physical way, but life had treated them so differently. Like holding a stuffed animal that had been loved by a child for twenty years next to an identical one that had spent its life in a glass box. My mother, bony and tanned, hands trembling while clutching her own stabbing elbows. Her hair in the braid she'd probably done before work two days ago, all frizzed out around her crown. Lipstick barely clinging on the very corners of her mouth and smeared up under one nostril from nose wiping. Her sister, pale and fat and beautiful, her skin never marred by work or strife, her hair beehived elegantly.

I rushed to my mother and took her hands in my own. As I looked into her face, I knew for sure that I was dead. I saw the truth written in the anguish I found there. "I'm here, Mom. I'm here. It's okay." I told her.

My mother began to cry.

"It's okay," I said.

"It's okay," my aunt Rose said. "Come sit down now. I know it's hard."

She guided my mother towards the chair I still had pulled out and facing the door, and pushed her into it, not unkindly, but forcefully, as though she'd been having to push her into every action all day long and knew the amount of pressure required to produce results. I'm sure that's why she was there at all. Someone would have to push my mother forward, and she had no one else left. I think Buddy's mother had done that for him, for a time. I followed them, my hands still wrapped around my mother's, and sank before her to the floor.

"Can you hear me, Mom?" I whispered.

My mother, between hitching sobs, managed to say, "The house smells like her. It smells like her. It's like she's still here!"

"I *am* still here," I said, but she didn't hear me. She never heard me.

I don't say these memories out loud to Buddy, on the off chance he hears them. My mother's pain was too much like his own. Instead, I sigh, and lean my head on his shoulder. "I don't know, Buddy. How are *we* supposed to move on when we're still here?"

He doesn't answer or respond to my touch. I wonder if he'll ever truly hear me or see me. Maybe with practice. Maybe with ghost glasses. Maybe, I should leave him alone. My heart clenches. The idea of walking away from him now and not looking back, eventually forgetting these last few precious days...I can't do it. But, I've written five words to the man and already have him sitting on the kitchen floor in tears. That can't be good for him. *I* can't be good for him.

And what about Addie? Would it be helpful for her to have another conversation with her father? Would she understand that he can't stay and talk to her indefinitely? *Come and play with us, Danny.* I shiver. Is there a happy ending possible, or should I have just kept my big mouth shut? I should have just stayed in my mother's house. That's what ghosts do, right? They pick a house, and they stick with it. The's why I haven't been able to find any besides Addie in the first place. We pick our tomb, we stay, we rot into grotesqueries.

Maybe I should go home.

"Are you ready to try again?" Buddy asks, and his voice is low, it's like he knows I'm right here next to him on the floor.

He stands, and I do, too, but it takes me a long time to place my hand back on his. I almost don't. "I'm ruining your life," I whisper, and tears sting my eyes.

"Did you say something?" he asks excitedly, whipping his head around and knocking it against mine. "I thought I heard whispering."

"Yes!" I say, and then I yell his name, and Addie's, and my own, but the moment has passed. He doesn't hear anything else. I guess I'll have to be careful of what I say, too. That would have been an awkward thing for him to hear.

He clears his throat, and I assume my position next to him. "Okay, what next? Let's see...what do you want from me?"

I laugh. What *do* I want from him? Nothing, I guess. Just the company he gives. I smile at the side of his face, but I don't write that down. Instead, I focus on Addie.

Help Addie

"Is she hurt?" he asks quickly. "Is she scared?"

I'm quick to move his hand to clear the board and respond, I don't want him to panic.

Lonely

"What can I do?"

IDK

Buddy looks down and his face breaks apart in hysterical laughter, the marker sliding from our grip. "I.D.K? How old are you, Poppy? When did you...you know?"

The whiteboard seems to be working fairly well, and I've gained better control of his hand with each answer, so I try for longer and longer answers, with more detail. I tell him where I'm from and when I died and lots of little things. I tell him (vaguely), what I look like, what movies I like, my favorite foods. It isn't until the morning sun is trying its best to claw its way through the dingy kitchen window's glass that I realize we've been standing here for hours, which is fine for me, but he needs a break, and sleep.

You should sleep

Buddy reads the words and glances at the clock on the stove. "Holy shit. You're right. I'm sorry, I shouldn't have...do you get tired?"

I smile and move his hand again.

No

"Okay. Will you...will you stay? I mean, you'll be here when I get up?" He sounds embarrassed.

I'm embarrassed, too. I don't know why exactly, the night has just felt full of vulnerabilities. We're confidants now.

I'll be here

He's smiling as he sets the marker down. "Cool. That's cool. We'll talk more? When I wake up? And uh..." He gestures around the bare apartment. "Make yourself at home, I guess? There's some books, and... I don't know."

He walks down the hall and goes into a tiny bathroom, stretching out his neck and shoulder as he goes.

I sink to the floor right where I am and pull out my notebook. I don't want to forget a single moment of our conversation. I start gushing to the pages like a teen with a diary. Buddy likes pistachio ice cream. Buddy used to ride horses. Buddy's favorite movie is Jurassic Park. Buddy says it sounds like I am pretty...*was* pretty.

I gaze down at the words and start to cry.

The bathroom door opens, and I hear Buddy whisper, "Goodnight, Poppy. See you in a few hours. Well...not *see* you, but yeah. I'll be up soon."

I don't look up at him, but I hear his bedroom door shut softly.

I'd usually take this time to leave, to wander the neighborhood or find a library and do some research on some more potentially haunted places. Anything to keep me occupied instead of this constant reminder that I can't relax, can't succumb to that great relief of unconsciousness. But, I look at our whiteboard. That ten dollar tool that is my only link to my only living friend. *I'll be here*. I'll be here. What if Buddy wakes, and calls for me, and I'm not here? What if I go out and forget again? I've been careless.

So, I am here. I gaze around the tiny apartment. It's dingy and dusty. It smells like disuse. Like the guest room of a recluse. He has no personal effects anywhere, and no decorations of any kind. This is not a home for him. This is a storage unit, at best. His cab might not have photos of his family in it, but it told me so much more about him than this sad box ever would. Or, maybe, this place says a lot, too. Buddy doesn't have a home. His home died with his family.

I wonder if he'd like to talk about Rebecca. His mother didn't really mention her, and Buddy and I didn't either. The closest he got was asking me if I had been married when I was alive. It's difficult to have deep conversations when each answer from me takes so much time. The yearning to be able to just *speak* to him, for him to just *see* me, is so strong that it feels like a headache, dull and throbbing.

I won't admit to myself that I'm obviously developing feelings for him. I tell myself now that I'm pinning every single emotional attachment I can muster onto this one person, simply because he happens to be the only one available to me. I don't admit that it's a lie.

I don't want to snoop, but the time is dragging, just waiting for him to wake up. How long has it been, an hour? Maybe an hour and a half? He might not even be asleep yet. I'm sure he has a lot of thoughts buzzing, too. *Does he maybe* like *me,* like *me? Don't be stupid, you're an unseen specter, literally haunting him. You're not Rebecca.*

The kitchen cabinets are almost empty. There's a stack of paper plates in one, and three mismatched coffee mugs in another. One says, "World's Greatest Dad." Another displays the logo for the trucking company he works for. The third is pink, with a gold rim and white polka dots. My heart clenches, and I touch all three with trembling fingers.

Another cabinet has two flashlights, a portable radio, and batteries of every voltage. I start to carefully close the cabinet again (this one squeaks), but then grin, remove the radio, and place it on the counter by our whiteboard.

There's no television to watch, and I worry about turning one on, anyway. I have a feeling that Buddy would notice. He notices me. I can't help but grin at the thought. I rock back and forth in the weird little space between the kitchen and living room that I suppose it meant to house a small table. I'm so full of energy, I can't just gaze out a window and watch the day go by like I sometimes find myself doing. I can't even—

Buddy's bedroom door opens, and he appears. "Hello?" he calls softly. "I couldn't sleep."

I can't wipe the stupid smile off my face as I turn on the radio to static, and Buddy grins right back in my general direction

It's seven thirty-seven in the morning when Buddy's phone rings for the first time. We had just decided to go get some breakfast somewhere ("I don't keep any food in the house," Buddy admitted sheepishly), and trill of the phone sounds from his bedroom. We both stop dead in our tracks, me more than him I guess, and gaze down the short hall. It's like a literal wake up call. We can't just hang out and play house, August Waters is looking for us. Addie is waiting. I need to get Buddy to go home, and I haven't even asked him yet. How did I forget to ask him to go home last night?

"I guess I'll get that." He sighs, as it rings again.

I don't follow him into his room, he deserves his privacy, but I hear him murmur an answer, and then I hear that murmur raise into a panic.

I rush forward, forgetting the privacy. Buddy is charging out, and his face is both angry and frightened. "I'll be there as soon as I can. Don't let him in, Ma. Don't let *anybody* in that house. I'm on my way."

He hangs up and jams the phone into a pocket. "Who in the hell is this Waters guy?" he yells. "What did he do? What did you have him do?"

I stand there, completely ineffectual. I can't answer him unless he goes back to the board, and he doesn't seem inclined to do so.

"My mom is hysterical. She said there is a *mob* of people at her house. They're banging on the doors and broke a window. They're chanting and screaming at her!" His voice has been getting louder, his words are getting all smushed together. He takes a deep slow breath and closes his eyes. "They're demanding to see Addie."

August Waters talked to Addie. He must have gotten her on film, just like the Emerald House man! I flap my hands in front of my face like I'm trying not to cry, but it's really because I don't know how to express myself. This is *big*, I just hope it didn't cause too much of a stir. I don't want Buddy to get scared off. Not now, not when we're so close to a reunion. "Buddy. We've got to watch his stream. His video! He must have posted a video at your mom's house. He must have gotten Addie on film!"

Buddy is pulling his shoes on. "No breakfast. I've got to get up there. My ma is *trapped* in her own house!"

I race over to the radio and turn it on. "Talk to me!" I beg. "Please, let's make a plan."

He gives the blaring radio the briefest glance. "I don't have time for this. You put my mother in danger. Made her cry."

"Wait, Buddy, please," I say, but he's already walking to the door. I follow him quickly before he can shut me inside. Does he even care if I go with him?

I slam right into his back on the other side of his apartment door. A roar of sound hits my ears.

There are dozens of people gazing up at us from the parking lot a story below. As one, they all start to cheer when they see Buddy. "What...what the fuck is this?" Buddy whispers.

"We found you!" A man calls among the din. "August needs you!"

Buddy opens his door again and steps back inside. He almost locks me out, but I stop the door with my foot and slip in beside him. He puts his back against the front door. He's shaky and sweaty.

"Hey," I say. "Hey, we can figure this out, it's okay—"

Sudden pounding from the other side of the door makes him leap away from it like it's on fire. "Jesus! They're animals!"

"Buddy!"

"Addie needs to talk to you!"

"You've got a ghost! Show us the ghost, Buddy!"

This last proclamation sends a snap of realization running through him. I watch his face change again. The tiniest little creases along his eyes, the change is there. They're spelling out *fear*, now *sorrow*, now *resignation*. I put my hand over my heart. "Don't send me away. I didn't mean..."

"Poppy," he says slowly. "I don't want all this."

"No, I know, I know. It's just a mistake. I can fix this, I just need to talk to Mr. Waters, I'm sure I can..."

He sighs. "I've got to get to my mom's. These people." He pauses, lets their yells filter through the room. They're pounding on the walls, tapping on the glass. "It's all too much. I've got to get her out of there."

"Just talk to me for a second, please!"

"You can come. I believe you. About..." He swallows. "About Addie, I mean. But this isn't right. We've got to figure out how to...how to fix all this."

How to get rid of me.

I gasp. How could I have entertained any thought of sticking around with a living person? Of course. He wants to get rid of me. He probably wants to get rid of his own daughter, too. We're not natural. We're frightening. Someone breaks the glass in one of the front windows and cheers and jeering rumble through the icy air drifting inside.

"Fuck!" Buddy yells. There's no more time, we have to leave right now, before these fans start crawling in like zombies.

Buddy flings the door open wide. "Get the hell off of my stairs or you're *all* gonna be ghosts."

People are filming, laughing, cheering.

He starts pushing through the crowd. Nobody seems willing to actually confront him, and people move backward out of his path. They're going to follow him, I realize. Whoever he goes, they'll be following.

Someone yells, "Wait, August is on his way!"

Buddy pauses for the briefest moment, I'm sure he's considering how great it would feel to give August a punch on the nose on camera and have them post *that* on their feeds, but in the end his mother's immediate need moves him forward. There's a small knot of people gathered around his cab, which is parked at the back of the small parking lot near the dumpsters.

"Don't touch that," Buddy says through gritted teeth as we approach. His face is purple with anger and embarrassment. People are shoving their phones directly in his face, screaming questions at him like he's a celebrity. I'm grateful I can't be seen, even though it's disappointing that even within this group of obviously hardcore supernatural enthusiasts, not a single one of them seems to share August Waters' gift. This isn't a case of just assuming I'm part of the crowd. I've got my arm looped through Buddy's to keep from getting separated. It would be obvious who I am if they were looking for me and could see me. The mysterious "Poppy."

We shove through the crowd of cell phones attached to waving arms and ignore every single question hurled in our direction (I will say that some of the questions *are* directed at me, even if they can't see me. There's the occasional, "Are you here with us, Poppy?" Thrown into the mix.), and I climb through the driver's side door quickly while Buddy is telling the arms and phones. "I'll be closing this door whether you're in the way or not, so think fast."

They think fast, and remove arms and fingers in time, but as soon as the door is shut, the hands start banging and knocking. I cover my ears and close my eyes. It's horrible and overwhelming.

The engine rumbles to life, and I can dimly hear Buddy shouting, "They'd better move!" And we rock forward. I chance a glance up. We're rolling slowly through the crowd, and people are parting last second like zipper teeth as they realize he doesn't intend on stopping. Once we get out of the lot, I let my hands slide down off of my ears and leave them trembling in my lap. I'm afraid to look at Buddy. I feel the anger coming off of him in waves of heat.

There's about three minutes of the worst silence before he says, "I didn't ask for this. I deserve privacy. My mother deserves privacy. And Addie, God. If she's there, she deserves privacy, too. We're not a sideshow. We'll go to the house. You tell Addie whatever you want to tell her. But then..."

Tears have been sliding down my face silently since the moment he opened his mouth. "Please," I whisper. "Let me try to fix it. I'm sorry."

"But then," he resumes, "you need to go. You can't just latch on to a random person and make yourself at home. It's not fair. You can't just tell some random celebrity about my life without my permission!"

"Buddy," I try again. But he can't hear me. Of course, he can't hear me. I shouldn't even be here. Who do I think I am?

"If you understand what I'm saying, turn on the radio." He brushes a tear off his cheek with venom as though it personally offended him, too.

It takes me almost a minute to push that stupid button, but I eventually get it done. A fresh wave of guilt surrounds me, and another set of tears blur my vision as John Denver tells us about Annie. Buddy has a few more tears fall, too, I think from the semi-regular snuffling sound I hear beside me. But I can't make myself look over at him.

August Waters: *All right, guys. That was. Incredible. I just can't believe it. Addie was no different to me than any other kid her age. She is* fully present *in that home, no ifs or buts. The guy at Emerald House seemed kind of vague, kind of distant. Confused. He was definitely not as impressed to be talking to me as I was to be talking to him. He was apathetic.*

Addie is so excited to talk. She's thrilled I can see her. She wants to be seen. But, guys. I can't ask the questions I want to ask to a little kid, you know? I don't want to scare her, and I don't want to make her sad. She knows she's dead, but I don't want to keep bringing it up. She's great for all this evidence, full of energy, but I need to talk to an adult ghost. I've got to find this "Poppy." If you know Buddy the truck driver, put the pressure on! If he wants to talk to his daughter, he's got to talk to me.

Chapter 12

We can only make it about a block away from Buddy's mother's house before he has to park the cab, no more room for street parking any closer. He pulls in behind a green station wagon with an *"I Want to Believe"* bumper sticker. The road is lined with cars and RVs, and there are people milling about the pavement like ants. Two police cars are flashing in front of the house, and orange sawhorses have been placed to block traffic in either direction. There are signs littering the ground. A news van looms on the far side of the sawhorse barricades, and just as many people and vehicles attempting to approach the house from that direction as well.

"What in the hell..." Buddy murmurs. He doesn't get out of the cab right away, instead he turns on his cell phone (he's had it off due to the constant stream of calls and texts), and dials. "Ma? Are you alright? I'm here I just..." He listens closely as she talks. I strain to hear her words, but don't catch any. "Okay. Let them know to let me through."

He gets out of the cab, and I scramble after him.

"Hey! Hey! Isn't that the guy? The dad!"

Here we go again.

I grab Buddy's elbow and allow him to pull me forward at a jog as he approaches the barricade. An officer steps out of one of the cruisers, saying something on his radio. He points at Buddy as the crowd gathers behind us, picking up volume as it congeals. "You the son?"

"Yes, sir," Buddy says.

The officer waves the pointing finger to the house. "Head on up, be quick."

Buddy steps around the sawhorse and jogs across the lawn, me on his heels. The pristine snow of Christmas is gone, the whole yard has been turned to muddy sludge by dozens of stamping, trespassing feet. Anger that was missing at the dingy apartment surges through me. This is his mother's *home*. How *dare* they treat it so disrespectfully? I feel Buddy's forearm writhe as his fists clench and unclench. He must be having similar thoughts, of course he's not forgetting that it's all my fault this is happening.

"Ah, shit," Buddy says, just as we reach the door. "The damn white board. I left the little one in the truck. Back to paper, I guess."

I *don't* want to be slowed down by having to write on paper, it was a lot more challenging. A second officer is waiting at the door, and ushers Buddy quickly inside. I follow, wait for the officer to lock the door behind us, then unlock it again and slip back outside. I make a mad dash for the cab, pushing through the regathered crowd. The officer that pointed us inside has not gotten back into his warm car, he's now standing guard at the barrier. There must be at least fifty people here.

No one is left standing at the cab this time, everyone has moved towards the house. I have no problem retrieving the smaller whiteboard. No one in this crowd sees me, either. By the time I've made it back to the barricade, the single officer is in trouble. He's on his radio, and the crowd is pushing close. Just as I'm stepping around, a woman near the front yells, "He can't stop all of us!" And launches herself over the sawhorse like she's diving into a swimming pool. She tumbles onto the icy pavement on the other side and then stands, arms raised in triumph. With her victory, the others take courage.

Damn. I left the front door unlocked for myself, and now it could allow any of these people access. I bolt across the grass, skid on refrozen mud, and land hard on my knees. My tights tear open and blood wells from long scrapes. As I'm clambering up to my feet again, the crowd of enthusiasts rattle the ground around me in their approach. I rush for the door, my breath coming in stitches from the pain, the cold air, and the fear of this ridiculous herd mentality.

I slam and lock the door shut behind me, and immediately there's pounding on the other side. I'm face to face with the other officer, on his way out for support. He has his gun drawn. I'm hit with a sense of unreality. I caused this. What if someone gets hurt?

I listen closely for Buddy's voice. I think I hear him from upstairs and place a foot on the first step. I look down and realize my knees are no longer torn up, though my tights are.

"Poppy!!!" A squealing voice is accompanied by thundering tiny feet. I look back up just in time to see Addie's smiling face for a moment before she's wrapped around my waist. "You came back!"

I hug her back as best I can. "I did! It's so good to see you, Addie. How are you? Are you okay?"

"There was a man here that said he was your friend, and he could see me! And he said he'd come back but then all these people were banging on the windows, and it's been so scary, but they were yelling *my name*! I thought maybe they could all see me, but I opened the door for a minute and yelled and none of them could see me. Why are they yelling if I can't even answer? Anyways Gramma is real upset she doesn't want all those people in the house, and they won't go away they've been here all day, and I guess they must be friends with your friend. Do you know all these people? Can you make them go away? I don't want them scaring Gramma anymore, I hate it when she's scared. Did you see? Daddy's here! He said that he needed to talk to Gramma and they went upstairs but I thought I heard someone come in and I thought it might be one of the people who can't see me, so I was going to come tell them to *go away* but it's you!"

Addie finally takes a breath. I take one with her, I'm exhausted just listening to all that. She's talking a mile a minute and dancing around and grabbing onto her clothes, fidgeting incessantly.

"Hey, let's go find your grandma and daddy," I say, instead of bothering to answer any of the questions peppered into the tirade.

"Poppy?" Buddy calls right at that moment. "Are you here? Geez, I hope she didn't get stuck in that nightmare out there."

Addie stops dead and goggles at me. "Can Daddy *see* you?"

I laugh. "I wish! We came up with another way to talk. Here, come see."

We dash to where Buddy and his mother are sitting at the kitchen table, me completely wrapped up in Addie's infectious enthusiasm. The crowd and Buddy's frustration with me both sink into the shadows in wake of the girl's brilliance. Buddy has a notebook in front of him. I scoot it out of the way and place the dry erase board there instead. I take the pen from his hand.

"Hey!" He says and then looks down. "Oh. Thanks."

I set the marker down next to the board and he picks it up.

His mother looks confused. "What?"

Buddy allows a small laugh. "Nothing, Ma. Alright. So, I'm going to put my hand here, and Poppy will guide it. She'll write messages to us. You ready, Poppy?"

"I want to try, I want to try!" Addie says, pushing in front of me.

"Here, watch me do it once and then you can try, okay?" I pull out a chair next to Buddy and pat it.

"Hmph. Okay." She flops dramatically into the chair.

I stand over Buddy and place my hands over his. "I'm going to tell them you want to try. Watch closely!"

Addie leans forward, nose inches from the board.

Addie wants to talk

Buddy looks down at the words, and I feel his grip on the marker loosen. "It's okay," I murmur, even though only Addie can hear. I trace a shiny scar on the back of his hand with my thumb unconsciously. To Addie, I say, "It's a little scary for them still." Scary might not be the right word, but I don't know how to express their sorrow and hope in a way appropriate for a five year old. Buddy's mother starts to cry.

A shot rings out from outside, followed by an uproar of dozens of screams.

"Jesus!" Buddy jumps up from the chair and grabs his mother by the shoulders. "Get down!" He guides her to the floor, kicking chairs out of the way. I grab Addie so she doesn't get knocked down by the chairs.

"What do we do?" his mother cries. "What do they want?"

"Don't worry, it's going to be okay," Buddy says. He sounds confident, but his eyes are sweeping the windows, listening, listening. "Let's just. Let's just play this little game down here on the floor. Okay." He clears his throat. "Addie?"

"He's talking to me!" Addie cries. "Did you hear?"

I can't help but smile. "Isn't it wonderful? Go ahead." I nod at Buddy's hand.

She scrambles over to him and grabs his wrist. She pauses for a second, then looks up at me. "I don't know how to write many words."

"That's okay! How about drawing a picture? Is there a picture you can do pretty well?"

"Hmm..." She considers.

"Is she here?" Buddy's mother asks.

"I'm not—wait. There! Look."

The two of them watch in awed silence as Addie guides his hand, her tongue sticking out in concentration. I wait, too. She draws two dashes, then a wide crescent. A smiling face. Then, she moves his hand to the bottom right of the board and starts to write again.

Addi

The "A" is huge, and each consecutive letter gets smaller. She runs out of room before she can fit the last one, so she drags his hand back up, smearing the other letters a bit. Above the A, she places a giant E.

"I ran out of space," she whispers. "Should I try again?"

I grin at her, as both Buddy and his mother stare down at the little white board as though it's made out of the most precious material in the world. "No, they love it. They know you're here."

The whole room seems to suddenly be underwater with the weight of realization. Neither Buddy nor his mother seem to be able to tear their eyes away from the sprawl of letters, and each of them has a hand clasped over their mouth. The resemblance between them in this moment is unbelievably striking.

Buddy clears his throat as though he might be ready to form a word or two, but three sharp raps on the front door bring us all back to the severity of the situation outside before he can push anything through.

"I'll get it," Buddy's mother says automatically, as though it's a normal day and it might be a postman.

"No, no, I should get it," Buddy says.

They compromise by both going. Addie grabs my hands, and we creep to the stairs and peer down to the foyer. Buddy opens the door only a two inch crack and peers through before ushering an officer inside. I don't remember if this is outside cop or inside cop. "Ms. Frances?" He tips his hat.

"Call me Sharleen, please. Is everyone okay?" *Sharleen*. I'm glad to have a name for her, finally. It suits her. I'll try to take better care of it than I did my own name.

"No one is hurt. We've received some backup from the city. There's been some arrests."

"Jesus," Buddy says. He looks like he'd like to open the door again and investigate, but the officer moves subtly to block him.

"One person fired a weapon into the air, you probably heard that. He says he was trying to get the crowd's attention for us, but discharging a firearm in a crowd is obviously a very serious offense, regardless of intentions. The arrests seem to have done a great deal of help to break up the gathering, though. Everyone is moving on."

"Well, that's good news." Sharleen sags a little. I didn't realize how much tension she'd had in her posture when they'd moved to the door.

"They might be back. We're going to keep an officer on patrol here for the next few hours, but..." But they can't stay indefinitely. That's what that sentence implies. I need to find the ghost hunter and have him call off his dogs.

"I need to call that ghost hunter and give him a piece of my mind," Buddy says as soon as he shuts the door on the officer.

"I don't know if that's a good idea," Sharleen says. "He films everything. Puts it all on his little channel. We don't want to make things worse. You should probably calm down first so you can be professional. He's in Illinois now. I told him I'd call when I was ready for him to come back."

"Oh, we don't want to make things worse?" Buddy turns on her. "Well, you could have fooled me, inviting him into the house and letting him use you. Use Addie like a TV prop! What were you thinking?"

"Why are they fighting?" Addie whispers, as Sharleen puffs right back up, ready to match Buddy's tone.

I bite my lip. "Hey, Addie? Want to come outside with me for a minute? I brought you something!"

Addie's eyes flick between her father and grandmother, face tense. Sharleen is currently shouting that it was *his* little ghost friend that brought August to her home. Buddy interrupts to tell her he had nothing to do with it and that he's not even sure who I really am.

"Uh, it's hard to go out..." Addie says. Her voice is soft and distant, barely an echo of the girl who was talking so fast a few minutes ago.

Sharleen is saying she's not really even sure she believes any of this anymore, how does she know Buddy wasn't drawing on the board on his own? She's saying her friend Mary says that August is a fraud, and maybe it's all a trick. She's saying Tom from church says there's a demon in the house, and using their grief to terrorize them.

"I'll hold your hand the whole time, and we'll come right back in," I say. "We're just going to go to the truck."

Buddy shouts that he's not crazy, and that Addie isn't a demon. He insists that if Sharleen had listened to him in the first place, none of this would be happening. Sharleen cuts him off to say *he's* never around to hear his daughter's ghost crying in the house, and maybe if he'd been around more, none of this would have happened. In fact, if he wasn't gone all the time, maybe Rebecca and Addie wouldn't have been out driving on such a snowy day, running errands that *he* could have been running for them. Buddy's retort is nothing more than an angry sob.

I grip Addie's hand. Her eyes haven't left them. "Is this my fault?" she whispers.

I have to get her out of here. What was I thinking, mixing a kid up in this? "How about I carry you?" I ask desperately.

Thankfully, she acquiesces to this and climbs up into my arms. The raised voices follow us all the way out, accusations flying. I hear my new name spit from Buddy's mouth like acid as I shut the door.

The street is thankfully mostly deserted. Yellow tape is now strung between the two sawhorses, which have been moved into the yard to allow traffic to pass. I step slowly and carefully through the icy mud, I don't want to fall with her in my arms. "What happened out here, like a party?" Addie asks.

"Kind of." I wish that I'd had more practice with kids while I was alive. I don't want to treat her below her age and understanding, but how much information is too much? I have no idea what's appropriate for a kid still small enough to carry.

"Are you mad at me?" A tiny sniffle follows the question, and my heart breaks.

"Oh, oh no, Addie. Of course, not. Nobody is mad at you." I break my promise and set her down in front of me to look at her. I wipe a tear away from her cheek. I've seen moms do that in the movies.

"Were all those people here for me?"

"Yep." I smile. "Because you're very special. They want to see you."

"They can't see me. I'm dead." She wrinkles her nose to dislodge some tear snot and wipes it up her forearm.

"People like Mr. Waters are, I think, very rare. But he's managed to show people that you're here, even if they can't see you. That's never really been done before." We start moving towards the cab again, hand in hand. I won't let her get lost. I won't let *us* get lost either.

"That's why Daddy's mad?"

"Kind of. He's not very happy with me, either. In fact, I might not be able to come back to visit for a while. I really want you to know that it's not because I'm mad at you and it's nothing you did wrong. I just...I shouldn't have ever really been at your house in the first place."

"Why?"

"Well, I didn't ask, I just invited myself. That's—"

"Very rude," Addie says promptly.

"Oh?" I can't help but laugh a little. I open up the passenger side door of the truck and Addie leaps inside.

"Yep! One time I walked home with my friend Ashley after church and stayed at her house for lunch. I told Mommy I was going and she said okay, but we didn't ask Ashley's mommy first. Ashley's mommy called and told Mommy that it was 'very rude'." Addie sits in the driver's seat and was tugging on the wheel, pretending to drive, but as she finishes the story she stops dead. "I forgot about Ashley."

I settle into the passenger seat. "But now you remember her." I am about to tell her to write down that story about Ashley so she doesn't forget again, but clamp my mouth shut. *I don't know how to write many words,* she'd admitted. Instead, I take out my own notebook and jot down:

Remind Addie: Remember your friend, Ashley? You went to church with her. Her mother was very rude.

She doesn't need to remember a grown woman calling her rude. I replace the book and rummage around under the seat. "All right!" I say, doing my best game show host voice. "For present number one!" I drag out the ceramic unicorn, leaving a trail of glitter on the floor mat. "Ta-da!"

Addie's eyes go round. "Wow!" She reaches for it.

"Now," I say, holding it slightly out of her reach. "This isn't technically a toy, it's more to look at. It's fragile. But," I place it in her outstretched hands. "If it breaks, it breaks. It's no big deal. Don't forget that, okay?"

She nods, gazing in reverent wonder. It may be the tackiest thing I've ever seen, but it was a good choice. I can actually see the fuchsia sparkles reflecting in her eyes. I want to bring her every single gift in the world.

"I should've saved that one for last, this other stuff might be boring." I stand up and rummage behind the seat until I find the mall shopping bags.

Addie squeals. "New clothes? For me?"

I nod. "I hope you like them. There's also a to-play-with pony!"

"I'll like them, I'll like them! I'm sick of this dress." Her head whips around to face the house. "Do you think they're done yelling? Can we go back?"

"I think we can go back," I say cautiously. "If they're still talking, you can just go try on your new clothes for a while, okay?"

"Are you really not going to visit anymore?"

I feel myself get clammy. I feel a little sick. Where will I go from here? What can I do to stop losing myself, if I can't focus on Addie? If I can't stay with Buddy? Will I find someone else to stick to like a parasite? My memory has been so much better since I've been with Buddy. If he won't have me around, I might lose everything I've managed to regain. "Maybe not. I'll talk to your daddy about it, okay?" Will I? Will he even give me the opportunity to?

"Do you have a house to go back to?" she asks. We're walking slowly back now, and she's hugging the unicorn to her chest like it's a stuffed animal. I'm carrying the shopping bags, but I've still got a hand on her shoulder, guiding her. "Do you get scared when you leave the house like me?"

"I don't really have a house of my own anymore," I say after some consideration. "Kind of like your daddy. He comes back here sometimes, or to his apartment, but most of the time he's just driving around with no house of his own."

"Do you have a truck, too?"

Just leeching off your dad's, actually. "Nope, but maybe I'll get one. They're pretty cool, right?" I open the door. Silence greets us, but it isn't the silence of peace. Addie's teeth are sunk into her bottom lip in apprehension, but her little shoulders ease as we cross the threshold.

We creep up the stairs, even though we both know it isn't necessary. Sharleen is on the couch, alone, clutching the whiteboard with Addie's drawing. "Should I go draw with her?" Addie whispers.

"Maybe not right now. I think she might ask you to, though, after she's had some time. Why don't you go try on your new clothes?" I hand her the bags, and she rushes down the hall with them, unicorn securely under one arm. I hear a door open and shut softly.

"Poppy?" Buddy's voice calls from the kitchen.

I feel like a misbehaving dog as I sidle around the corner. He has his back to me, leaning forward against a counter. I don't bother saying anything.

"If you're here, I want you gone. Don't follow me, and don't stay with my family." He doesn't turn, and his gaze must be focused on the empty counter in front of him, if his eyes are even open. His words are precise, like he's been reciting them in his head. "Just go."

My heart lurches. I can't just go, not now! Not when I have Addie to talk to. Not when I have Buddy, to sit with, to sing with, to write notes with. What if I forget he likes pistachio ice cream? How long will it take me to forget his dimples? We spoke! Buddy *knows* me, doesn't he?

Or maybe, I just know him. Just like I know the couple who lived in my farmhouse. Maybe I only feel like I know him because of all the time I spent beside him, unseen. Maybe I'm nothing more than an unwanted presence, after all. The hurt is almost more than I can bear, and my legs feel full of water. My lungs, too. I gasp for air I don't need.

I can't stay here, not now that I've been expressly told to leave, but I don't have to give up. August Waters is in Illinois, Sharleen had said. My home. I wonder if he lives in Chicago? I could go home, and I could find him. He could help me sort everything out with Buddy, I'm sure. He can be our mediator.

Saying goodbye to Addie would feel too final, so after staring at Buddy's turned away shoulders for too long, praying he'd change his mind and call me back, I slink past the hall she's down on tiptoes, hoping she'll remember that I said I might not be around for a while. I hope she doesn't forget me. I hope I don't forget her.

The cold hits me more forcefully as I step out their front door this final time. The front yard looks even uglier. I don't even know where I am. I think maybe I wrote down the address, the town, in my notebook, but I don't bother to get it out right now. What good would that do me now? I don't have a map.

I don't even have my map of *my* city. The front yard looks a mile wide between me and the street, and the idea of walking to the ghost hunter seems impossible, even though I have nothing but time. The sun is setting, and I turn my back on it and start walking. I don't even bother moving across the yard to the gravelly road, I just walk through the yards. As the crow flies is fine with me.

I've barely made it anywhere before a coal of panic in the pit of my stomach has a bright flare. "The ghost hunter," I murmur aloud, but I can't remember his name. I pause under a fragile looking naked maple tree and retrieve my notebook flip through its pages.

A man saw me on the train today. I trace my fingers over the indentions of my writing. I hope I'd had the presence of mind to write his name down somewhere in here.

And so, I've come back to the beginning. I sigh. At least he should be much easier to find, now, once I remember his name. Andy? Austin? I'll be able find his stream on any stranger's phone, or at the library. He'll announce where he's headed next, I can meet up with him, if I have enough time to get wherever that might be. Unless, of course, it's Sharleen's house. I'm not allowed there anymore. I crush my notebook against my chest, wishing it was Addie and Buddy in the embrace.

Crowd Dispersed by Law Enforcement, Two Arrested

The small town of Garden Grove, Iowa, woke up to a shock on Saturday morning when dozens of people appeared in a convoy and made camp on a residential lawn.

The crowd had signs and chanted, demanding to see "Addie," the supposed ghost girl caught on camera by ghost hunter, August Waters.

"We just want to talk to her," said a woman in the crowd, asking to remain anonymous. "They can't keep something as special as her hidden."

Garden Grove doesn't have its own police force and had to request back up from the neighboring town of Osceola. The home's resident could not be reached for comment, but was heard begging the crowd, "leave me in peace."

Chapter 13

It's so, so easy to lose myself in the monotony of walking. I hold my notebook clutched before me, a talisman. I talk out loud to myself, a habit it took ages for me to get out of, in the early days. I'd forgotten that until I started doing it again. I used to think that maybe I was just suffering from some kind of delusion. That maybe something horrific had happened, or maybe I'd just had a bad fever, and my mind just disconnected. Maybe I wasn't dead. Maybe I just pushed everyone I knew away or got lost. Maybe the woman whose house I inhabited, whose sickness I witnessed, whose eye color and chin I inherited, maybe she was a stranger, or a nurse. Maybe I invented her.

Maybe I hadn't been trying hard enough to draw attention from others. Maybe they were ignoring me just like they'd ignore any vagrant shouting at them. It's so easy to look the other way and pretend you don't notice them. I used to do it too. Maybe they donate to charities or even some very special ones volunteer at shelters, but they're not going to talk to a woman covered in urine muttering to herself on the train. I think maybe I spent a long time convincing myself that might be the case. I was just another person that somehow fell through those ever widening cracks in society, and I couldn't crawl back out again.

I started stealing, wearing nice clothes and makeup, keeping my hair glossy. I kept up with fashion. I didn't talk to myself anymore. I was polite. I was still invisible. That was the only time in my afterlife that I truly considered the idea of giving death a second opportunity to find me and finish the job. I spent a long time gazing into my own eyes that night. Could I do it? I could not. Even after death, the idea of ceasing to exist was the most terrifying idea. I vowed to keep the body I was trapped in safe and healthy for as long as I could manage, and I've mostly kept that promise. I get to keep so few promises.

My thoughts dance around that phrase. *Cease to exist*. Will I still be in there? When I finally become the monster I've been keeping at bay? Will my consciousness, my essence that I don't even truly have a name for, will she be locked inside?

I think about the spider in the farmhouse, with all of those hideous grasping hands. What might it have been? Who might be trapped in there, forever searching, reaching, touching.

What will I become?

It's a dangerous thought to dwell on while I'm all alone and so far from my city. But, oh, how I can't help but dwell.

It's full dark, and the stars are more beautiful than I've ever seen. I don't know if it's the low temperature or the lack of light pollution, or both, but every little pinprick of light up there seems fully alive and the blackness in between doesn't look like the flat blanket of two dimensional dark that I'm used to, but the actual expanse that it is, stretching away from me forever. I get a jolt panic in my stomach when I look straight up, like at any moment I might start falling. Thankfully, my path is finally considering leaving the endless barren fields of untouched snow hiding viciously stabbing dead corn stalks, and a town is on the horizon.

I change my trajectory ever so slightly to aim for a gas station on the north side of the town. It looks like the only business that's still open this time of night, whatever this time of night might be. The ever repeating landscape is skewing my perception of the distance. How far is that gas station? A mile? Two? The only sounds are my crunching feet and regular loud breaths, vapor puffing up and clouding my vision for a moment on every exhale. I stop for a moment to wipe the condensation from my freezing face and slow down my breaths. No reason to hurry. I hardly have anywhere to be.

Crunch, crunch.

I pull my sleeves away from my face slowly. Did I hear that? More steps after mine? I hold my breath to listen more closely. I assume there are animals out here, rabbits and the like, I'm not really sure what animals are out and about in the winter. In the city, the rats and pigeons are out year round. I spin, scanning the ground in a circle around me.

There's someone else standing in the field, maybe thirty feet behind me.

I say, "someone," for lack of a better phrase. It's certainly not a "something," because it must have moved. I most certainly stood where it is standing now only a moment ago. The stars are bright, and my eyes are well adjusted to the darkness, having been walking in it all night. I have no trouble seeing them.

My mind says "scarecrow," though it doesn't look like any scarecrow I've ever seen. It stands at least seven feet tall. Its parts are all in semblance of a human, but the proportions are very, very wrong, and very unsettling at this size. The head is perfectly circular from the front, and a full third of the thing's height. Even from this distance I can see the clumsy stitching holding the front and back panels of rough burlap together. Red yarn hair jabs straight up in a fringe from the top of the stitching, stretching another foot into the air, and the same yarn has been clumsily looped through the face to make a childish smile. Black buttons the size of my open palms are stitched on for eyes, and they catch the starlight as the thing finally breaks its stillness and tilts its head just a bit in my direction. It's a handmade child's doll, but for an unimaginably enormous child.

My first instinct is, of course, to run screaming into the night in the opposite direction. I take two steps backward, and it takes two steps forward at the same time. How long has it been following me?

My second thought is: *This will be me.*

I wrestle with myself. Should I attempt to communicate? How long has it been wandering out here? I take in the doll more closely. Its arms are shapeless tied off knots of burlap, short and stubby, with no joint. Its legs are the same, only a little longer. It wears some kind of either smock or overalls, that I think might be blue if it weren't so washed out in the starlight. It's a very old doll. Maybe a very old ghost.

I take a shuddering step towards it.

It takes a step back.

This gives me some courage, and I manage to stammer, "Hel-lo?"

There is an unknowable amount of time where the doll and I both stand motionless and silent. My courage is leaving me. It's so utterly *wrong* to look at. I jump back when it decides to move on its own for the first time, taking one awkward wobbling step forward. It's whole body rocks and tilts wildly with each step. It is not a thing that was ever meant to stand without the guiding hand of a child.

"Hello?"

It's a perfect, exact mimicry of my own voice. The pitch, the tone, completely identical, like a recording played back. "Oh...no," I mutter. Can't do it. Not tonight. Not alone. I turn slowly back to face my destination, that brightly lit gas station.

Crunch. "Hello?"

I start walking briskly.

Crunch, crunch, crunch.

"Hello? Hello?"

I start to jog as best I can over the uneven terrain.

"Oh...no." The words are still my own, and as quiet as I said them, but much too close for my liking. The crunching comes faster, louder, more erratic.

The mile or so away the gas station seemed to be a minute ago now seems like five, ten. It might be on the moon.

"Hello?"

I turn to look back. I don't know why.

The doll has gained on me, I'm not sure how on those stumpy impossible legs, but it's looming, only two or three feet behind, wobbling closer. Its giant moon head is blocking out the light of the stars.

My boot catches on a jagged corn stalk and I feel the sole tear partially away from the upper. I come down and bend the sole backward with my weight, throwing me face first into the snow.

"Oh...no," the doll mutters, and tumbles on top of me.

I think I'll be crushed beneath its weight but am happy to find it stuffed with not straw, but maybe corn husks. It's light for its size, and malleable. I'm far more damaged from my awkward tumble to the icy ground. I shove it off of me and stand as quickly as I can. My palms and knees are burning with scrapes. I turn to continue my escape, sure to be slower now on my ruined shoe.

"Hello?"

I bite my lip and look down. The monstrous thing is flopping like a fish on land. Its little arms and legs can't get that giant head off the ground. I hover in indecision. I can't just leave it like this, can I?

I move in a wide arc around it, to look down at its face. "Hey. Can I...help you?"

It stops its fruitless flapping and rotates the wide flat disc of a head sideways to (presumably) gaze up at me with those buttons.

I squat down. "What's your name?"

At the question, it begins to jitter obscenely, like it isn't corn husks inside, but thousands of cockroaches. I shoot back up and take and involuntary step back. My skin is crawling. I should have kept running.

"whatsyournamewhatsyournamewhatsyourname"

The voice (my voice) doesn't come from its thread smile. It comes from somewhere under that blue smock, or maybe from everywhere. It doesn't stop. It repeats the phrase with zero pause besides the ones in my own cadence. As I stand there gawping, it pushes its head against the ground and raises its midsection into an arch, little arms waving.

"whatsyournamewhatsyournamewhatsyourname"

It heaves itself forward, and is suddenly standing huge before me, my own words blasting me in the face. As it looms above me, panic consumes me completely. I reach down and rip the sole the rest of the way off my boot and hurl it directly at a button. I don't wait to see if it has any impact, I turn and start hobbling toward the gas station as fast as I can manage. The crunch of its footsteps immediately follows, but my words are sounding further and further away. My panic is clawing me, completely drowning out my tiny rational voice asking, *what could it possibly do? Why can't you stay and help?* The thing is just too big, too wrong, too unnatural and downright frightening on purpose. Why do they all have to be so scary? I'm not a brave person. I don't know if I was while I was alive, but whoever I was then is completely lost now. I don't share anything with her anymore, not even her name.

I lose my footing again as soon as I step from the crunching grass onto the slick asphalt and grab onto the back of a green station wagon for balance. It has an "I Want to Believe" bumper sticker. It seems fleetingly familiar.

"Oh...no." I look back toward the field and see that the doll has not pursued me onto the strip of grass that separates the field from the station. It stands, perfectly motionless again, at the very edge of the tilled earth. "Oh...no."

I take out my notebook, and scribble.

Scarecrow, due east of Addie's town. Cornfield.

"I'll come back," I call. "I'll come back and help."

The doll doesn't move, but as I turn and limp towards the outrageous normality of the station, I dimly hear my voice: "Help."

NEW HAUNTING FOOTAGE FROM PARANORMAL INVESTIGATOR

August Rivers has officially taken the internet by storm with his newest livestream, capturing what seems to be the ghost of a five-year-old child. Experts are coming up empty as they attempt to debunk the footage. Ms. Shirley O'Bannon is quoted as saying, "This is the most compelling footage for the case of life after death we have ever seen. It's truly spectacular footage."

Our reporters have found the child in question to be Adeline Frances, child of Rebecca and Sean Frances, of Iowa. Rebecca and Adeline tragically lost their lives in a vehicle collision three years ago. Sean Frances could not be reached for comment.

August Rivers' new television series, rumored to be his ghost hunts on a bigger scale, is set to begin filming this summer.

Chapter 14

This isn't a giant truck stop like the one I met Buddy for the first time in, this one just has snacks and drinks, and a few racks of traveler friendly items. It seems raucously loud in here for the time of night it must be, and I pin the noise on a group of four young adults, calling back on forth to each other over the aisles. They seem hyper and giggly, like they've just returned from a live concert. The middle aged clerk is busying herself with a novel behind the counter, occasionally blessing the group with a scowl over the top of the yellowing pages.

It's warm and bright in here, but I'm shivering convulsively. I think it must be more from the encounter in the field than the cold walk. On the bright side, my injury theory is holding true, as I crossed the threshold in the station, my hands and knees returned to their regular, pre-cornfield tumble state. I flex my fingers.

The same can't be said about my poor boot, which has served valiantly but is definitely beyond saving. The other one isn't looking so hot either, to be honest. They weren't really made for walking. My tights are still torn from my fall in Sharleen's yard earlier (yesterday?), and I smell vaguely like tilled earth from my scarecrow encounter. I need a bath and some new clothes.

I'm perusing a spinning rack of flip flops shaped like fish and personalized key chains when I hear, "I wish August would have shown up. That would have made the whole trip worth it even if we didn't get in."

I accidentally knock a keychain that bizarrely reads, "Amandas are princesses, but Mandys are Queens!" to the floor in my haste to move closer to the speaker.

It's a man, probably a little younger than I was. He's wearing a smelly leather jacket covered in pins that is definitely too small to fit over his protruding belly, so I can read his t-shirt, or, I should be able to read his t-shirt, but it's a band logo in a font so severe it's illegible. He's got fine, unwashed long hair sticking to his sweaty neck, and thick glasses that were in style when I was a child. He says, "Maybe we should just head to his next haunt and try to meet him."

"I can't," whines a younger girl, abandoning a bag of pork rinds she'd been making fun of. Her intricately applied eyeliner probably looked amazing twelve hours ago, but now it's smeared down the side of her acned face where she's obviously been sleeping. Whatever she might be wearing is completely hidden under a giant army jacket that hangs past her knees. I eye her combat boots and wish I had a pair. "I have class tomorrow. I've gotta get back."

"Just skip, who cares?" asks the man. "College is for sheep."

The girl bites her lip, unwilling to argue.

"Yeah, come on, babe, where's your sense of adventure? This is a quest, remember?"

I roll my eyes before I can even focus on this new speaker, who has sidled around the rack I'd been perusing. This one is another man, more my age, probably. Definitely the oldest of the three. His hair and beard are dyed a crimson red, and he is wearing red tinted sunglasses. Inside. At night. My eyes have perhaps made a full roll at this point.

These three were obviously part of the group harassing Sharleen and Addie. If I hitch a ride with them, maybe I can learn where August is headed next, or, if I'm very lucky and eyeliner girl is very unlucky, they might even take me right to him.

"We're done!" calls a fourth voice, and the other three drop whatever they're holding and sprint towards the exit.

Startled, I dash after them as quickly as I can with my shoe situation. The clerk stands just as I'm running through the door, the last of the group. "Hey," she calls uncertainly, and then, "Hey! Stop!"

Unsurprisingly, we are climbing into the green station wagon. It appears Leather Jacket may be the owner, as he hops into the driver's seat, gasping for air. I dive into the middle of the backseat, knocking fast food wrappers and half empty drink containers to the floor. Eyeliner hasn't even fully closed the door I dove through before we're peeling away into the night. The car immediately slides on the icy pavement and fishtails, bumping one of the concrete barricades that protect the gas pumps.

"Watch it, you want to get us blown up?" Sunglasses yells. He's sitting on my right and Eyeliner on my left. The mystery fourth person is in the passenger seat, digging through a backpack on the seat beside them. It's too dark to make them out properly, especially compared to the full fluorescent view I've gotten of the other three, but they are small, their head hidden completely behind the wagon's low headrests.

"It's fine, it's fine," Jacket says through heavy breaths. "What'd ya grab us, Toph?"

"Hmm," the small person, apparently Toph, says. "I got hot fries and pretzels, energy drinks...jerky. About twenty candy bars. She couldn't see the candy bar aisle."

"Any beer?" Sunglasses asks.

"You don't need any beer. You're already an asshole," Toph replies.

"You guys," says Eyeliner. "I really don't like this. Why don't I just call my dad? I'm sure he could lend me—"

"Your dad will call the cops on us and say we kidnapped you. You know how he is," Jacket says.

"You mean he knows how *Stephen* is." Toph's voice is muffled by the backpack—she's basically halfway inside it—pulling out the snacks.

Eyeliner has already given up her argument again and leans the smeared side of her face against the window, completing the puzzle. She mutters, "We didn't even need that stuff." But no one hears her except me.

"What is your problem with me today?" Sunglasses says, punching the back of the seat. "And don't call me Stephen. It's Onyx."

"You're too old for a new nickname." Toph surfaces from the bag. "Among other things." She looks pointedly at Eyeliner, and as she turns, I finally get a glimpse of her face. She's older than I thought she'd be, maybe in her thirties. Her face is pointed, and every feature is small. Her hair is short in a way that says she has a shaved head but also forgets to keep it shorn. She has an outline of a star tattooed or drawn over one entire eye socket. She turns and holds Stephen/Onyx's eye for a long enough time that I assume there's some history between them, and all the heartache that belongs to history.

"So..." Jacket says too loudly, reminding everyone he's still there, and also that they're in *his* car. "Where am I heading? Back to Champaign for our civilized student? Or onward to St. Louis to speak with the Speaker?"

"Can you maybe...drop me off on the way?" Eyeliner leans forward and whispers.

Onyx reaches across my lap and grabs her upper arm. Too tightly. I scowl. "Hey, it's just one more day, then we'll get you back to school. It wouldn't be on the way to drop you off. Besides, you don't want to miss your chance to talk to him, do you?"

There's a car on the highway behind us, filling the top half of the car with bright white headlights, so while Eyeliner is leaned forward, her face is illuminated so well that I can see tears starting to form in her eyes, her bottom lip starting to tremble. She leans back into darkness, breaking out of his grip.

"Hey!" Onyx reaches across me again, more aggressively, and reaches toward the girl.

"Knock it off." I say and bat his hand away.

He leans back, sulky.

"Everybody, shut up!" Toph screams, holding her arms out like she's trapped in a glass box. "I felt something."

The mood in the car shifts dramatically. Both the other back-seat passengers lean forward, all animosity forgotten. Jacket unconsciously lets the car slow to a crawl and the car behind us zooms around, horn blaring.

"Pull over," Toph says.

"What?" Jacket says.

"I said *pull over*. Now."

Jacket does as he's told and guides the car to the shoulder. He puts on the hazard lights and the *click-click* of them fills the car, but Toph reached over and snaps them off again. There are two minutes of full, tense silence.

Finally, Toph clears her throat. The others lean even closer. I find myself squished shoulder to shoulder. "Please, spirit, use my voice and body to guide our way. I feel you near."

I look from Eyeliner to Onyx with a raised eyebrow. Is she talking to *me?*

"Um. Well, hello to you, too, I guess." I say awkwardly.

Toph's head drops to her chest, her shoulders go slack. She inhales in a sickly, wheezing way that sounds painful. Like a gasp before death. She says, in a deep, rasping voice that is barely recognizable as her own, "You must go, my children. Go to the Speaker."

What the hell is going on here? I crawl up over the seat to look at her more closely. She gives another horrible breath and says, "I am here with you now, and will know if you disobey. You will suffer."

Her eyelids flutter. Her body goes rigid. She gasps with her own small voice like she's coming up out of deep water. "It's gone," she says.

The others applaud and cheer and high five one another.

"So, we've gotta go!" Onyx says. "The spirits want us to go so we can communicate!"

I consider just getting out of the car and walking in that moment. I wonder how they met. An internet chatroom? Probably. I wonder if this Toph character is charging the others for her "services." Definitely. One thing is for certain, the only spirit in this car is me. Toph is full of shit.

But, I only have one shoe. I need a bath. And they're heading where I'm headed, so might as well stay. I'm glad I'm here to continually be in between Onyx's grabby hands and this poor girl sitting next to me. I wish I could somehow tell her that she's not going to find whatever she'd looking for with this group. From their little comments as we continue down the road, I gather that she's lost someone close to her that she'd like to find. She must think they're out here somewhere, wandering. Maybe they are, but I hope instead she finds herself, and her voice, and tells this creepy old guy to fuck off.

Leather Jacket is called Simon, it turns out, and he's a know it all. Also, supposedly a skeptic, just here to prove that August's video are fakes. I saw him when Toph was putting on her little act, though. He really *does* want to believe. He keeps turning up the volume on the stereo to listen to bands I've never heard of and don't really understand, and Toph keeps reaching over and dialing the volume back down to almost inaudible, saying the music "disrupts the energies." She's done two more little puppeteer tricks while I've been in the car, though neither were deemed important enough to pull the car over again.

She's also regaled the group with tales from all the places she's been, all the people she knows, all the miracles she'd witnessed. They hang on her every word, Eyeliner's eyes full of stars. I've decided, in my two hours spent with them, that Onyx is in love with Toph. They were obviously an item in the past, and he hasn't given up on her. I've also decided that Toph digs him up whenever she needs something from him. Onyx probably only brought this young, pretty girl along as some kind of barrier to keep himself from getting screwed over as badly this time.

I watch Toph as she waits for some kind of lapse of faith in their mission to arise before she puts on a little show to keep them believing and excited again. I watch her silently prepare for each act, a sip of water and a roll of her neck to loosen up the muscles. She's a straight up fraud, in everything she does. If these other three weren't so blinded by hope (and in Onyx's case, maybe love), they'd see it, too.

They talk about August Waters constantly. He's almost like some kind of god to them, a beacon showing them there's a world beyond the not so great one they've lived in so far. I get to hear about several of his streams in great detail, with colorful commentary and good natured bickering between Simon and the rest about the legitimacies. Simon and Toph both agree to listen to a few interviews August had done recently over the stereo, during which they attempt to find hidden meaning behind each mundane word he speaks.

I also hear Addie's giggle.

By the time the sun is rising, I'm ready to jump out of the car as it seemingly crawls down the interstate at seventy miles an hour. Each second with the group is grating on me worse than the last. Eyeliner (who not a single person in the car has spoken to or about by name throughout this entire journey) has taken off her shoes to curl up and sleep more comfortably against the window. I pick one up. They're my size, dang it. Could I steal this poor girl's shoes? No. I couldn't. She's having a bad enough day as it is. I sigh and place it back on the floorboard.

"Welp," says Simon. "We're here."

I lean forward. There, on the horizon, I see the Gateway Arch. Unexpectedly, I start to cry. I miss Buddy so much already. I don't like these people. I feel like I want to go home, and surprise myself by realizing "home" means the passenger side of his cab to me.

"It makes me feel sad," Eyeliner murmurs. I didn't realize she was awake.

"What does?" Simon asks. Both Toph and Onyx are passed out, Onyx snoring lightly.

"The Arch. I don't know why. I just look at it and feel sad. Homesick."

I wipe my tears from my cheeks and clear my stuffy throat and nose. Is it me? Maybe she can't chat with me like August might be able to, but does she feel me here beside her? Probably it's just wishful thinking, and we're both just feeling homesick. I touch her hand, and she doesn't react. "Sorry," I whisper to her. "I'll be gone soon."

Simon hollers for the other two to wake, and they both groggily join the conversation again. Toph cracks her window and lights a cigarette, Simon reminds her she agreed not to smoke in the car. Chaos ensues for a minute, everyone yelling at each other, which ends with the compromise of Toph smoking in the car. They each dig through the backpack and have breakfasts of warm energy drinks and melted candy bars (the bag has been sitting too close to the heat vent all night). All in all, it's a disappointing morning, and not the heroic adventure Onyx had talked up while they were robbing the gas station.

Simon punches an address into the GPS from August's "tour" website, and we leave the highway and start crawling through the city streets. It's rush hour, and the traffic is dismal. I want to get out and start walking, but Simon doesn't keep his phone in a holder like Buddy does, and I can't see the address we're heading for. Only a little while longer.

"How much longer?" Onyx whines. "I've gotta piss."

"Lovely." Toph groans.

"What? Everybody pisses."

Simon looks at his lap. "Supposedly nineteen minutes. But we're early. Want to stop?"

Everyone agrees. Eyeliner wants to redo her face, Toph needs cigarettes (Eyeliner offers to buy them nervously). It turns out that the nearest gas station is four miles back the way we've come from. The entire car groans, me included.

"Well, I need to get gas, too. Otherwise, we're all walking." Simon pulls a U-turn and cuts off a pickup truck without a second thought. We slide around the backseat until I'm basically on Onyx's lap. He smells awful. Not that I can talk, I know I look and smell worse than any of them, or I would if anyone could see or smell me. I worry briefly about meeting August in these conditions and decide it's time to break away from my taxi.

I lean forward over the front seat until my shoulders are between Simon and Toph's, and snatch Simon's cell phone from where he has it jammed under his thigh. I sit back and hastily scribble the address into my notebook, before realizing that the address is for the gas station. "Shit." I try to go back and find the previously entered address, but this map app is different than the one Buddy has, and I'm clumsy with it. The phone shouts, "In five hundred feet, turn left onto cypress avenue."

I freeze, like the occupants of the car might suddenly realize Simon's phone is in my hand instead of where it should be. Of course, nobody notices. I've spent so much time with Buddy that I've almost forgotten that the average person would let me grab onto the steering wheel and direct the car straight into oncoming traffic without ever noticing me. I can do whatever I want and say whatever I want, and here I've been sitting quietly and respectfully in a car full of assholes. I put my feet up on the seat in front of me to prove that I can and take the next few minutes figuring out how to use Simon's phone without worry.

Finally, I figure out the address. I double check by inserting it into a search engine, which shows me several results about the house's supposedly haunted history, and also many telling me that the famous August Waters will be streaming from there this evening. Satisfied, I write it down.

The GPS finally guides us into a parking lot, and I hop out and stretch with the rest. I take my shoes off completely. It'll hurt my feet less to be barefoot than to continue to walk awkwardly on one sole. I deposit them in the trash and walk away from the group and the car, not looking back even once.

Host: Welcome back, and here we are with our most anticipated guest of the hour, paranormal investigator, August Waters. How are you doing today, Mr. Waters?

August Waters: I'm doing alright, Jeff. And who's your friend?

Host: My...what?

August: Ah, I'm just joshing you, man.

Host: Oh, haha. Ah. Anyway, you're enjoying quite a bit of new respect these days from both skeptics and believers alike. Can you tell us a little bit about your newest video? About Addie?

August: Well, you've all seen it. Addie is caught on film laughing and speaking, manipulating objects, and there are even a few frames where her form is fully visible. There's no denying it, there's the ghost of a child in that house, and she is present and capable of communication.

Host: Are you planning to meet with Addie again? To ask her some of the harder hitting questions?

August: Unfortunately, the owner of the house is, understandably of course, pretty freaked out. As of right now, she doesn't want us to come back.

Host: What? She doesn't want to hear from her granddaughter? You'd think she would be ecstatic.

August: Well, you know how a certain type of old person is. She started thinking maybe it's 'demon' or whatever, and now she doesn't want to take any chances.

Host: A demon? Have you ever come across anything like that?

August: Nah, dude! Demons aren't real.

Host: You say that like many people say, "Ghosts aren't real."

August: Not after they see that footage of Addie. Listen folks, I might not be able to get to talk to Addie again, but I've got high hopes of finding her 'friend,' a potential ghost traveling with Addie's father. I've now found that his real name is Sean Frances. Sean, if you're out there, you are being haunted, and I can help.

Host: Is being haunted dangerous?

August: No, but he has something really precious following him around that I'd like to get a chance to speak with. It's imperative. We've got to find Sean 'Buddy' Frances.

Host: Haha, alright. That brings me to my next question: There have been reports of your fans being...a little assertive in their attempts to see Addie. Have you heard anything about that? People bothering a woman in her home? I even heard the word 'mob' thrown around...

August: I haven't heard anything about that. People are excited, *Jeff*. This *is* life changing. Death changing, too. No wonder people are a little excitable about it.

Host: Well, I'm sure you can't wait to give them more footage with your new show!

Chapter 15

The gas station is at a fairly busy intersection in an all commercial area. There's a Walmart on the opposite corner, and a hotel shares its parking lot. Perfect. As I walk barefoot across the several lanes of traffic, I feel that pang again. I remember walking to the Denny's. I remember our server's face. I remember Buddy chose a blue crayon and asked the server if they could see the "Hi!" we'd written there. I smile. I'm so glad I remember. I've just got to hold those memories tight. They're slippery, but manageable.

I watch over the hotel manager's shoulder as they enter a guest for check in. I try to do it myself, but must be missing a step, I can't get to the screen where I'm supposed to scan the key card to make it work for the door. I have to wait to watch twice more before I finally manage it on my own. I miss the days of physical keys that fit into toothed locks, this magnet stuff is confusing.

I open the door and breathe in the overly cold hotel room air. It's a very particular smell. It's interesting how it lessens the longer a person stays in the room. Do we get used to it, or is that first blast just the smell of emptiness, and we fill it up by temporarily living there? Well, I don't *live* anywhere. Not anymore. But that smell of air conditioning, even in the winter time, of slightly damp carpet and newly laundered sheets, it still does make less of an impression every time I open the door in the same room.

The shower is the most amazing thing I've done in a long time. I honestly can't remember the last time I showered, which is very much not like me. I've just been...what have I been? I've been busy. I've been away. There's a hair dryer attached to the wall, but no hairbrush of course, so my hair doesn't look as nice as I'd like, but at least it's not covered in dirt. My face is clean, pale, sad. I pull a sad clown face at myself, dramatically downturned lips, eyes rolled up. I let out a little moaning wail of anguish. There. Proper ghost. *Attic Spider.* I shiver at the comparison, the memory.

I don't want to put the filthy and torn clothes I was wearing back on, so I steal the robe out of the wardrobe that has the hotel's name embroidered over the pocket. I wish I had shoes—my feet will get all dirty again on my way to the store.

I keep my hotel key card. Maybe I'll come back here and put on makeup and wash my feet before I go find August. I want to look presentable and smart. I want him to listen to what I've got to say about Buddy's family. His fans look at him like some kind of deity, I'm sure they'll listen if he lays down the law. Maybe this will be a learning opportunity for him, and he'll be more careful about the information he divulges about his cases in the future.

The ground is freezing under my bare feet, and I have to tread carefully so as not to cut myself on any rough patches. St. Louis hasn't gotten the snow that Iowa and Illinois have been covered in for months, but it's still uncomfortably chilly, especially wearing satin. The knowledge that I won't freeze to "death" and that my feet will heal does calm my anxieties tremendously, but I also have to admit that I'm a tiny bit disappointed. *There's no way out.*

I take my time in the store. I try on several outfits and many shoes, for once thinking about function over style...at least for the shoes. My clothes are always going to be cute, first and foremost. I wander to the cosmetics and peruse and brush my hair right there in the aisle. I pick my stray strands from the tines and place them in my pocket before returning the brush. I'm not a monster. Yet. An image flashes into my head of me as a Cousin It style creature whose sole purpose is to leave long hairs that aren't yours on your brushes and in your showers. I laugh but then banish the idea as thoroughly as I can. What if it comes true?

The last thing on my short shopping list is a new coat. I've saved it for last because I'm excited, I love outerwear. I'll attribute that to memories of my life walking in the city, even though the only walk I can clearly remember is that last, sticky hot night. There are a lot of nice options here, actually. Since I don't pay for anything, I usually go right to fancy department stores, but it seems there's really nothing wrong with a Walmart coat. After an hour or so of trying on every one, I choose a long faux wool duffle coat with big, square pockets. There's a large pocket in the inner lining that I think will be perfect for my notebook, which is the most important feature.

I panic a little when I pat myself and realize my notebook is not with me. But of course, the hotel robe I walked in wearing had no pockets. I must have left it at the hotel. My panic returns as I realize I don't have my keycard. I distinctly remember thinking to bring it.

I quickly choose a purse and store the cosmetics I decided on, and retrace my steps along the giant store, heart thudding more urgently with every empty expanse of floor. I see the robe I carelessly flung off and kicked to the side under a row of bathing suit covers (summer is coming eventually, I guess), and rush to it. I run the fabric through my fingers and, there. A rectangle of hard plastic within the folds. There *was* a pocket in the robe, after all.

My heart doesn't cease its panicked thrumming. A little voice in my head is reminding me over and over, *you're forgetting.*

You'll lose yourself. Hair monster. I start to run. I need my notebook. I need to refresh.

The hotel door opens at my keycard's touch, even though I was sure it wouldn't, that I'd have to search every room to find my things. My ruined clothes and shoes are laying just where I left them. My breathing starts to even out. Everything will be fine.

My notebook is not with my clothes. It's not in the pockets, it's not set aside anywhere in the room. It's not here.

I must have left it in that awful station wagon, when I had it out to copy the address August is heading to. "This is fine," I say out loud. Sometimes, I guess it's okay to talk out loud. Sometimes I just need someone to reassure me, and it's going to have to be me. "I'll just go find the car. I know where they were going."

But, I *don't* know where they were going. I wrote it down in my lost notebook, but I certainly don't remember the address now. Not even the street name.

In the lobby, there are two ancient computers and a fax machine in a little glass box of a room near the front desk. My key card opens the door. After several horrendously frustrating minutes trying to figure out how to use the hotel's convoluted login process, I have access to (albeit horribly slow) internet.

I type "*August ghost hunter*" into the search engine and come across mostly news articles. The headlines are sensationalist, he's a messenger of God, he's an alien, he's actually dead. I don't click on any of them, searching for his actual website. The list of tour dates I find is frustratingly vague (that he's currently in St. Louis is all he's officially told his fans), and without remembering the house address, I realize I'm going to have to deep dive into forums. I groan.

The forum threads hurt, just like I knew they would. There are dozens of paparazzi style photos of Buddy, some of which were at times and places that I know I was accompanying him, which makes everything feel worse. In fact, here's what looks like a still of surveillance footage from Denny's. Our server must be in the forum. And Addie's obituary appears several times along with her school photo. Sharleen and Rebecca are both also being exposed, dissected, discussed. It doesn't seem like any participant thinks of them as real people, they're more like fictional characters without feelings, or at best celebrities. It's disgusting. I scroll through as quickly as I can until I come across a sub thread with a link to another website titled: "Where's August?"

Finally, a list of addresses, complete with names of the families that live at each address, and people that may or may not be haunting those addresses. I feel gross using the list, but find what I'm looking for. The printer costs seventy five cents per page (credit card only), so I hop up and dash towards the front desk to procure a pen.

I swing the glass door open and slam it straight into a woman carrying camera equipment walking down the hall. "Oh geez, I'm so sorry," I say out of habit. "Are you okay?"

She stumbles slightly and looks down at the arm that I've just smashed into, but is oblivious to me. She looks kind of familiar, but I can't quite place her. She has what my mother would have called "a face for the pictures," definitely someone to be remembered, very beautiful. She's dark skinned, and has long braids in varying shades of purple tied into a thick ponytail, and purple lipstick to match.

Just as her name comes to me, it's shouted. "Amethyst! Are you still in here?"

She turns back to the direction of the elevators around the corner, equipment jangling slightly on its straps. "Here!"

"Did you grab the headlamps?"

I know that voice. I gasp.

Amethyst gives a long suffering sigh and stomps back down the hallway. I follow, pen forgotten and now unneeded. August Waters stands before me, holding the elevator door open with his leaning body. His arms are crossed, and he's carrying nothing.

He lets Amethyst into the elevator and the doors start to close, but he remains in the hall with me. "Hey!" Amethyst calls through the sliding door. "You could at least take this stuff to the van!"

The door shuts completely, and August says, "Whoops." unconvincingly. He starts to stroll towards the lobby, and I fall in step beside him. After four or five steps, he says, without turning to look over at me, "Look. I'll give you my autograph if you don't tell anyone where I'm staying."

"Fame not all it's cracked up to be?" I ask. I'm keeping up with him, but follow his lead and don't turn my head as I talk.

He stops, so I do, too. He glares at me. "Do I know you?"

"Not formally." I stick out a hand to be shaken. "Poppy."

Instead of taking my hand, or even looking at me more closely, his eyes sweep the hallway, as if expecting a camera crew to be filming. "Oh, yeah? You're like the fourth 'Poppy' that's introduced themselves to me this week. Nice gag. See you on the stream."

I grab hold of his jacket as he starts to turn away. "It's actually me this time. Don't you remember me, from the train?"

Now he stares at me. "How did you know about that?"

I can't help but grin like an idiot. I can't believe he's actually here. I guess I was due for a little good luck. "It's difficult to forget the first time someone makes eye contact with you in almost sixty years, you know."

"Holy shit. Holy. Shit. It really is you," he says. He runs a hand through his hair, and it falls perfectly back into place. Another face for the pictures. "Alright, we're going to have to get this on film. My guys are packing up, but—"

"Let's hold off on the cameras for a bit, okay? I need to talk to you. About the Frances family."

The laugh that comes out of him immediately makes my blood boil, and he waves a dismissive hand. "Old news. We don't need them anymore. Some government agency hit me up and said they might need my cooperation running some tests in the house to get more info on the kid and I said sure thing, but they won't allow it to be filmed for the show so that's back burner shit. They can figure out how to talk to her the hard way."

"I'm sorry," I stammer. "What? Did the Frances' agree to that?"

August gives an uninterested shrug. "Does the government ever ask for permission? Anyway," he leans in close and puts an arm around me, like he's telling a secret. "I was really only hanging around there in hopes of meeting you. We've got a lot to talk about. I could put you on the show, hell! You can be my co-host! Think of how cool it would be to have a ghost helping the ghost hunters. You'd be like Blade!"

I shake my head, try to break out of his grasp. "No, I really just wanted to—"

"Alright, your highness, here's all your shit. Get in the van, we're going to be late." Amethyst clatters past us, carrying way too much equipment, a scowl marring her features.

August opens his mouth, but I stomp down on his foot. "Hey! What the—"

I cover his mouth with my hand until Amethyst rounds the corner, then release him. "What is your problem?" He swats at my hand, then feels his face like I've accidentally marred him with ectoplasm or something.

You. "Let's just keep this between us for now. I'm not ready to be on camera...yet," I say, adding the lie of "yet" a little too late.

I can see him turning over possibilities and outcomes in his head, just by looking at his face. He's so calculating, it's frightening. "Okay. What do you want?"

This is it. Can't screw it up. "It's a big ask, but I want you to cancel your hunt tonight and take me to Indianapolis instead. We can talk more on the way. Just you, no crew." These are not the words I thought I was going to say. I *thought* I was tracking him down specifically to ask him to get his followers to leave Addie and Buddy alone, but apparently, I had some other reasons, hidden from myself. Maybe more selfish reasons.

"Indianapolis? Why?"

He didn't immediately laugh in my face, so I'm taking that as a good sign. "There's someone you need to meet. I can explain on the way."

***August Waters**: Hey all, hope you're having a freaky Friday. I'm so sorry to do this to you guys, but I'm going to have to postpone our visit at Lemp Mansion. I know you're looking forward to it, and so am I! I'll let you know our rescheduled date as soon as it's available.*

You'll notice I'm coming to you live from the highway right now, and from my phone, no less. No crew with me today! But I promise, it's for an excellent reason. I have a very, very special guest riding shotgun right now. Do you see her? No, probably not, but she's glaring right at me. I promised no recording this meeting, but she's making an exception, so you all don't think I'm dead.

You probably assume she is, though, which is fine, because she is. That's right, folks. I've finally caught up with the mysterious "Poppy" I've been searching for. We're taking a little road trip! Poppy, is there anything you'd be willing to do to let our lovely viewers you're here with me now?

Hey, that's a nice trick. You hear that, everybody? Here, let me flip the camera around so you can see the dash. Poppy's changing the radio stations. And...now she's turned the music off. She must be done with this little interview. All right, I'd better focus on the road, or I'll end up like Poppy. I'll update you soon!

Chapter 16

"Have you ever seen a monster, besides that one on the train?" I don't know a better way to phrase it. Calling them monsters feels bitter in my mouth, now that I've worked out what they might be, but they're so varied in appearance that there's really no other way to describe them.

August gives a short laugh. A forced laugh. He's behind the wheel of his car, some kind of little sporty thing with only two seats and so low to the ground that looking out the window makes me a little nauseated. He's speeding, weaving between the more conscientious drivers like they're sitting still. "You're going to have to be more specific," he finally answers.

He's seen them. I wasn't sure if he did, without me bringing one straight to him and then locking them in a train car together. I know that other living people *usually* don't, but I don't fully understand the parameters of August's gift. But what I really want to know is if he has realized what I have realized about the monsters. It's only taken me a few weeks of ghost hunting to figure it out, and he's been at it for quite some time. "Say you go to a house that's supposedly haunted, hoping to find a ghost, and you find something, alright, but it's not human, it's-"

"A foot tall, normally proportioned man in a top hat with no face that walks on the ceiling like it's the floor?" August says in a rush, almost a shout. "That drops down onto your shoulders if you walk underneath him?"

There's a long silence. I don't know why I don't feel like he's done, like I shouldn't answer.

"Or maybe you mean like a floating, lidless, singular eyeball that just hangs out on the staircase and swivels, watching you as you walk by?"

I open my mouth, but before any sound comes out, he goes on.

"Or, do you mean like a shadowy person-shaped thing that pretends to be a regular shadow of the furniture or whatever until you look away, but then you can see it reaching for you out of the corner of your eye whenever you turn your head?"

"Yes," I say quickly, before he can tell me about any more horrors. His childhood must have been...not always fun. "Yes, like that. I see them, too."

He almost rear ends the car in front of us as his attention leaves the road and focuses on me. I slam my hands on the dash and say, "Ahhh!" helpfully.

It does the trick, and he weaves deftly to the next lane over, not even tapping the brakes. Once we're in the clear, he says, "You do?"

"I do. Have you ever wondered what they are?"

He scoffs his annoying scoff. "You said it yourself. Monsters."

"Monsters aren't real, August."

"Ghosts aren't real, *Poppy*." He enunciates my name as though it bothers him that I used his. Does he expect me to call him "Mr. Waters"? "Ghosts are real to me," he continues. "So why not monsters, too? I just figured they were ghosts, too. Like, good spirit/evil spirit kind of deal."

I frown. I think of the scarecrow, standing at the edge of the field. *Help,* it had said in my voice. *Help.* "Ghosts are just people," I say, wistfully. "Do you think you can talk to me because I'm exceptionally good? I don't think the monsters are inherently bad."

"Oh, yeah? Tell that to the creepy Lilliputian trying to gouge my eyes out."

I fall silent. How can I explain? "I think the monsters are just ghosts, too."

God, that awful laugh of his. I almost wish I was back in the smelly station wagon for a second. "Well, if that's the case, why aren't there any live monsters terrifying living people?"

He's not understanding, or I'm just bad at explaining myself. He's going to have learn the same way I did. He'll have to see for himself.

"Can you do me a favor?" I ask after a few minutes.

"Am I not doing you a favor right now? When are you going to do *me* a favor? You won't talk about the show at all?"

"Yeah, yeah. We'll talk about it." We won't talk about it. "I was hitching a ride with some of your followers last night, and I left my notebook in their car. It's very important to me."

"Then why did you leave it in their car?"

I close my eyes. Every second I spend in his company, I miss Buddy even more. "I forgot it. I forget a lot of things. That's why I have a notebook."

"Oh, yeah?" he's suddenly interested. I open my eyes to find his bright green ones piercing me, searching. "Is that, like, a personal problem? Or like a ghost problem?"

I sigh. "Do you think you could maybe ask for it back? I know their names. Their first names, anyway."

"Sure, sure. They'll love that. The fans love to help with the show. Hey, maybe I could bring you to them, we could pick it up in person? If," he adds, mockingly apologetic. "You'd agree to be on the show, of course."

I need my notebook. "Well. Alright, I guess."

We've been driving for almost two hours now, and he hasn't asked another thing about me. Not how I died, not where I lived, not anything. I try to tell myself that he's just saving it all for the show, that he wants genuine real time responses between us when his viewers finally meet me, but I can't make myself believe it. I really think he just doesn't care.

His telling me about the monsters is the only time I've gotten a response from him that felt genuine. I almost ask why he doesn't really go into depth about these occurrences up on his stream, but I already know the answer, and I already know that he'd lie anyway. The truth would be that he's frightened of them and wants to pretend they don't exist. I can't blame him for that. I don't even know how many years of my own existence have been spent just trying to avoid them and avoid thinking about them.

"I think," I begin slowly. The minutes have passed without me keeping up with them, I have no idea how long it's been since he asked about my forgetting. It was only him mocking me, anyway. He wasn't expecting an answer. "That it's a ghost problem. The forgetting, I mean."

He turns his chin toward me to show interest but keeps both eyes on the road. "Oh, yeah?"

"Yeah. I think that something bad happens to us if we forget too much about who we are."

"Explain."

"I am. I'll show you when we get there."

"Why are you being so cryptic? I'd think you'd be dying to tell me literally anything. Ha." He flashes me a grin of perfect teeth. "Dying."

I roll my eyes. "I'm not a five year old."

"Hey." He rocks the car around a sedan in the middle lane and then glances at me. "Could you see her? Or hear her? On the stream? The little girl."

"I didn't get a chance to watch it, but I heard her laugh on the audio when some of your fans were listening," I admit.

"What?! Come on, my crowning achievement and you didn't even watch?"

"It's not like I have a phone. Besides, I can talk to her any time I want, how special would it be for me?" I shrug.

"This is *huge.* Isn't this the proof that you're here? Everyone on earth is going to want to talk to you!" He's yelling now.

"To say what?" I ask, and my voice is getting louder, too. "To ask if their dead families are happy? To ask what heaven is like? To ask the winning lottery numbers? I *don't know anything.*" Tears sting my eyes. I feel like I've just professed my darkest secret. "I don't know anybody. I don't know the secrets of life, or death. Addie is the only other ghost I've ever spoken to." I start to cry.

He's quiet for a long time. Maybe my tears embarrass him, or maybe he doesn't know what to say. I don't really care either way, I'm just focused on my own wave of misery. "Well," he finally says. "That's a disappointment."

I squint at him through my puffy eyes. "You mean...you mean for your show, don't you." It's not a question. I've waited so long for this opportunity, for someone to finally comprehend my existence. The disappointment in this man is shattering.

"Well, yeah. But don't worry. It'll still be good. You're still plenty of draw, just being dead and all."

"What the fuck is wrong with you?" I ask. I don't really use that "f" word. My mother never allowed it in the house, and I just never got into the habit, but sometimes, certain words are called for.

He looks genuinely startled. "What?"

"Do you have any empathy at all? Do you even realize when you're being completely insensitive?"

The Laugh appears. "You sound like Amethyst."

"Do you even realize the grief and headache you're putting the Frances' through? Buddy might lose his job. He and Sharleen have had their entire lives turned inside out, everyone knows their business-"

"Hey, that's *your* fault as much as mine!" he yells. "How else was I supposed to find you with only that weird ass email to go off of?"

"There are people camped out in their yard! They can't leave the house without being ambushed! And *Addie*," I say, and actually slap his shoulder in my frustration. "She's scared! She doesn't understand. And there's all these people outside with signs, chanting *her name*. How can you just leave them like that? And, now, the government is getting involved?"

"None of that is my problem!" He hits the steering wheel. He's going over ninety miles an hour. I should have waited to start this argument, but it just came spilling out. "I just showed up and filmed a ghost. That's what I've always promised to do. What people do with that information isn't my responsibility."

"The least you can do is ask your fans to leave them alone," I say. My voice has a begging tone that I'm embarrassed about.

"It's too late for that," he says. He's starting to settle down too, now that I'm finished attacking him. "They know she's there. They're never going to let up, now."

"So, tell them she's gone," I say. I'm surprised how easily it came to me.

"What do you mean?"

"Tell them...tell them she passed on, went to the light. Whatever. Tell them you exorcised her."

"You want me to lie? To my fans?" August sounds deeply offended, and I can't tell if he's joking or not.

"Yes. I want the Frances family left alone. That's my condition. For the show." I don't expect an answer from him right away, so I lean back and turn my head away from him, look at the landscape flying by. It's flat, getting dark, and makes me queasy. I shut my eyes.

"I'll think about it," he says cooly.

I suppose that'll be good enough for now. I'm tired of talking to him already. I try to imagine an eternity of these car rides with him, of spending my nights with the red eye of a camera pointing at my face while he and I profit off of miserable invisible souls like me. I feel sick. But I'd do it. I'd do it for Buddy to be happy. I miss him.

Chapter 17

August parks the car. It's full dark now. A siren wails nearby, getting closer. The only people around are shuffling shapes in the shadows. "Jesus," he mutters, scooting down a little in his seat. "This place has really gone downhill since I was a kid. Why...why do we need to be here?"

He's nervous. Good. When he's nervous, he's honest. I clear my throat. "I...found someone. Someone you used to know."

He jolts up so fast, he bumps his head on the car roof. "Charlie? You found him? But you said Addie was—"

"I didn't talk to him," I admit. "I was...he was...I just want you to come see him." I'm nervous, too, to be honest. I don't particularly like August, but I don't want him to get hurt. I briefly considered the implications of bringing him to see the Fat Man, but I didn't really consider the other dangers that a live person might experience. I look him over. His blonde hair gleams in the moonlight. His clothes are designer, fashionable, branded. He's slim and pale. Anybody could push him down and take his lunch money, if they wanted.

"Well, shit. Is he inside? I hope he remembers me. You said you dead people forget easily, right? I mean. He was my friend for years..." He trails off, and I assume he's remembering the times he shared with Charlie. But then he adds, "Can I *please* film? This is it. This is the reunion my entire stream is based off of. I've got to document it."

I bite my lip. "August," I put a hand on his arm, look seriously into his face. "I really don't think it's a good idea. You can do what you want, of course. But, well. Let me just show you."

"I'll record but not stream," he says excitedly, popping open the door. "Then I can just decide later if I want it out there or not. Hey, Poppy," he says, and puts a hand over mine that's still gripping his arm. "Thank you for finding him. I mean it. This means a lot."

To your stream. I can't help but think, but I offer a weak smile. "Don't thank me yet."

We walk across the street. August turns on his phone camera as soon as we're close enough to the chain link fence to read the sign, his flashlight blares across the lies written there. "I'm here at the grocery store—"

"Shh," I say. "When I was here last time, there were people trying to sleep in front. Don't bother them. Turn that light off until we're inside."

August grimaces and replaces the phone in his pocket. "Sleeping? Here?" he hisses.

I don't bother to reply, I just slip through the bent back links in the fence and hope he's following. He must be, because there's a clanging of metal and "Shit!" as he gets stuck in the jagged edges. Things are much as they were last time, complete with the dingy tents propped up to one side. I motion August towards the window I'm familiar with.

"I'm gonna get all cut up," he whispers.

"It's safety glass. Besides, it's clear along the bottom." I hop through into the blackness and overpowering smell of disuse.

August tumbles in beside me. "Do you think there's anyone inside? Like. Anyone living?"

"There wasn't last time." I shrug. I'm enjoying being able to speak at a normal volume while he continues to whisper, but that's a small power I'm about to lose. I don't want to startle the

Fat Man. I still continue to walk with confidence I don't feel, to give myself a little bit of an edge. August grabs the back of my coat like we're in one of those fairground haunted houses.

"Why would he be in here?" August asks, his face so close to the back of my head I feel my hair move. "*You* wouldn't stay in place like this, would you?"

"I was staying in the same hotel as you, actually," I murmur. I need to somehow prepare August, and I need to figure out how to bring Charlie back, if that's a thing that's possible. How do I remember the things I've forgotten? My notebooks, of course. My recorded memories. "Okay, I need you to be ready to talk to him. Do you have, like, any fun memories you could remind him of? Any moments that you two shared that made an impression on you?"

"Oh, geez. Yeah, I'm sure there are things he must remember. We went to the zoo together, we saw 'Cars' together...Hell, he's the one that taught me subtraction."

I nod. "Perfect. When we see him, remind him of all those good times, okay? And, August," I stop and look back at him, he's stooped down so our noses are almost touching. A loud metallic scraping noise comes from the dairy section. "He's...different, now. Dangerous. Keep some distance, okay?"

I turn to start walking again, but he hangs tight to my coat and doesn't move. "Wait, what? What do you mean?" He forgets to whisper.

The scraping noise comes again, followed by a loud clang of metal hitting concrete.

August digs in his heels and clenches tighter to my jacket at the noise. "Wait, Poppy, what was that? I... I don't want to do this. We should come back tomorrow morning at least, right? No need to wake him up."

"He doesn't sleep," I say. My voice is cold and foreign to me. Maybe I'm the one without empathy right now. "The dark doesn't matter. Come on. You can turn your light on if you want. He knows we're here."

"He knows? Wait, wait, hang on." He can't stop me from walking, he's getting pulled along, clinging like a child.

"Your light, August. Your camera. Don't you want to film?" I raise my eyebrow and pull a smirk. I can't help but feel a teeny bit of glee at his obvious fear. As long as he doesn't get hurt, I think he deserves getting cut down to size, at least a bit.

"Ah, shit." The showman in him overcomes, and he pulls the phone out, presses record. "Okay, okay. Um. I'm here with Poppy. Here in Indianapolis, at the grocery store where I first met the Fat Man. It, uh...well. The age of the building is really showing, let's say. It's a dump. Abandoned. Uh...Poppy tells me that, uh..."

A gurgling groan erupts from the back corner of the store. August screams and pans his phone in the general direction of the noise. The wall that was in shambles when I left last time has been partially rebuilt, which means that it might be the Fat Man who builds it, shutting himself away. My heart aches for him, if any trace of him remains. I can't decide if I want it to be that way, or if it's better for it to just be a mindless creature.

Oh, no... The Scarecrow had said. Oh, no.

August's yell has gotten the Fat Man's attention, and I hear the telltale sound of it dragging its body across the ground. *Soon we'll know. Now, we'll know.*

"What is that?" August screams. "Oh, God, oh, God. What *is* it?"

He has his camera panned to a low spot in the rebuilt wall of debris, and there, I see the Fat Man's bulbous eyes. Its gaping, horrible mouth. Those blocky misplaced teeth.

"It's Charlie," I say. I can hardly raise my voice above a whisper. I hope he hears. "It's what's left of Charlie. He's forgotten."

The Fat Man lets out another horrible gurgle and reaches its long arms over the top of the low wall.

"No!" August shouts, still training his camera upon the monster. His voice quavers, and a twinge of pity wracks through me. He really did love Charlie, I think. No matter how much of a twerp he's been to me, once, he'd been a boy, and Charlie had been his best friend. "No, that's not him. That's not him."

"He's just the Fat Man now, August. You've got to *remind* him. Tell him who you are. Tell him about the zoo. You've got to try." Tears are streaming down my face. August *has* to be able to bring Charlie back. If he can do it, maybe there's hope for all of the lost monsters. Maybe there's hope for me, if I forget.

The spindly arms throw pieces of the wall at us. Metal racks and shelving rain down and clatter to the ground in front us. Its breathing fills the silence that follows.

"Ch-Charlie? Is that you, bud?" August calls, softly. "That's not him, Poppy. He was just a guy!"

The Fat Man's arms reach out again, and it drags itself forward through the wall, the debris like falling leaves around its mass. It's suddenly much, much closer to us. August squeals and yanks me back several feet by my jacket. "He's in there, I know he is." I insist. Something in me is more sure of this than anything else. So sure, I wonder if it's something I knew before, and forgot. I blink away the confusing thought. "Keep trying, August. Tell him!"

"Charlie, remember when. Uh, when I was little? I'm August. Remember August? Aw, fuck this." I feel suddenly lighter as the pressure on my jacket disappears. With it goes the phone's flashlight.

"Shit. August!" I call. I turn and see the retreating light bobbing back and forth as he pumps his arms in his sprint for the broken window.

I flap my hands in indecision. I really don't want to leave here without some answers. I *need* to be able to get through to Charlie. I *need* this to not be the end of his story. We can't end like this. I hear the thing dragging its body closer, its labored breaths. "Ch-charlie?" I call softly. I dance around, looking for a vantage point I might be able to talk to him from that he might not necessarily be able to reach. I can't see anything, it's too dark without August's flashlight.

The Fat Man brushes one of those delicate hands across the ground in front of my feet. He's about to be very near. "Fat Man? Remember the little boy you used to stay with? He'd call you Fat Man? Remember, you met him right here in the grocery store. He was shopping with his mommy and he waved at you. Remember, Charlie?" I dance out of reach of the grasping hand, and I can feel the heat of rancid mildewy breath. I can barely see glimmers in the darkness, no amount of my eyes adjusting is going to let me see in here.

The Fat Man is patting his hands along the floor again. He seems far less agitated now that the light has been removed. He drags himself forward in small increments and feels his way slowly.

"You and August went to the movie theater together," I ramble, stepping backward quickly as I speak. "You saw a cartoon about cars. Remember going to the zoo, Charlie? Do you remember little August's favorite animal? What's your favorite animal, Charlie?"

I'm backing slowly towards the entrance. I keep saying Charlie's name over and over, along with "Fat Man," in case that jogs his memory. I'm getting louder, more confident as the Fat Man repeatedly does not reach out and snap me in half or grind me into paste. But, as I reach the ruins of the checkout lanes, the Fat Man stops creeping along after me all together. I no longer feel the flutter of those weird fingers at my feet, and the sandbag scrape of his body is gone. The only noise that keeps him in on my radar is the ragged breath.

"Charlie?" I call again softly. "Are you okay?"

I jump back another three feet as the Fat Man gives out a huge gurgling roar.

"I'm sorry, I'm sorry!" I cover my ears, the sound is horrible.

As he calls again, I realize that the noise is exactly the same, not random gurgling.

"Awwwwwwww-ghwaahhhtt"

"August!" I cry. "Yes, August! You remember him? You remember!" I desperately wish I had my own light. I'd like to be able to look into this thing's eyes and search for Charlie inside them. He *must* be there. We can get him back.

"Aww-ghwat"

"August!" I turn and run for the broken window, skidding on pieces of glass and particle board. "August, hurry! He wants to…" I shove myself through the frame. "Talk to you."

He's not out here. I wander up and down the storefront, but he's nowhere to be found. I hear the low roar of an engine starting nearby. He wouldn't. "August?" I call again. I dash for the gap in the fencing and stick my head through, just as his headlights fire to life. "Wait!"

He revs the engine, and peels away out of the parking lot, leaving the stench of his new tires getting needlessly chewed up. He left me. He left Charlie. He didn't even look back.

I clamber back through the window. "Charlie?" It's a drowning black pit in here without August's flashlight. Just solid dark, too deep to swim through. I was only outside for a moment, but I can tell by the heavy slides that the Fat Man is already making his way back to his sad, lonely lair. The moment is gone. I did well with him, I think, even without August, but I'll need to return in the daytime, or with a light. I'm not even sure I could find my way back to the dairy corner in one piece in this inky soup. The sound of the Fat Man dragging himself around is replaced by careful, considered clangs of metal on metal, of things being pushed and moved with delicate fingers. The Fat Man is rebuilding his fortress. "I'll come back," I whisper, not wanting to disturb him again. "I'll come back, and we'll get this all figured out." Another promise.

"Okay," I say to myself as slowly and calmly as I can manage, once I've reappeared in the dazzling light of the night sky. I sink down to sit on the curb, the "coming soon" banner draped behind my back like wings. "I just need…I just need a pen. No big deal. I've just got to write down everything I can remember. It'll be okay. I remember plenty."

I stand and start walking without any inkling of what direction I'd like to go. My first thought is to go back to…to Addie's house. "Shit," I mutter. What's Addie's grandma's name?

I tell myself that I had only recently learned the woman's name, and it's not a big deal I've forgotten. I knew her as Addie's grandma. As Buddy's mother. It's fine. What's not fine is, I also don't remember that name of the town she lives in. Besides, Buddy told me not to return. I'm unwelcome, and unwanted.

There is nowhere meant for me.

Just get a pen, I repeat in my head like a prayer. *Just a pen. Not that hard, that's all you need, no big deal.*

August Waters: *Welcome back! I'm sorry I left you all hanging with the whole Poppy stream. We had a little...tiff. She's scared to be on camera, I guess. Doesn't really appreciate how important this footage is for living people. I'm guessing maybe she's losing a little decency, what with not being alive and all.*

I know you all have been asking for her. I'm giving her space right now, but hopefully in the future, she'll reconsider.

In other news, I've got a long list of spots I need to check out. You all have been drowning me in them! I've been in talks with that other super secret definitely-a-Netflix-show project, and they want me to preemptively scout out locations so that we don't waste any time on false leads.

But I know you guys, my true fans, understand the importance of being there every step of the way. So, for the next few weeks, I'll be streaming locations with you, before they make it to the big screen. Well...to the TV screen. So, make sure to subscribe.

I see your comments, I see 'em. I'll ask effing Poppy if she wants to come, if that's what you all want. Everybody loves a girl ghost hunter. Ain't that right, Amethyst?

Amethyst (*off camera*): *I just handle the lighting, don't drag me into this. Go find your co-ghost.*

August: *"CO-GHOST." Babe, that's gold.*

Chapter 18

"Hello? Hello??? Poppy? Are you here?"

I look up from my seat next to the free paper dispenser. I don't think it's the paper dispenser I've been trying to find. It doesn't feel quite right. I remember there was something important at the dispenser, something I left behind, but there's nothing in this one. I also have a tickle of memory about something *else* that was on the platform. Something bad. But, there's nothing bad here. Maybe later, maybe tomorrow, I'll get back on the train and try the next stop.

I've been feeling all out of sorts for a few days now. An insidious creeping *wrongness*. I was, at first, sure that I was on my way back to the brownstone I lived in with my mother. I know I consciously thought, *I should go home. I'll feel better at home,* but I never did find the house. They all look so similar, and it's been so long, and besides, I don't even live there anymore. My mother doesn't live there anymore, either. My apprehension remained. I must have been confused, meant to go somewhere else and lost track.

I was a sleepwalker. I kept patting my pockets for something that wasn't there, circling the neighborhood I haunted when I was alive. A letter, maybe? A map? A notebook. I had a notebook. I keep it with me. Where did I put it? Certainly not in the house, that didn't feel right at all. But I know I had one. I see it, opened before me on concrete, covered in tiny letters written in ballpoint pen. The concrete it lay upon had a thick line of yellow paint. A train station platform.

I meandered back across the city, with the dim thought of a train station my only light to see by. It's been another disappointment so far, hours and hours wandering up and down the lines. But there's *something* tickling my brain about this station. I stare at the closing train doors, and picture myself standing inside, looking out of the car, my forehead pressed against the window. Something was here. Some*one*. Maybe if I just sit tight, I'll remember.

"Poppy? Hello? Is there anyone here that sees monsters?"

There's a man turning circles within the shuffling crowd, arms spread wide. What is he doing? He calls again.

"Poppy? Remember me? Remember Addie, and Buddy?"

I squint at him. The names send the hairs on my arms shivering. *Buddy.* That seems kind of familiar. I think my mother had a parakeet called Buddy.

The man sighs and wanders over to a bench and sits. He has his feet planted far apart, and leans his head way down like he's trying to get over a wave of dizziness. He's a young white guy, dressed smartly and has blond hair styled like the men I see on billboards for cologne. He wears an earbud in one ear. As I watch, a teenager runs to the man, hands up in recognition, or confusion, I can't tell. The man accepts a cell phone from the teenager and stretches it out away from their bodies as they momentarily lean close. A picture together. The kid yells, "Thanks!" in a rush a breath and darts away to waiting friends.

I'm trying to decide whether it's worth the effort to stand and examine the man more closely when he suddenly whips his head towards me, like he felt me staring at him. "Hey!" he yells.

I look behind me.

"No, you!" He points at me.

My jaw drops.

"Ha! I knew you'd be here! Poppy!" He jumps up from his seat and jogs over to where I'm sitting on the ground. He sits next to me in the filth, ruining his slacks. "Do you remember me, Poppy?"

My eyes fill up with tears. "You. You can see me?"

"I can see you. How long have you been sitting here? You want to go grab a coffee or something?"

I sniffle. What is going on? I've been invisible for so, so, long. Years and years. Who is this person acting like he knows me? Who is Poppy? That's not my name. My name is… "I think I'd like a coffee," I say.

"I thought you might be forgetting things," the man says. He stands and offers me a hand. I pull myself up using it. "You said if you don't write things down, you start to forget. Couldn't get your notebook back, though, sorry about that. One of the kids from the car stole it and says she returned it to an address that was written inside. Do you remember writing down an address?"

I have absolutely no idea what he's talking about. In fact, I'm pretty certain he might have me confused with someone else. I fall into step beside him. I'm suddenly self-conscious. I don't remember the last time I washed my hair or changed my clothes. "I don't usually look like this, I don't think," I mumble.

"No, I don't think you do. At least, you didn't last time we hung out. You've had a rough few weeks."

"Who's Buddy? Who are you?"

He pushes open a door and gestures me through and we're out on the street side of the station. "I'm August. August Waters. I'm a…a supernatural investigator."

"The ghost hunter," I say, surprising myself

He laughs. "Yes! You remember me?"

I stagger as the weight of the last few weeks' memories crush down on me. The Big Bird. Buddy. Addie. Charlie. The ghost hunter. I push August Waters' helping hand away from me. "I don't want to talk to you." I turn back towards the station. I feel like I might throw up. A whole life crashing down around me. I need to reprocess this. All of it. *Oh, Buddy.*

"Hang on, hang on. I'm sorry I left you. I've been trying to find you ever since, I promise. I just...I just got freaked out, okay? You weren't really fair, you didn't prepare me for, for all of that." He's got his hands on my shoulders, staring into my face intently. I don't even think he's blinking. I feel my breaths getting shallow and quick. I feel like I'm drowning. I forgot. I forgot about Buddy. Addie. How could I, how *could* I?

"How are they?" I whimper. "You've talked to them? Are they okay?"

"What, you mean the Frances'? They're...okay."

The beat between those last two words is a moment too long. He's lying. He can tell that I know. "I haven't talked to them recently, okay? Your friend *Buddy,*" He spits out the name like poison. "Won't let me. It's a whole mess, honestly. I didn't mean for everything to get so out of control, okay? The internet, it's a beast. People are insatiable on there. Everything just snowballed. I never would have done this to that family on purpose." He's stumbling over his words, stuttering, gesturing. Placating.

"Then fix it," I say, simply.

"What?"

"If you didn't mean to hurt them, *fix it.*"

He rubs the back of his neck and gives me a little laugh that sends rage into my heart. "How am I supposed to do that? I can't put this thing back in the box, Poppy. Everyone knows about Addie now. She's a legend. Everyone wants to see her, wants to meet her-"

"She's a little girl, Mr. Waters. She's not a science experiment, and she's definitely not a sideshow for you to parade around." I shrug off his grasping hands, but don't leave just yet. "Tell them it's fake."

He goggles at me. "What?"

"Tell your viewers it's all fake. Tell them Buddy's mom is an actress. Rig up some fishing line and move some stuff around on camera. Whatever you've got to do."

He laughs again, a full hearty one that makes a passing woman glance over at us, confused at who August is laughing with. "No," he says. "Absolutely not. I've just gotten my big break! Netflix is going to have me do a series!"

"You're a monster," I say. "And speaking of monsters, you *left* me. You left *Charlie.*"

He runs a nervous hand through his hair. "Yeah. Um, look. I'm sorry about leaving you. That just really freaked me out, you know? That blob was the most disgusting thing I've ever seen in my life."

"That blob was *Charlie*. And he called for you. And you," I wipe my eyes angrily. "You weren't there."

A shadow of pain mars August's features for a moment. He reaches up and gently touches the bridge of his nose, breathes deep. "He did?"

"He did," I spit. "He needs you, and you left him." I try to turn away again.

"Wait, Poppy. I just want to chat with you about some things. I think maybe we could figure out a way to *help* you, and Addie, and others like you. Maybe even like Charlie. We could be a team!" He grabs me by both shoulders and spins me around to face him, searching my eyes. I hate how grabby he is. You'd think that after decades of no human contact I'd be thrilled to feel his fingers on my arms, but they feel like teeth. His eyes are greedy. He makes me sick.

"Fix. Your. Mess." I repeat.

"You're not really being fair to me here."

"Take your hands off me," I say firmly, "And consider yourself officially haunted."

"Poppy, I am *begging* you." August groans.

He's just walked into his brand new, posh penthouse apartment. It's got a gorgeous view of Lake Michigan I've never seen the likes of, in all my years in this city. I have just finished demolishing all of his expensive video and sound equipment and leaving the pieces in cryptic messages along the bamboo floors.

FIX YOUR MESS

I've also left the clawfoot bathtub overflowing for the past three hours and cut fun designs in the fronts of almost every single shirt he owns. I've only been following him for about thirty six hours. Haunting maliciously is surprisingly fun. These kinds of antics would never work on the average person, of course. They'd explain even the most outlandish things away without considering a ghost might be responsible. But August knows exactly who to blame. I've been having an excellent time.

"You're lucky I've been nice," I say. "I haven't done anything to mess up your reputation yet. You can either be a fraud, or I'll come up with something much, much worse."

"What are you going to do, sing Henry the Eighth?"

The reference is lost on me. "August. Do the right thing. That family is *suffering* and it's your fault."

"That's not fair! All I did was show the world the truth!" He kicks pieces of microphone across the room. It obviously wasn't satisfying enough, so he picks up the biggest remains of a camera and hurls it. It smacks into his huge flatscreen TV, and the screen spiderwebs.

"Wow, I guess I could have just let you do all this on your own," I snap.

He comes toward me, fists clenched.

I laugh. I laugh right in his impotent face. "What are you going to do, kill me?"

He hits me, square in the jaw. I rock back and fall to the floor. I taste blood. My head is vibrating.

"Oh, shit," he says. The rage has left him. "Are you okay? I didn't think—"

"Do you ever think, August?" I mumble. I'm still sitting, running my tongue around on my teeth.

The answer to that question, I now find out, is yes. While I'm sitting there, focused on the damage he's done, he's considering the implications of that punch. He realizes what it means, and the glimpse of malicious resignation I catch on his face as he swoops toward me is terrifying. He can hurt me. He could get rid of me...maybe permanently.

"Wait," I start, a new quaver in my voice. I put my hands up to block him, but he's too fast, too determined.

He scoops me from the floor and throws me over his shoulder like a sack of laundry.

"Hey! Hey! What do you think you're doing?" I start kicking wildly and elbowing the back of his head, but I can't break free of his grasp. "Put me down!"

I hear the sound of the sliding glass door to his patio being unlocked, and suddenly a gust of chilly air flings my hair into my face.

"August?" I ask meekly. My stomach is flipping continuously as I realize my entire body is on the wrong side of the railing.

He wouldn't. He wouldn't do this.

He releases me. I don't even see his face before I'm already falling, already way out of reach for him to change his mind. I fall sixteen stories to land on the sidewalk in front of the overpriced cookie shop at the base of his apartment building. I would have assumed, if I had considered what it would be like falling sixteen stories prior to actually doing so, that I would have had quite a few thoughts on the way down. It turns out that the time it takes to fall that far passes very, very quickly, and the only thought I very clearly remember having outside of a terror so visceral, I think my heart actually stopped long before I hit the ground is: *I'm going to make that man wish he had never been born.*

It hurt. It hurt to land, and I felt my body explode to the concrete around me. It was quick, I admit, but it'll be difficult to forget that feeling. I find myself almost glad it happened, because now I don't have to wonder any more what would happen if it did. No more intrusive thoughts about this particular fear, and I guess I don't have to be quite so careful all the time.

I stand up, and it's much like standing up the night of my death, except, thank goodness, this time I'm not leaving a body behind. The pavement is crisp and clean behind me, power washed to perfection. The air smells of chocolate chip cookies. I brush myself off and make my way to the lobby of August Waters' apartment building. I walk behind the concierge desk, rummage in a filing cabinet, and acquire the maintenance key fob. I ride the elevator up, humming to myself a little. *Maybe I'm humming "Henry the VIII."* The doors open and I step right back into August's life.

He's not in the living room, or the kitchen. He hasn't bothered to clean up the very expensive trash pile I left for him. I wander down the hall to his bedroom. The door is closed. I hear him in there, maybe laughing.

"Knock, knock," I say.

I open the door, and he's sitting on the floor, elbows on his knees and hands grasping his hair. He's not laughing. He looks at me, at my clothes, and I look down at them, too, absolutely soaked in fresh, red blood. Maybe *all* my blood. His face cracks apart, horror and guilt written in every line. His breathing changes, turns into quick little sobbing gasps. His eyes are pinned to the horror show of my body, unable to be torn away.

Finally, he whispers, "I don't know why I did that."

I sit down facing him. The steady *tap-tap*ing of blood dripping from the ruined hem of my dress and onto the floorboards is the only sound for a moment. He stares dully at the puddle forming underneath me, at my bright red hands, starting to dry around the edges. I bite back a lot of the things I want to say, and find myself with nothing suitable. The physical damage I've sustained might be long gone from my body, but it'll be haunting those handsome green eyes of his for a long, long time. He can't take it back. He'll have to learn to live with himself, and the things he's capable of.

"I'm sorry," he says. "Did it hurt?"

"Yes," I say. "A lot."

He starts to cry again. "I looked over. I saw...I saw."

"What you did?"

He puts his head down. "Can you forgive me?"

I take my time answering, leave him in suspense. Can I? What just happened has been so freeing for me, not that I'll ever admit that to him. I could almost *thank* him, if I wasn't so furious with him about other things. "If you do what I'm asking you to do, then yes."

He sighs. "I don't know how to do that, Poppy."

"Don't worry, I'll help."

"No," August says for the eighty fifth time. "No. I'm not doing this."

I sigh and try a different approach. "Look, this thing that you've shown people, this gift that you've given them, they can't handle it, August. If you keep doing this, people are going to see your proof and do horrible things."

He snorts. "Don't exaggerate. What would they do?"

"Well, maybe they decide there's no heaven. I don't know that, of course, but they might decide that. Maybe the promise of heaven was the only thing making them not commit unspeakable acts."

"So, a few nut jobs go crazy. You take something off the Taco Bell menu and there's going to be a guy that decides there's no heaven." He's pacing around the room, gesticulating wildly, while I'm curled up on his sofa. There aren't any pillows or throw blankets for me to ruin with my gross clothes, it's all sleek lines and hard angles in this space. I hate it. I did, however, help him clean up some of the devastation I'd wrought with his belongings after his guilt got the better of him and we started brainstorming.

"Maybe," I continue. "Someone, or probably some group, will decide you must be some kind of demon, to speak to the dead. Maybe they assassinate you."

August pauses at this one, but ends up just shrugging. "I'll hire security."

"Maybe," I say. I wasn't going to bring this up again, but I will. "They decide maybe death isn't such a big deal after all, so they decide to throw a person off a high rise balcony because they're annoying."

He doesn't say anything.

"Maybe," I say, sitting forward, making sure I have his full, undivided attention as I lay my ace. "A certain ghost who already has a penchant for communication with the living goes ahead and spills that little detail, and ruins your career anyway."

"God, you are *such* a bitch." He stops pacing and flops down to the other side of the sofa, rubs his hands down his face in exasperation.

I grin. He's going to do it.

"You'll help me though?" He sits forward, leans toward me. "You said you would, if anyone ever hired me for-"

"*Yes*, for the tenth time. It's not like I have other obligations." I sigh.

"Alright. Let's...let's get this over with." He sighs.

August Waters: Hey, kids, me again. This is another very special, unscheduled stream. I, uh. You'll notice the crew isn't here with me today, I've just got the tripod up. I need to tell you all some things.

What you saw. At the Emerald House, in my sessions with Adeline Frances…they're not…man, this is difficult. Let me start again.

I can't really…I don't…I don't see ghosts. I mean, not any more than any other person, I don't think. I have my memories of the Fat Man from when I was a little boy, but. Well, I was a little boy.

However, I'm a pretty good stage magician. Magic tricks are a secret hobby. What you saw of that little girl, and at the Emerald house, they were evidence of these tricks. A-hem. My crew had no idea, they weren't in on it. They believe in their work. Sharleen and Sean Frances had no idea, and I owe them my deepest apologies for using their tragedy in my…act.

It's all been smoke and mirrors, guys. All tricks. I'm coming to you live right now because I want to show you firsthand what I'm capable of, so that you believe me. Tell me what you want to see in the comments, and I'll make it happen before your eyes.

Chapter 19

"Alright, here's a comment telling me to flick the lights on and off. Starting with the easy stuff, huh?"

We've set up August's equipment (that I didn't destroy) right here in his living room. The sun is setting, and the whole space is filled with a magical low light. August tells me that it was this time of day when he toured the apartment for the first time, and the reason he bought it. He sounds so sad when he says it, and the tiniest trickle of remorse crawls around my stomach, making me wince. He won't be able to afford this place anymore, after tonight.

I clench my jaw. He'll be fine. He'll have other opportunities, maybe something that doesn't involve accidentally hurting people.

I can't believe he actually went through with it. His stream is live, and there's no taking it back. He gave up his dream. I dash across the room and toggle the light switch a few times.

"There we go, see? This building just completed construction three months ago and there isn't an ancient burial ground for miles. No ghosts." August is basically spitting the words. I worry he might cry, or worse. "Next one, let's see. Make a chair levitate. No problem."

I run back and grab one of his shiny dining room chairs by its back legs and wave it in a circle behind August's head. This is actually very thrilling for me. Years. Decades. And I've never gotten a single manipulation of an object noticed (*before Buddy. Oh, Buddy.*), and now, thousands of people are noticing me. Watching me. They think I'm fishing line and tricky camera work, but still. They see me. I can't believe, after all my attempts, all it really takes is for the viewer to be *expecting* me to be there. They just need to believe in me.

"There you go. Ta-Da." He's getting bitter already. I better make a quick exit from this place when the stream is over, or he might do something horrible. Again. "Alright. You want to hear a voice? That's a tricky one, usually requires a little set up, but I'll try." He glances at me.

I balk for a second. Will they hear me? *They're expecting me.* My palms sweat and my hearing goes a little fuzzy. People might *hear* my voice! "Hello?" I call loudly. "Can anyone hear me?"

August squints at the screen. "Did that work? Yes! Excellent." *Holy shit.*

"Alright, you probably get the idea. One more and we'll wrap this up. I'm feeling pretty bummed, sharing this with you all, to be honest. I've worked really hard on this, and I'm proud. But showmanship and straight up lying can get really blurry, and I was starting to get the ick. I should never have pretended to see a kid. That was...that was definitely over the line." He clears his throat. "Alright. I'm seeing a lot of support here and also some really pissed off people. That's all valid, and I thank you all for joining me on this journey." His cadence gets stronger as he goes, falling into his comfort zone in front of the camera. I think August Waters will definitely pull through this setback. He's made for the pictures, after all. "I'm seeing a lot of people asking to see a full bodied apparition. That needs some really special lighting, it might still be a little bright in here for it to work..." He risks a tiny glance at me.

I move into frame and hold my hands up in a shrug. I have no idea how to turn suddenly visible, obviously.

"Okay." August moves over and puts an arm around my shoulders. "I want you all to look very closely. I'll try to help direct your focus by standing here. Stare at my arm, and if this works right, you might suddenly realize that my arm is actually around a woman. She's waving at you. Look close."

I smile and wave awkwardly.

I see the screen fill up with comments.

Why is she all bloody?

Is that an actress?

She's so scary!

My eyes fill with tears, and I dart out from under August's arm and off screen. They see me. I'm real. They all had their ghost glasses on, for that moment. There's now footage of *me* on the internet. The weight of it is too much, and I sink to the floor.

"All right. I think that's enough, you all get the idea. I know you have questions, I know you're mad. There's going to be fallout from this, so you know... Be on the lookout for changes to my filming schedule, ha. I just couldn't keep going in good conscience. Have a creepy night."

He turns off the camera. "Alright, Poppy. Let's go." He frowns down at the heap of me. "What's your deal? I did what you asked, you should be happy."

I sniffle and look up at him from the gleaming hardwood floor. "Where are we going?"

"I don't want you here!" He laughs. "You're cramping my style. Tell you what. I'll buy you a cell phone. Get you a data plan. That way we can keep in contact, and you can use the internet."

"You'd do that?" I sniffle, try to wipe my eyes and make them sting more with the dried blood I forgot was on my hands.

"Well, sure. It's not all bad." He leans forward and offers me a hand up and even a tiny smirk. "I actually kind of feel all right. We're square now, right?"

I nod and take his cool, dry hand in my own, let him heave me to my feet. I actually feel pretty good, too. Some of my endless existential crisis is absent. I exist. People saw me. This man is holding my hand. All this time, my issue has really mostly been a matter of perception. Plus, yay! A cell phone! "Square." I grin at August, then let the grin falter. "I won't tell anyone about...I won't tell anyone."

"Cool. Let's go. Actually." He looks me up and down, then inspects the hand that recently released mine. "I'll give you some clothes, too. I don't want, uh. I..."

He doesn't want my blood and filth all over his car. I've been ruining everything I touch in the apartment...purposefully at first, I must admit. "Can I use your shower first, too?"

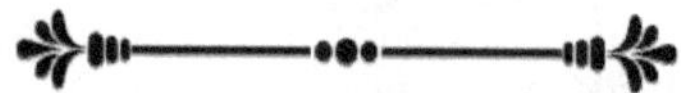

"So," August says, leaning over the center console to show me the phone he just purchased for me. "This is your text message app."

"I know how a phone works, dude."

"Don't say 'dude,' it's weird. Aren't you like eighty?" He hands me the phone.

"I think I'm like twenty-four or twenty-five, actually," I say, opening the internet browser. "I want to see the stream."

"Ugh," August throws himself back against the driver's seat. "I can't watch it. It'll kill me. You know my phone is off right now? My agent, the crew, everybody and their mother calling me trying to figure out what the fuck is wrong with me."

"Yeah, that must be terrible," I mutter, thinking of poor Buddy. I'm still playing with the phone, the marvels of the world held in my hands. My very own cell phone. Wow.

"You really don't care what this means for me, do you?" he asks. "You came to *me*, remember? You *asked* me."

I sigh. I *do* feel bad, the guy is actually starting to grow on me. He didn't mean to hurt anyone, really. He was just trying to make sense of his world, to share his gift, probably to not feel so crazy. I put a cautious hand on his shoulder. "I care, August. I really do. You did a very kind, noble thing, and you can't even vlog about it. But it matters to me. And it matters to Addie. What do you think government creeps would have subjected her to? *You* put a stop to it. You get to sleep at night knowing you saved her from that."

He drums his fingers along the steering wheel. "Whatever. Let's go. I'll drop you off at Sharleen's."

"Wait," I say, and tear my eyes away from the screen. "They don't want me there."

He laughs. "You think they won't know what you made me do? They'll want to thank you."

Will they? I hadn't even considered. Would Buddy possibly forgive all of the trouble I caused? Would he maybe want to speak to me? My heart flutters at the possibility. I'm never going to be Rebecca, obviously, but maybe...maybe I could help with Addie? Maybe I could be useful, be like part of the family? Maybe at least a friend?

"That would be wonderful," I manage.

August pulls away from the curb without another word.

I turn my focus back down to the device in my hands. I begrudgingly close the web browser. I have more important things to do. I need my notes, even if it means accepting a digital format.

I start at the beginning. I notate the day I died, and then exit out and download a new app, a record keeper. It was fifty eight years, five months, and three days ago. I feel better knowing. I thought that number might be forever lost to me. I think, vaguely, that since I know the day, I should be able to very easily look up my death in the newspaper microfilms at the Chicago Public Library. I'm certain there must have been a little blurb about it. Back in those days, a single tragic death was newsworthy, even if it was an accident. I should be able to look up my name, so easily. Why did I never think to do that before? Or, *have* I done that before?

My next note: *Look up death day in library*

I take my time, going as much in chronological order as I can remember. My mother (look up her name, too. That might be more difficult, as I've forgotten when she died, exactly), our house (I have no idea where it is anymore, maybe Berwyn?), my relatives (vague, faceless possibilities). I write about my fascination with the train stops briefly, and how they were important to me, but I don't remember why.

I look down at the screen. None of this seems important to me anymore. None of this is who I am anymore. I want to write about Buddy. I want to tell the story of our time on the road together, and all the things he said, and what his favorite coffee and doughnut is, and how his dimples crease so deeply when he smiles. I want to talk about the songs he loves to sing to. I want to talk about the books he's read and reread and loses himself in, every time. I want to talk about him.

And I want to talk about Addie. I want to write down all the questions I have for her. What she remembers, what she's scared of. I want to know her favorite cereal so I can make sure it's always in the house for her. I want to learn how to do her hair however she likes it. I want to find out all her favorite colors, I want to let her paint her own bedroom, I want to give her the rest of her childhood that she deserves. I want to know the things I think she might know that I don't. I think she's more powerful than I am, more in tuned with her abilities to manipulate the world around her. I think she might understand the monsters, and I think she might be able to help me save them. I think she might know how to not become one.

My hands hover over the mostly blank screen for a moment longer, and then I start to type, all in a flurry and with many, many errors that the phone does its very best to correct. I hope it's legible when I'm done.

"Are you even listening to me?" August's voice interrupts my thoughts, and I accidentally type "to me" on the document.

"Mmm?" I say, without looking up.

"Why don't you learn to drive? I don't want to come all the way out to bumfuck every time you need a ride."

"Maybe Buddy will bring me to you," I say absently, mind back on the notes.

"Maybe?"

I sigh and look up, irritated at him for derailing my train of thought. But he really is helping me out a ton here, I need to be more thankful. "I'll get to you. I know how to take a bus, at the very least. Hey," I look around. "Where are we?"

"Oh, welcome back. I've only been talking to you for two hours. Where do you even go?" He's parking the car. "Here, get out, I'll show you."

It's the middle of the night, and the only light I can see is from the car's headlights, illuminating a mostly gravel road with no paint. I squint out the window. August has already gotten out from the driver's side and is coming around to my door. I pop it open for him. "Little detour?" I ask. I'm feeling little apprehensive. Maybe I should have been paying a little more attention to the road, or at least to my driver. Did I upset him, getting so lot in my own head?

"I just have to piss. But, there is something neat here I wanted to show you. Kind of like Charlie."

"Oh, did you see something here?" I hop out.

"Mm-hmm. Camping with my mom. Here." He holds out his hand. "Let me put my number in for you, in case we get separated."

I hand him the phone casually and take a few steps toward the edge of the road. "Where are we, exactly?"

A hard kick to my tailbone sends me sprawling into the shallow ditch. There's a few inches of water hidden in the tall grass, and I splutter for a few seconds before pulling myself up to my hands and knees.

"You really think I was going to help you? After what you did to me? Fuck you. I hope you never find your way out of here," August says. His voice is cold and hollow.

"Wait, wait!" I cry, but his car door is slamming. I hear rocks being kicked up as he pulls away, slowly enough to not spin out and find himself trapped with me. "Wait."

I sink back down into the muddy, icy water, and lay there until the sun is overhead, just thinking of everything I should have done differently, starting with not taking the train south the day I ran into August Waters.

In the daylight, I see that he has dropped me into some kind of forest preserve, like a dog he didn't want to be able to follow him home again. I guess that's what I am. But I have no intention of following August Waters anywhere. I never want to see that smarmy face again, as long as I...exist.

But how long will that be? I finally muster the energy to drag myself out of the ditch. I'll need to start walking if I'm ever going to make it back to Addie's house. August lent me a tracksuit. I look ridiculous, but the clothes are comfortable and fairly warm. I still have decent shoes. I can do this.

I feel like it was exceedingly mean for August to get me that phone and then take it away from me. I didn't ask him for one, why would he add that extra layer of cruelty? I realize that, maybe, he didn't plan to do this. He's short tempered, not rational. He probably got me that phone and started our journey with the full intent of bringing me to Addie like he said he was going to. What changed his mind?

Was it just the realization setting in that we ruined his reputation last night? Was he planning on somehow salvaging the situation and realized on the way it wouldn't be possible? Or, maybe, I really just wasn't grateful enough for everything he was doing for me. I should have been more attentive to him during that drive. I wonder what he'd been saying?

This train of thoughts feels good for me. I feel present. I feel angry and hurt. I feel like a person. The forest is coming alive around me. I hear the animals moving around in the underbrush and the birds calling to each other, and I remember vaguely, the zoo I grew up near. It feels like a lifetime ago. I remember spending nights there, long after I had died, listening to the lions snore. I remember wondering if dogs could sense me, because sometimes they'd look at me on the street as their owners walked them by, and they'd *look* at me look at me like people never do. I sat in the zoo and wrote down the musing in a forever lost notebook. Maybe one day, I'll be able to test that theory.

I follow the gravel road for most of the morning, stepping over yellow gates with padlocks on them a couple of times. I think it must be some kind of maintenance access road, but I haven't seen any vehicles or signs of any kind. I'm completely alone.

It *is* pretty out here, though. I'm not much of a nature girl. I've spent almost all my years in the city, with only brief escapades in the surrounding corn and bean field countrysides, and those visits are murky in my memories. This is completely different. I can only see a few yards in any direction for the naked winter trees and occasional dark green pine pressing in around me. I don't mind them, they're a comfortable kind of close. It smells clean and new and alive. There's not a lot of snow, just some tiny melting piles along the shallow ditches every once in a while. It's not really quiet, like I'd expect. The breeze rattles everything and the birds chirp. There's constant rustling. It perversely reminds me of traffic. I suppose he could have abandoned me somewhere worse.

I wonder if he was telling the truth about being here before, about seeing something out here. I'm inclined to believe he was, why bother lying? I think I vaguely remember one of his streams mentioning a camping trip with his mom. I start to inspect my surroundings a little more carefully as I walk, secretly hoping to find his monster.

I don't find it before I find a path, cutting across my road. It's a walking trail, with a "Caution: Motor vehicle crossing" sign set on both sides of the road. I bite my lip. Should I continue on the road, or cut onto the trail? The road has been frustratingly unhelpful in terms of signage, but if the hiking trail is for the public, as it seems to be, it might give me a little more information. As the day gets warmer, I might even be lucky and come across a person I can follow back to civilization.

I decide to turn left after a mental coin flip.

The walking trail is not paved or gravel, it's just a dirt trail. There are puddles of mud with icy edges dotted along it, and birds bathe and flutter in them, ignoring me completely. I was already fairly certain from the many times I'd had to step over pigeons that birds either had no interest in me or didn't notice me, but I make a mental note anyway. With it comes a flash of memory. Me, hunched down in the living room in the brownstone apartment, my nose pressed against the painted wire of my mother's parakeet's cage. "Please, Bertie. Don't you see me?" I whispered. "Pretty Bert, Pretty Bert..." I sang. My eyes filled with tears then, and do now as well. Birds can't see me.

I'm only about ten minutes down the trail before I come across a low sign that tells me I am at the 1.5 mile marker of the "blue" trail, whatever that means. It doesn't say how long the blue trail is, but I'm making some kind of progress.

My tracksuit is almost dry, and I'm starting to warm up from my exercise and feeling pretty good, pretty comfortable. August can't stop me. I'm in too deep. I've got people I care about, and he wronged me. I'm not going to forget their names so easily as I forgot my own.

My name. My new name. I stop, put my hands on my knees. *Shit.* It's...petunia? No. No. It's Poppy. I shake my head and start walking. I need to be more careful.

"Poppy. Addie. August. Buddy," I say, keeping time with my footsteps. There's no one out here to hear me. I can talk out loud. Maybe it'll help. "Poppy," *step*. "Addie," *step*. "August," *step*. "Buddy." I am two miles into the blue trail. "My name is Poppy," I say. "My name is Poppy, and I am two miles into the blue trail. I'm going home."

At the four mile marker, the trail opens up into a parking lot on one side and a fishing pier on the other. There is one pickup truck in the lot, and two figures sitting on camp chairs at the pier, their fishing poles leaned up against the weather beaten wood railing.

I hustle over to them. They're both older men, maybe sixties, maybe seventies. They've got matching flannels (one red, one blue), matching overalls (both blue jeans), and matching ratty old baseball caps, each one supporting a different team. They aren't talking to each other, just gazing out at the water in the most comfortable silence I could have ever imagined. *Old friends,* a snippet of song plays in my head. *Sat on their park bench like bookends.* I miss Buddy.

"Hello!" I say and step up between them.

Neither of them respond. Good, I'm tired of being seen right now. I sit down between their tackle boxes (one grey, one green), and rest.

They "fish" (neither of them catches anything or seems disappointed by that fact) for most of the afternoon, with hardly a sentence spoken between them. The time passes by me like a butterfly. I gaze at the sparkling water and listen to the rustling trees and the gentle breathing of the people around me. It reminds me of my train journeys in so many ways, but nicer. I sink down into a quiet existence, barely present. The closest thing I get to sleep. The wind sighs, the sun taps my face, promising warmth in weeks to come. I feel okay. I barely feel at all.

"Welp," red flannel says. And with that, they both begin the ritual of standing, stretching, grunting, and packing up their gear.

I stand and stretch too, and wander toward the truck they must have ridden in together. There's no room in the cab for a third person, so I climb up into the bed, make room between a rusting toolbox and some wadded up tarp, and wait. It's another five minutes before they finally meander over and store their things beside me. It's another five minutes after that before they're both settled in the truck and it putters to life.

I've never ridden in the back of a pickup before, and I'm disappointed that it's nowhere near as fun as it looks. I slide around with every bump and the slipstream off the top of the cabin buries me in howling wind, sending my hair flying straight into my eyes despite my attempts to hold it back. We can't be going more than twenty five miles an hour, I can only pray they don't get on the highway, or I'll have to just try to lie as flat as I can and hope for the best.

Luckily for me, no high speeds are involved. The ride is only about twenty minutes before we pull up in front of a cute little farmhouse with a picket fence and blue flannel takes his leave. All of his fishing equipment remains in the pickup—this must be a regular thing. The forest looms dark and cold in the distance, but here are all the winter fields I'm used to. The ghost hunter must not have taken me *too* far off course.

I take my chances remaining in the truck bed, hoping that red flannel man lives closer to a town. I considered getting out of the bed and into the cab when we dropped off blue flannel, but it seemed like the truck barely slowed down to let him out, and I didn't want to get left behind. Luckily for me, the rest of the ride is very short, and on less bumpy roads. Red flannel lives in a blue cottage that seems to be right on the edge of a tiny town. There's a water tower, but no words are written on it. When the man parks, I call, "Thank you!" through the little sliding window into the cabin and then tumble out onto the street.

Nothing seems obviously familiar to me. My experience with small farming towns is pretty sparse, so each looks much the same as the last. I could be in Iowa, but it could just as easily be Illinois, or Indiana, maybe Missouri, but it does seem to be a little flatter than I remember Missouri.

I stop walking. Wait, what city was the ghost hunter's apartment in? Was it in Chicago? I can't, for the life of me, remember. It seems so long ago already, and the time before I was in the apartment feels fuzzy. Did he come to me, or did I come to him? Where was I?

I tell myself this doesn't matter, and spin back toward the pickup truck. I sweep around the back and check the license plate. Illinois. There. At least I know where I am *right now*, and that's the most important thing.

I wander vaguely in the direction of the water tower, assuming it to be the center of town. Maybe there's a library, and I can print myself a map.

The thing I mistook for a water tower is actually some kind of machine to deposit grain into train cars. I wander down the residential streets into the night before I finally find the library, disguised as a regular little house, across the street from a large church and a tiny post office. I might have overlooked it entirely if not for the green street sign with a stick figure holding a book and an arrow pointing towards the house. Of course, it is evening, and (I think) a Saturday. I wouldn't expect the library to be open until Monday. And even then, I have to hope it's not some kind of bank holiday.

I reach the front door. Closed on Sundays *and* Mondays, of course. Should I break in? I jiggle the handle, just in case, but it's locked up tight. I sigh and sink down onto the little house's stone porch. I haven't seen any stores to speak of, no hotels, no restaurants. Nowhere where people might be congregating. The street is deserted. I pull my knees up under my chin and wait for Tuesday.

Ghosts Aren't Real After All

A stunning blow was dealt to the paranormal enthusiast community last night in the form of a confession vlog by internet sensation August Waters. His recent "proof" of lingering spirits sent him outside of the fringe community of ghost hunters and into prime time spotlights with guest appearance on everything from the Tonight Show to Good Morning, America.

Even people that had no interest or belief in the supernatural had their heads turned by Waters' incredible video evidence, but according to his stream last night, it was all a charade. Waters confessed that his "ghosts" were created using stage magic, and proved it by recreating the feats performed by the supposed specters while standing in his own dining room.

It's disappointing, to say the least, even though the effects he was able to produce on command were no small feat. Fans are enraged and devastated. William DiAngelo, the creator of the superfan website: , shut down the site today. The link now only displays a page that reads, "August Waters is a fraud. The hunt for the truth lives on, but it does not live with August."

Chapter 20

By Sunday afternoon, I'm feeling restless. I get up to stretch my legs, maybe I'll just take a quick walk around the block. "Buddy," I say. "Addie, Poppy. My name is Poppy."

The church across the street is having service. I almost went over, but felt the need to stay at my post. However, as I move past it, the doors open wide and I'm hit with clumsy organ music, chatting and laughter. People with brightly colored dresses and khaki slacks peeking out under winter coats spill out into the sunlight, all small talk and disingenuous compliments to one another.

I pause. I don't have to wait for the library to open, of course. Any one of these people has a computer at home, a phone in their coat pocket. I could just follow someone home like I always do, unseen and uninvited.

I spot a woman gripping two teenage girls by their elbows, nodding and smiling as politely as she can while also steering the girls toward their car as quickly as possible. I choose to go with them for no other reason than there is most likely room in the car for me.

As soon as the mother unlocks the car, I hop into the middle of the backseat. The girls have a brief moment of shoving and grabbing to reach the front seat first, and the shorter of the two wins.

"God," groans the taller girl, as soon as her door is shut behind her. "Catherine is *such* a bitch."

"I like Miss Catherine," the shorter girl says dreamily. "Just because she asked you not to pop your gum doesn't make her a bitch."

"Girls, stop saying 'bitch," the mother says, more sigh than actual words. "But Leigh, for the record, your sister is right. Catherine is a bitch."

All three of them giggle, and I immediately love them each with all of my heart.

By the time we've made the very short drive back to their single wide trailer, I know that the taller girl is Jessica, and has a crush on a senior boy named Josh, which the younger girl, Leigh, finds to be the funniest thing on planet earth. The mother's name is unknown, but she has promised both girls pancakes for lunch in a town called Champaign before they go grocery shopping. I perk up. Champaign is a familiar name to me. Far from home, I think, but still familiar.

The family is all rushing to get changed into "human clothes", as Leigh so aptly calls them. I wander around the house, touching random things, looking at photos on the wall, reading the reminders stuck to their refrigerator.

The mother has left her phone on the kitchen counter, so I snatch it up to find out where I am. Fairmount, Illinois. It's only a tiny speck of houses in a massive green field of nothingness on the map. And there, to our west, is Champaign. A college town, I suddenly remember, and a straight shot south from Chicago.

I'm not invited, but I decide that pancakes sound good for lunch, so I wander back outside to take my place in the car, which the mother has forgotten to lock, or maybe never bothers to lock on this safe little street. Should I take the front seat? I wonder what would happen. I shrug and hop in the passenger side.

When they tumble out of the house, a tornado of laughter and bickering and mascara and secrets, both of the girls get in the backseat without comment. I'm excited for the car ride, ready to drown myself in their conversations, but I'm disappointed. Each child is immediately immersed in her own cell phone, and the mother puts on classic rock and doesn't sing along. It's a long half hour.

Lunch is better, with each of the three ordering a different ridiculously sweet pancake, and me eating off of every plate. My favorite is a cinnamon swirl, topped with bananas. It seems familiar, and I feel like it would be good with bacon, though no one ordered any meat... I say goodbye to the family as they head for the grocery store. I have a bad feeling about going in the store that I can't quite explain, the thought of it sends a shiver down my spine.

Instead, I make my way to a bus stop at the end of the block. From here, I'll be able to take a city bus to the commercial bus terminal, and from there, I'll be able to head north to Chicago. No problem. The bus arrives within the hour, and I find myself on the highway and heading home before I can even consider what I was doing so far away in the first place. The bus is dark and mostly silent besides the discordant low hum of several peoples' headphones set at a high enough volume to be heard throughout. Not even a crying baby to contend with. I lean my head against the glass and try to sleep, but the bumps are too frequent, the bus is too cold, the seats aren't comfortable enough. Instead, I stare out at the billboards flitting by and think of home.

When I finally get off the bus in the south suburbs of the city later that night, a wave of relief overwhelms me. I sink to the ground outside the liquor store that the bus, for whatever reason, stops in front of, and everything feels more familiar. The traffic trundles by and I inhale the smell of asphalt and oil and dirty snow. I'm back. Finally. I feel like I've been gone for a hundred years. How long was I away? Days? Months? Why did I ever leave? I want to wrap the whole city around me like a blanket.

I know that my most frequented train line has a stop only a few miles from here, and I know how to get there. The confidence I feel makes me giddy. I'm going to be alright. The forgetfulness I've been so worried about won't touch me here. I practically skip down the dingy streets. I'm going to go home.

I'm wearing such strange clothes. They're too big, and itchy, and certainly not my style. I pull at the collar of the jacket while I walk. I know this part of town doesn't have much in the way of shopping, but once I set eyes on my house, like a traveler in an airport making sure their gate is real before they set to wandering, I'll go find something new. Something that feels like me. As I walk, I think about what stores I might go to in the morning.

I pat my sides to find my notebook. I should make a list of the stores I'd like to visit tomorrow. I frown. I don't feel the familiar edges of a notebook anywhere on me. I must have left my notebook at home. It's not like me to do that, but it's okay. I'll be there soon. As I walk, I say my list out loud, so I don't forget. I'm like a little kid going to the store sometimes. "And a stick of butter, a carton of milk, a dozen eggs," I say out loud at the end of my list. I try to laugh, but for whatever reason, my mood is slightly soured by the grocery list.

Here it is. My beautiful train station. The long blue sign on the empty platform reads, "Hazel Crest to Chicago" with a little arrow pointing. My stomach turns in a little knot. Have I forgotten something? Something important? I stare at the letters, begging them to give up their secrets. They don't. I pretend like I don't have a sinking feeling, and snuggle up against one side of the glass enclosure to wait for the next train north.

Taptaptap

I jump up, arms raised ridiculously like I'm about to hit someone. Somebody was tapping the glass above where my head was resting, from out on the windy open walkway beside me. I had been off in my own head, concentrating. Thinking of something I was supposed to do when I got home...

Taptap

I see it this time. An upside down, ruby red, human mouth, grinning at me in the darkness as it swings back and forth, just a few feet away. As I try to comprehend the rest of the creature's form, it turns slightly, and kicks a spray of salt and grit at the window with its giant, taloned bird foot.

Taptaptap

The thing is a nightmare, my poor mind is working overtime trying to label it with a sane, human label. But another part of me, a stronger, louder part, tells me more important information. *Don't let it know you can see it. It is invisible. Don't let on.*

I force myself to turn my face away, and to lean as casually as I can back against the glass. The thing out there in the dark only tries to get my attention one more time.

Taptap

And then it makes a strange, honking noise. Maybe a sad sound. Maybe a lost sound. I close my eyes and silently beg for it to just go away. What *is* it? Why is it here? Why do I feel like I know it, like I've seen it?

I hug myself and shiver. Something isn't right. Something is off. I suddenly feel like maybe I'm dreaming, or maybe I am running a fever. My breaths start coming faster and faster, and I can't seem to get them under control.

The last train arrives, and I run for it, as fast as I can manage on the newly refrozen ground. I ease into a plastic seat, and pat my pockets again. I realize that I don't have my purse with me, and I have no money in my pockets, no train ticket. I think I usually have a monthly pass...where could it be?

It must be at home. I nervously wait for the conductor to come by. I'll have to plead my case, explain my forgetfulness, promise him that I'll come back tomorrow and pay my fare. What if he makes me get off at the next stop? I'm still a long way from home, it would be a terrible walk in the cold, in these clothes.

When the conductor makes his rounds, I avoid eye contact, pretend to be asleep. I've seen it work for others. He sweeps by me without a second glance, and I exhale a relieved breath.

The train's gentle rocking and stops and starts send me into a peaceful daze, gazing out the window. I just keep telling myself, *almost there, almost there.* I feel like it's been a weird day, or maybe a weird could of days, but everything is kind of hazy. Did I maybe go to a party? I remember having pancakes with some friends. Maybe we partied a little too hard last night, that's all. It doesn't matter. I'm almost home.

I have to walk the last few blocks from the nearest train station to my house. I run my hands along my upper arms as I walk, trying to keep out the cold. I wonder what time it is. I feel like it might be close to dawn. My sleep schedule is so messed up, these days.

I'm halfway down a block, and I stop, and turn a full circle. Did I make a wrong turn, somewhere? Which way is my house, again? I put a hand up to my temple, and squint down the road. No, no, this isn't right. This is the way to work. I laugh a little to myself, but not too loudly, I don't want to wake up anyone sleeping. I can't believe I walked on autopilot for so long!

I start to turn around, and glance down the alley beside me. There's a garbage truck there, its mechanical arm picking up the full cans and shaking them until the contents are purged into the truck's open, waiting jaws.

I look at the ground, see it rising up to catch me as I plummet. *No.*

The ground has no choice but to catch me harder than I would have preferred, and I land badly on my wrists and knees. I can't move. I might stay, forever, in this spot where I was supposed to stay on that day all those years ago. Some things come back to me. I've been here before, in fact, I think I was here very recently. I always end up here. Every time I forget, I start again right here. A reset, right where the sidewalk intersects with this nameless alley, amongst the hundreds of identical nameless alleys. My last place. My home.

I pat my pockets again. I need my notebook. I *need* my words, reflecting back the light of who I was, what I wanted, where I was going.

"Come on, come on," I whisper, grabbing fistfuls of hair on each side of my head and pulling them tight. "Just think. *Anything.*"

Maybe it's hours I sit there, and maybe it's only moments. But, instead of remembering anything, I forget the last thing. I forget that there's anything to be remembered. Behind is a void, and ahead, uncertainty. Everything else is gone.

When I stand, my tears have dried and my muscles have unclenched. I'm only standing because sitting was uncomfortable. Now that I'm standing, I figure there's nothing better to do than to start walking.

I walk.

Amethyst*: Hi, all. I finally figured out August's password. I'm not here to talk about what August said, although I will quickly tell you that, in my heart, I don't believe what he said to be true.*

I think it's more likely that he was paid off, or coerced, or even threatened, to say what he said. August really did...does, see ghosts. I have no doubt in my mind he does. This isn't why I broke into his computer. It doesn't matter whether or not he sees ghosts or not, none of this fucking matters.

I'm here because I need help. I need your help, his followers, his friends. I haven't seen August since before he made his final video. No one has. Not me, not Johnny, not his mom. He hasn't come home. The police are not helping. They say that he's obviously "lying low" after that video, and that he'll come around.

He wouldn't lay low from me. I'm worried. I'm worried that maybe something bad has happened, that maybe he's been kidnapped or...I don't know, fuck. I just. I need help. Please, help me find August, okay?

We can use his gotghosts email linked below because I don't know any of his other passwords. Just email there if you've seen him, please. Thanks.

Chapter 21

I no longer know how many days have passed since my death, the only thing I'm definitely sure happened to me, and the details of how and where it happened are lost to me as well. I find myself curious about these things. It seems like the kind of information a person should have about herself. I make a mental note to try to figure it out.

I know, though, that the clothes I'm wearing are uncomfortable, and dirty, and I don't like that, so I change them. I follow an old man into his basement apartment and use his facilities while he watches a recording of a basketball game on a tiny television. His microwaved dinner sends a wave of something through me, it touches my heart in a sad and familiar way. Is it nostalgia?

My reflection startles me in the tiny bathroom. I look different than I assumed I would look, or maybe than I remembered I look? I run my tongue along teeth that don't seem familiar, and my entire body seems to be fuzzy at the edges, as though the tiny medicine cabinet is covered in steam. I wipe my had along it, and it comes away dry. I'm distracted by my wiping hand, which seems subtly unreal even outside of a reflection. My nails are long, sharp, and dirty. I turn away and run myself a bath.

I spend too long in the tub examining my skin, my fingers, toes. My hair seems longer and darker than I think it should be, but I remind myself that it is wet, and that's to be expected. The room darkens around me as the sun sinks, and I realize it's past time to move on. There's a compulsion to leave, to leave, to leave. To just keep walking and to never return. I will heed it, because I have no other plans.

I catch my reflection in my peripheral as I stand, dripping, from the tub. The two eyes that glare back at me are pinpricks of yellow, foggy light, like headlights in the distance in the dark.

After selecting some new clothes, a lovely little bag, and a pretty book to jot my thoughts down in, I decide I'd like to take the train. I find my way to a station without any effort, and briefly wonder if this is something I used to do often. This isn't a thought I deem important enough for my new little book, the crisp pages are too nice.

The train has quite a few commuters this time of day, and I casually touch each of them as they enter the compartment. I'm sitting close to the exit specifically for this reason, but I'm not sure why I am compelled to do it. Something is niggling. I frown, and shiver, to banish whatever might be poking my mind. The static of the overhead recording. "*The next stop is: ninety fifth street,*" is like a lullaby.

When I run out of train line, I begin to walk. I have no qualms about leaving the city, and no thoughts of returning there. The compulsion just says, "Go." It says nothing of ever going back. As I walk, it seems that my stride is different than it used to be. I notice that my shoulder bag dangles in front of me, instead of bouncing on my hip as I see other people's bags do. Regardless, the day is sunny, there's the hint of a promise of spring in the air, and it's a good day for a nice, long walk.

I don't talk to myself as I walk. I find I have very little to say, without knowing anything. But there's that squirming in my gut again. At even the consideration of trying to recall *me*, the me as I think I knew her, there's a sensation almost like nausea, or the idea of nausea, maybe. I have to let her go. The notebook remains untouched, and I am intent on arriving at the next destination, whatever that might be.

I don't know how long it's been. I no longer remember starting this journey, or if I have a destination. Every time I look into my bag, which I suppose must just be something I do out of habit, I am newly surprised to find a cute little blank book in there, with a pen attached. I do not mar its pretty pages. What would I say?

Besides, my fingers seem like they might not be the right shape for holding fancy little pens, like the one attached to the notebook. My nails are too long, too pointy, almost more like barren tree branches than fingers. My knuckles gnarl and burl like wood as well.

Eventually, I abandon the little shoulder bag and its book completely, dropping it sadly into a puddle of melting snow on the highway's shoulder. My shoulders hunch up at the wrong angle to hold it in place as I shuffle down the road, and I'm tired of constantly hitching it up, tired of it swinging in front of my face and blocking my view of the ground in front of me. It was holding me back, but seeing it lying there fills me with a sudden pang of the worst (and first) loss I can remember. My eyes fill with tears and I let them fall without embarrassment. The tears feel like tiny daggers, full of sharp edges. It is utter devastation. I feel like I'm abandoning my whole life, but I don't understand why. It's only a moment, though, before I'm able to scrape my wooden arms along my cheeks and move forward. The book's pages were blank, anyway.

It's dark when I decide that I would like a ride. Is it the first darkness of my journey? Every darkness is the first. Every moment is the first. Whatever I had left behind is forgotten, and being sad about it is also gone. All I know now is that my steps have become short, and slower than I would like them to be, and the cars that fly by me are like the wind.

My path is illuminated before me, which doesn't surprise me, as this is my first night and it has always been this way.

I also know, now that I have need for it, that I can easily make the living take notice of me. It's funny, how simple the feeling is. It's like having water put in my mouth and knowing to swallow. It's like putting one foot in front of the other to get where I'm going.

Soon enough, what I can only assume is my own silhouette is blossoming on the pavement in front of me as I'm haloed by the headlights of an approaching car. The shadow is blurred and strange, especially around where I assume my head must be by the illumination of my own eyes.

My spine is arched forward like a question mark, and my head hangs low, in front of my chest. My arms joint strangely and twist around me, maybe with dozens of fingers, or maybe just distorted by multiple light sources. My hair trails the ground in front of me, I realize now, staring at the pavement.

I turn as the car approaches. I'm standing with one foot on either side of a dash of yellow line that's so much longer when you're standing upon it than when you see it fly by from a vehicle. I know I've seen them fly by. My head spins at the thought, but I banish it and focus myself on the car.

It screeches as the driver slams on the brakes, and the back end dances precariously back and forth a few times before the whole car manages to come to a shuddering stop just a few feet in front of me. I relax myself, and slip back into abyss of being unnoticed.

Screaming is coming from inside the car, and it gets louder as I open the back door. "You see that?! Right there in the road! I thought—"

"No, Adrian, all I saw was you almost killing us!"

I close the door quietly and go about the business of making myself comfortable on the bench seat. It's full of suitcases and plastic totes, and the floor is full of discarded cardboard coffee cups.

"You were asleep! There was a...car or something facing us in the middle of the road."

"There was?" There's a scoff. "Then where is it?"

"I...I don't—"

"Get out. I'm driving. You're obviously *too tired*."

I watch the argument impassively. I have no desire to know who they are, or where they're going. I don't care if they're siblings, or friends, or lovers. I didn't even say hello as I entered the car. I just need to go.

The bickering continues for a few more moments, the driver insisting he's fine and the passenger insisting she take over. I swallow what feels like sand through a throat already dried out and rotting from lack of use. I focus. "Go," I say.

Both driver and passenger let out gasps of surprise, and then stare at each other, stare at the radio, and with obvious apprehension, the back of the car. They see nothing, because I don't feel like being seen right now.

The passenger, whose hand is on her door handle to show she is serious about driving, relinquishes it. "We should just...let's just get out of here. I have to pee."

Without discussing events, they drive. The silence between them fills the car like thunder, but it doesn't touch me. I'm hardly even here. I'm just a hitcher.

When they finally pull into a truck stop that's been beckoning them with billboards for miles, the relief of both of them washes over me like a warm gust of air. They feel safer here. Under the fluorescent lights and cheery unoffensive music, within the eyes of other late night travelers, weary, but with that hint of excitement and adventure around each of them, there can be no untethered voices in the dark. There will be no mirages of strangers needing assistance, poised like a Venus fly trap in the middle of the road. Inside, everything will feel familiar, even if they've never been here before.

My face scrunches up in confusion as I consider this. Will it feel familiar for me? Will *anything* ever feel familiar for me, ever again? Curious, I unfold myself from the confines of the over packed car. In any case, I'll find somewhere more comfortable to ride from here. This will be the end of my journey with this driver and his passenger, may they never encounter me or anyone like me again.

Music plays softly over the overhead speakers inside, and I'm surprised to know the words. They come unbidden to the tip of my tongue, and I sing along. "Hold me closer, tiny dancer. Count the headlights on the highway."

The smells inside *are* familiar, and so are the beige speckled tiles that my feet stick to slightly as I pick up each shoe. Years of mopping spilled soda and trodden in grease has left a film that can never be undone, present in this building and every other one like it.

There is a rack near the door of sunglasses, and I move to inspect a pair more closely, but my fingers are all twisted together now (or maybe they always were), and I can't move them in the ways I think I should be able to. I can't pick up a pair. I couldn't even wipe my eyes if I were to cry.

I don't know if I am able to cry.

The sign for the restrooms suddenly looms like a warning. Should I gaze at my own reflection, see the thing I am? It feels unfamiliar, this form, but I can't quite figure out what else I might have been like. Surely, not one of these small frightened living people? I turn away from the sign, intent on ignoring it. On forgetting it.

Instead, I wander. Would I like to eat something? Do I like to eat? It certainly seems a popular thing to do, as many of the shelves are full of food. I lick my dry, rough lips with a drier tongue. The sound it makes is like branches rustling in a breeze. Maybe later. Maybe I'm not ready.

I wander further, and come across an aisle of nonsense. There are toy cars that can be driven by remotes, and t-shirts with silly phrases, magazines showing hundreds of white, white teeth. There are...there are. There.

There is a statue of a unicorn. A foot tall, and painted with glitter that has drifted off like so many autumn leaves to collect on the glass shelf it sits on.

It turns out, I am able to cry.

I do so now, and I feel my sandpaper eyelids attempt to blink away the moisture. I'm not sure why the ridiculous thing should trigger this kind of feeling in me, a loss so profound. It must mean something. I try to pick up the glittering mass with my stiff, wooden fingers. I can't really manage it, but I think if I can just scoop it up into my arms...

The unicorn crashes to the linoleum. Its horn lays in two pieces beside it, and one of its rearing front legs. Glitter continues to shimmer down long after it has crashed, like snow.

As clear as though the speaker were standing right beside, maybe within me, I hear the phrase, "If it breaks, it breaks. It's no big deal."

I lower myself to the tiles beside the broken thing, my limbs creaking ominously. *I* said that. I said that to someone. I have not always been the Hitcher. Before, I must have been a person, a person that gave a silly gift to someone.

I just have to remember who.

Chapter 22

I've been successfully curbing my instinct to move on for a while now. This is important, and as long as I have this broken unicorn, I'm not losing sight of my intentions. I've been haunting the truck stop, bright lights and cheery music be damned. It's not bad, actually. I snack on processed, packaged foods, take the first cup of coffee whenever the attendants brew a fresh pot, read the magazines, watch the people. I do love watching the people. I find myself creating little backstories for them which may be true or may not be, and I wish them well when they leave the oasis and continue their quests.

I am changing. My hair, which dragged along in a tangle at my feet when I arrived, brushes my shoulders now. My fingers can flex and move. My back is straight, my neck mobile. I can't be sure, because in all this time, I haven't gained the courage to view my reflection, but I think my eyes might have lost their incandescent glow. It's never dark enough in here to test them.

I feel different. I'm sad, and vulnerable, and very, very lost. I feel like a child accidentally left behind on a family trip (a scene I got to witness recently, along with a happy and tearful reunion a few minutes later), but I don't know who my missing family might be. But there's also a sense of adventure, and a sense of discovery in that sadness. I'd like to think I saw it in that child's eyes for the moments he was alone. Of course he was scared, but wasn't it all a little exciting, as well? A story to be looked back on fondly once he was again safe? I gave this unicorn, this glitter bombed talisman, to someone very important to me. I just need to find myself, and then maybe I can find them. I repeat that magic phrase in my head, then test out my voice.

"If it breaks, it breaks."

The sound that comes out of me is gravelly at first, tires crunching on a dirt road, but over time I find a voice that feels right, feels familiar. I think it might be mine.

I've changed clothes, and the pickings are slim at a truck stop. I'm not ready to leave this place yet, too anxious for the potential of losing this kernel of memory out there in the breeze. I'm wearing camouflage leggings, and a pink sweatshirt that reads, "Ain't NO Girl, Like a COUNTRY Girl," and it makes me laugh. I don't think it's the kind of thing I would have usually worn, but it makes me feel very, very human. I like that feeling.

I carry the shattered unicorn under my arm like a security blanket as I wander the store, when I feel like wandering. It's morning, and the sun is warm again today. Its heat radiates through the glass panes of the sliding doors, but the warmth is still negated by the rush of chilly air every time the door swishes open and shut, so I retreat back into the confines of the snacks as another customer approaches across the cement.

I'm hovering by the brightly lit doughnut display. Every morning, a truck comes by and delivers a fresh supply. I like the blueberry ones, but they're a popular choice. I feel bad depriving any actually hungry person of their deliciousness, so most days I've trained myself to wait until the evening before taking one, if there are any left. Not today, though. Even though it can't be noon, I see there's only a solitary blueberry to be found amidst the obviously inferior chocolate and vanilla ones, and I decide that I *must* have one today.

A person shuffles in front of me to select a doughnut. I peer over his shoulder. "Don't you do it, don't take that...aahhhh." He's chosen my doughnut. I sigh, not willing to take it from him, even though I definitely could. I stand behind him as he clumsily places it into a little white bag using the flimsy wax sheet. "You know, the chocolate ones are in season, I think." I sing to him, but he is not interested in changing his mind. He turns.

My unicorn slips through my fingers and shatters into a dozen shards at my feet.

The doughnut thief is a Black man, slightly shorter than me, but large. He wears no winter coat despite the cold day, just a sweatshirt and joggers. He's probably in his late twenties, maybe early thirties. His hair needs a trim, it puffs out from underneath his baseball cap. I have seen dozens of similar looking men come in and out of this truck stop since I have been haunting it, but not this man. This is the most beautiful man I have ever seen.

I know him. I must know him. My eyes fill with tears and my now empty hands start to shake. "Hello?" I whisper. Will he see me? Will he know me? Will he tell me who I am?

He does not see me. My doughnut wrapped securely in its bag, he turns and heads for the checkout counter.

"Wait!" Tears well up, and my whole body shakes. He has to see me. I *know* him. "Please don't leave me here." I grab onto his sweatshirt, but he moves on, as if I weigh nothing, as if I'm not even here.

I try to remember the night that I arrived here. That night, I did something new and powerful. I forced myself to be seen, or unseen. It had felt so easy, and natural, I remember. So simple that I didn't understand how I hadn't known how before. I try now. I try so hard. "Please, just *see* me." I say as the man pays for his (my) doughnut and gas. "I know you, I know I do. You must know me!"

To an observer (if I could be observed), I might look like a child, throwing a tantrum because he refused to buy me a unicorn statue when we only stopped for gas. Or maybe, I'd look like a partner, caught doing something unforgivable, begging him to be forgiven. Whatever I might look like doesn't matter, as I'm the only one to witness my begging, snot and tears and desperate pawing. It takes much too long before I realize there's no rush, I can simply leave with him, and continue wracking my brain in the comfort of his car.

Leaving the store is even more difficult than I expected. I don't know how long I was in there, but some part of me firmly rooted there, and that part is so, so reluctant to step out of those sliding glass doors. Some part of me insists that the world will definitely end if I go out there, and tries its best into sweet talking me to remain with promises of Doritos and fresh coffee and sticky tile floors. But I am stronger than that bit of me, and I'm now shuffling across the concrete, wondering why on earth I've stayed here for so long. I should have taken my unicorn and left with the first comfortable car owning person that liked the same music as me. I leave the broken unicorn on the ground near the doughnut case, a little memorial to me, from me.

I still clutch onto the man's sweatshirt, but I'm no longer yelling or crying. It's more like we're in a dense crowd, or a blizzard, and I don't want to get separated. We walk around away from the cars getting gas, to the other side of the building. On this side, semis are all lined up, idling like massive beasts purring. *He drives a truck, and it is purple,* my mind informs me. For some reason, the fact that this information has been so clearly and easily divulged to me is rage inducing. Thank you, memory, for keeping this little snippet safe for me. I don't know my own name, or where I was born, I don't know what happened yesterday or two years ago, but we are positive that this man drives a purple truck.

There it is. The sight of the thing doesn't fill any blanks in my past, but the recognition is there, and it's so strong I feel the hair on my arms raise. I'm not mistaken. I know this man, and I feel certain in the knowledge now that my "memory" about him is correct. I exhale in relief, and tears threaten again, but I keep them in check.

When I climb up on the passenger side and open the door, I know that I have done so before. That little squeak is familiar, I know how much pressure I'll need on the handle. The grey cloth interior is just the way it should be. Everything is right.

"Hello?" I call into the back as I sit. I don't know why, but part of me expects another person to be within. There's no answer.

The man climbs up behind the steering wheel and throws his phone on a little holder on the dashboard before settling himself in to the doughnut prize. I gaze at him for a long ten seconds, waiting for any kind of revelation. It doesn't come, and then I realize I'm just looking at him to look. My cheeks flush.

"Um," I say, and look around the cab. "Alright. No offense, but I don't remember your name." I snatch up a clipboard from beside him. "Sean Frances."

I frown. That's not right, is it? I stare at him. I throw the name at him over and over in my head, but it doesn't stick, it just bounces off. *Could* I be mistaken? Is this some other person that just reminds me of someone I used to know? No, it's him, whoever he might be. He smells like home. This cab smells like home. I live here.

When he's finished our doughnut, he reaches over and takes the clipboard out of my hands without a second thought, like I'm a piece of furniture. He notates a time, and then, I think, re-enters the same information into an app on his phone. He sends a text, which I don't mind snooping at over his shoulder, that reads, "*I'll be home tomorrow afternoon.*" He's ready to start driving.

My heart lurches with the truck. I'm afraid to leave. What if I can't retain this person I've become? What if I revert into that...that other thing, the least parts of me? I reach out and touch the man's shoulder. "Don't lose me, okay?"

The highway is hard for me. The monotony of the dotted lines, of the repeated billboards, the *same*ness of it all. It makes it difficult for me to focus. I turn in my seat and instead study the man, hoping for any further revelations. They come, but nothing that helps in the moment. He has a shiny scar on the back of his left hand. I can't see it from here, but I know it's there. I know there was a time when I held that hand in both of mine. He has a nice singing voice, I remember hearing him sing...

The radio. The radio was important to us. Why hasn't he turned it on? Who drives in silence for this long? I reach out and press the power knob. As Hall and Oates (oh yes, my classic rock memory has been nicely filled by my stay at the gas station) fill the silence, the man gasps and spins to face my seat.

"Poppy?" he asks.

"Look at the road!" I squeal, and put my hands up to my eyes. The semi is now barreling down upon a slow moving white van, which, for whatever reason, decided it suddenly needed to be in this lane.

I don't think the man heard me, but he must have had the same thought, because he does, in fact, look at the road and taps the breaks gently, until we coast along at a safe distance behind the intrusive van. He makes short, quick looks in my direction as he does so.

"Poppy, are you in here? If you're here, please tell me. I've been looking for you, I swear. I just didn't..." He pauses, blinking hard. "I didn't know where to look. I didn't find out enough about you when I had the opportunity. I'm sorry. I'm so sorry. I shouldn't have sent you away. I didn't...God, are you even here? What if I'm just..." *What if you're just talking to yourself? Again. You've been talking to yourself, haven't you?*

I stare at him, mouth hanging open. "Can you hear me? If I talk to you?" Poppy doesn't sound like my name, just like Sean doesn't sound like his. But it *must* be me he's looking for. How could it not be?

"If you're here, can you turn off the radio?" he asks, and he sounds like he's embarrassed. *If you're here, give us a sign.*

My hand floats back toward the knob, presses it gently. I hope I'm not accidentally impersonating someone named Poppy, but I do want him to know I'm here. I desperately do.

The man lets out an emotional huff, wipes a cheek desperately fast with a hand. "I'm so glad you found me," he says. I'm so glad he found me. "We'll talk soon, okay? I've got to work, but we'll talk soon. Just stay with me. Don't leave me. I'll talk to you. Wait!"

I jump at the urgency of the *wait*. He said it like I'm in immediate danger.

"I have something of yours. Some kid brought it to Ma's. She said the address was in it. I can't...It's hard for me to look at, but..." He wipes his cheek again, an embarrassed little flash of his wrist. "It must be yours. I keep forgetting about it. It's here, It's on the bookshelf by my cot back there." He nods over his shoulder to the sleeping compartment.

I unbuckle and unsteadily clamber over my seat towards the area portioned off from us by a curtain. Behind it is the man's whole life while he's on the road. A little bed, a shelf of books, a single photograph of a little, laughing girl with her beautiful mother. I left this photograph here in the cab, I can visualize me tucking into the visor above the driver's seat. The girl has the man's dimples, and one day, maybe a long time ago, I gave her a unicorn covered in fuchsia glitter.

"Addie," I say, as I touch her smiling face. "Her name is Addie."

"Did you find it?" the man calls.

I run my fingers along the spines of the books stuffed haphazardly into the spot he calls a bookshelf, but I may never find what I'm looking for, because my eyes haven't left the photograph. My entire existence is on the tip of my tongue, right there, right there, but I can't quite get to it. For now, I know that this little girl is Addie, and I have to keep her safe.

My fingers brush absently along the books and across something that is not a book, or maybe it's a very small one. I tear my eyes away from the picture. I am touching a little notebook with a pocket on the front for a pen to sit in. An elastic band holds it closed, and it is much used, dirty, the binding cracked. It's mine. I pluck it from the shelf and hold it in front of me as though it's made out of glass, or maybe glitter covered ceramic, begging to be dropped and shattered.

Here I am. I'm inside this book.

Where's August?

MODERATOR: *Hi all. I'm reinstating this forum at the request of Amethyst and Johnny. August Waters hasn't been seen or heard from since his last video update. They're worried about him, and I think, as his fan base, we should be worried about him, too.*

Johnny and Amethyst are both skeptical over the validity of the confession video. They think it's possible that he was forced to make it, maybe by a government agency, an individual, heck, maybe even a ghost. They believe August really does see ghosts, and they can't imagine he would have made that video of his own volition, especially without telling them.

What I'm saying is, August could very well be IN DANGER. We need to find him. I've set up a direct link to contact us with ANY information regarding his whereabouts.

If, on the off chance August is reading this: Call your mom, at least, dude.

Chapter 23

I turn the radio on and off several times to show my appreciation to the man. He laughs. I love that laugh. "I guess you found it? I figured it might help. Ma said that when that guy was hanging around, he talked about Addie being worried about forgetting things."

I clutch the notebook close and hang on his every word, hoping for more sparks of recognition, but they don't come so far. I'm apprehensive about opening the book. I will, but I want to drink in every moment and savor it, both with the man, and with the book. I don't want to divide my attention.

"That guy" means nothing to me, but the tone in which he said the words gives me a shiver of dislike all the same. If this man doesn't like someone, then I don't like them either. "Addie forgetting things," though, that phrase holds far more weight. That phrase is a bomb. She is like me, and she is afraid. That much I know now.

"I tried to look through it, but I didn't want to be a snoop," the man says. "But I don't remember any of it, even though I tried. Except one page. There's a page that..." He clears his throat. "There's a page where you wrote down Addie's name a bunch of times, so you wouldn't forget her. Thank you for caring about her," he says. And then he says nothing else for a little while except small secret sniffles, and I pretend not to notice them.

In the quiet, the urge to open the notebook is strong, but before I do, the man has collected himself. "You'd write to me, you know. You...hey! Why don't I just tell you about us, a little? Would that help?"

I gasp and lunge for the radio knob. I turn it on and off.

"Once for yes?" he asks.

I hit the knob once again.

He laughs. "Is that a yes, then?"

Once more.

"Well how do I know once isn't no? Hmm." He's smirking. "All right. So..." A deep breath, a long pause, and then he begins to tell me of our travels.

The more he tells me, the more I remember. As he talks of Addie, I know that that it was she who christened me as "Poppy," named after a friend's cat. The man and I learned to communicate in a restaurant with crayons he tells me, and I grin, remembering our poor server. When he mentions the internet sensation turned chaotic nightmare that was August Waters, my blood runs cold, and I recall the wind on my face as I hurtled from his balcony, and how much it hurt.

Things come back on their own, things the man never knew. I remember late night ghost hunting (and mostly not being successful) while the man slept. I remember trying to do Addie's hair on Christmas morning. I remember abandoning Charlie, being abandoned by August. All the things that have happened since I first decided to follow this man home are presented to me on the silver platter of my thoughts, even the things that the man wasn't there for. I remember how much I enjoyed his company, even if it was lonely sometimes, and I remember that I've missed him terribly.

The time before the day I followed the man to his truck (not today, but a very similar day, I think), is a big, open space of possibility. I have lived many lives and died many deaths in that space, I think, and perhaps the notebook still keeping my hands from shaking will show me those things. But for now, I am overwhelmed. I simply can't hold the weight of all of these things in me at the same time, and I'm afraid I might explode.

"And the kid at the Denny's." The man is laughing. "They must have thought I was completely bonkers. I can never go back in there!"

I smile, and watch him laugh, and let his words wash over me like the ocean. He hasn't told me his name, and I haven't remembered it, yet. It's okay. I'm home.

"They've just got to unhook this trailer, then I'm off for two days," the man tells me as he maneuvers into the truck yard. "We're going to go up and see Ma. I'm actually staying there right now, I broke the lease on that apartment. This won't take long, we can just stay here. I have something else." His words come fast paced and excited, and he infects me with his enthusiasm. He gets up, stoops, and pushes the curtain aside. He sits on the cot and pats the thin mattress beside him, beckoning.

I come over and sit. I loop my arm through his and lean my head onto his shoulder. "I've missed you," I say. "Even when I didn't know who you were or who I was, I missed you."

He doesn't respond, he's pulling something out from behind the passenger seat, where I know I'd stored Addie's things and even a bicycle once. He produces a dry erase board, only a little larger than a regular sheet of paper. A blue marker is clipped to its side.

"I've been doing a lot of talking," he says. "Do you have anything to say?"

He balances the board on his crossed legs and unclips the marker, holds it in his left hand just above the blank surface. I trace the shiny scar on the back of his hand before I envelop it in both of mine. What do I tell him? I run over the things that I don't remember, the blanks I'm trying to fill, and my hands start moving. They don't form a single question.

I missed you

He reads the words, and then brings his right hand up to cover his eyes. The whiteboard clatters to the floor. "I've missed you, too. I'm really sorry." His voice is fading into a choked whisper. "It was just, scary, you know? Not you, you aren't scary, don't..." He's looking at me now. Just for a second, I think our eyes meet. It's probably an accident.

"If you're wearing pink, I think maybe..." He falters again. "I think I just saw you? For a second, I swear." He excitedly grabs the board again, and I scrawl.

PINK!

I laugh and hug him tight and pretend he can feel me there, even though he can't.

"This is great. Maybe, with practice or something?" He grins. "Just wait, Addie will be thrilled to see you. I assume. You know she can't write a lot, but she...lets us know she's around."

We leave the yard trailer free, and head toward Addie, wherever she is. I'm not even really sure where *we* are. I feel like there are a hundred questions I'd like answers to, but the man is driving again, and I have no way to ask, so I open my little notebook.

Buddy. I breathe a sigh of relief as the name jumps at me from the first page I turn to. Oh, Buddy. How could I have ever forgotten you? "Buddy!" I cry. "I forgot your name, don't be mad."

Buddy cocks his head toward me. "Did you say my name?"

My eyes fill with tears. "Yes, can you hear me?" He can't. But he *did.* Instead of trying again, I toggle the radio.

He grins. "Once for yes. Hi, Poppy."

I try, with some difficulty, I have to admit, to shift my focus to my written words. They are scattered, indistinct. I obviously thought that a phrase or a name would be enough to trigger a more complete thought, but it isn't always the case. There's no timeline, hardly any dates. Things like "green car: I want to believe" are underlined, important, but without context. I'm going to have to take these, and the things I remember now, and try to arrange them cohesively. I need a plan, a system, an outline, anything. I need a memoir.

There are a good chunk of blank pages still left at the back of this book, so I write down key things to figure out, to fill in, to elaborate on. I never, ever, want to sink into that place I was. I shudder.

If I should forget it all, everything that makes me who I am, I still will not cease to exist. I will still wander here. I've seen others that have forgotten everything, or almost everything. I will detail them, and their locations, in the following pages, so that I might be able to help them remember who they were.

My own personal monster is a creature I will henceforth call the Hitcher. I will give all of these monsters, for that is what they are, even if they are only monsters of our own creation, names like this throughout my detailing. The names are only placeholders for a spirit's true name, and should I discover that name, I will keep it separate from the thing left when the spirit is gone. These monsters are not us. My time in that state was thankfully brief, but from what I remember, I did not possess my personalities, my fears, or my loves. There was only the creature, a thing to take up the space where I used to be.

I read over the words, and try to decide if they are true. *Was* I in there, when I was that monster? Was my transformation incomplete? I decide that, in the long run, it doesn't matter within the context of my own notebook, which is only for myself. If that is the way that I felt, then it is, simply, the truth.

"You doing okay over there?" Buddy asks.

I've been quiet for a while. It took a lot of effort to put down this fully formed thought instead of a haphazard scribble. Maybe I used to write like this, long ago, and it whittled down to the barest minimum over many years. But then, how many notebooks would I have, long filled? Where might they be?

"Poppy?" Buddy asks again, and there's the tiniest edge in his voice. He's anxious, he thinks maybe I've left him, or that he's imagined me after all. I can see it spiraling through his mind by the squint in his eyes as he listens for a response. What if I'm not real?

I quickly turn on the radio, and leave it on. Maybe we'll feel less tense. Buddy exhales.

"Sorry, just checking," he says.

The DJ announces an hour long music block brought to us by the generous accident attorneys of some firm in Des Moines, and the songs begin. I sing along to two songs before I realize something is different. Buddy isn't singing. We used to sing together, is something bothering him?

But, we used to sing together when he thought he was alone. Now that I *am* real, and he knows that I'm present, some things will be different. I assure myself that it's for the best, but I feel the ache of loss all the same.

It's late by the time Buddy pulls into a rest area. He tells me, or himself, that he lost track of the time and should have stopped ages ago, but he was just trying to get as close to home in one go as possible.

"It's only another two hours or so," he says through a yawn. "But I just can't do it tonight. Too bad you can't drive, eh? Wait. Can you drive? We'll talk about it tomorrow. Well, later today."

Before he gets out to wash up in the visitor center and stretch, he looks toward me. "I'll leave here at seven, *but* not until I'm sure you're with me. You turn that radio on and off three times when you are in the truck and ready to go in the morning, okay? I don't want to lose you."

My heart swells. I will definitely be in the truck, as there aren't many places to go from a rest stop on the side of the highway, but the fact that he will check that I'm here a wonderful feeling. I'm invited, I'm wanted, I'm a guest.

I go in the center too, just to wash my face and look at my reflection. It's been a long time since I've seen myself. I'm still nervous about it, but with Buddy nearby, it's easier. He heard me, maybe even saw my pink shirt for a second. He's not scared of me. I must not be a monster, right?

I am not a monster. I'm a woman, maybe in her twenties, maybe in her thirties. I have brown hair and blue eyes. Some freckles. I'm wearing a novelty sweatshirt and camouflage leggings. I don't have headlights for eyes or branches for arms, did I ever? My back is straight. I have no shoes on, just dirty socks. I laugh at the woman in the mirror. She looks ridiculous, and tired. She looks like she's been on the road for twenty years and is nowhere nearer her home. But, she's still going. I'm proud of her.

I open and close the cab's door as quietly as I can a few minutes later, worried Buddy may already be asleep, and doubly self-conscious about making noise after he's both heard and even briefly *seen* me today (I can't believe that this outfit, of all outfits, is the one I was seen wearing. Figures.). I'm right to be anxious, because he calls out from behind his partition curtain. There's a reading light on back there, filtering into the front of the cab.

"That you, Poppy?"

"I'm here," I say.

He doesn't hear me, but he pauses politely and goes on like he did. "I know you don't sleep, but if you want to rest, you can..." He falters and gives a funny little embarrassed cough. "What I mean to say is, you're welcome to be back here, too. You obviously won't bother me. You can come and go as you please."

I'm still not in the mental state to say for sure, but I think I have spent every single night completely alone for a very, very long time. It doesn't have much impact to say that I don't remember the last time I spent any significant amount of time laying in a bed. But, maybe...maybe there is a memory there. A deep memory, a very long ago place and time. There's a phantom scent of hairspray, and a blue chenille quilt. The quilt had roses on it. I touch the fabric of the passenger seat and try to remember how that quilt felt. The roses were raised, I remember brushing my hands along them.

"I'm not trying to be forward or anything, don't worry. Just hate the idea of you sitting up there all uncomfortable all night. Doesn't seem fair."

I come back to the present, and pull the curtain to the side. Buddy is propped up against the wall, squeezed onto the far side of the cot. He has a hefty sci fi novel open in his lap, and glasses he wasn't wearing while driving. They're cute on him. I sink down beside him and lean my head on his shoulder. He's holding the book low, probably because he's far sighted, but I imagine it's so I can read, too. He's about a quarter of the way in, but it's okay. Once I figure out which name belongs to which role, the story will be easy to follow. The sad main character will find a new purpose in helping some down on their luck new acquaintance. He won't want to help at first, because he's a loner, but he'll realize he has no choice, and the acquaintance will become a friend as they overcome the obstacles. There will also be hull breaches.

"I like to read for a few minutes before I try to sleep," Buddy says conversationally. "I used to have nightmares about Addie and Rebecca's accident. But if I read first, it's just dreams about whatever I'm reading about, usually. Minds are trainable, I guess."

Are they? I certainly hope he's right. Maybe mine's just an old dog. It's trying its best, but sometimes, it forgets. I snuggle up close, but can't focus on the words on the page. I just close my eyes and enjoy being next to another person.

***August**: Hi, Mom. And, hi, I guess, to any other people here to hate watch. Any friends left on here? Hi, if you're there. Or if you come back to watch this later to see what happened. Hi to the cops that will probably be watching this in a few hours. Hope you're all having a screaming Sunday. I assume this will probably be my last vlog for a while. Sorry I haven't been posting the last few weeks, haven't been in the mood.*

Basically, I want to tell you that my last video, my confession video, is my true lie. I was forced into making it, coerced, by certain people (and yes, ghosts) that didn't want my truth out there in the world. It was all too big, too much attention, too many lives getting turned upside down. Yada, yada.

I was silenced and humiliated for telling the truth. For filming the truth. Johnny and Amethyst know, at least. They know there weren't any tricks. They believe me. I love both of you for that. I'm sorry I didn't appreciate you more.

Even though I've suffered this indignation, I maybe am I little bit to blame. Maybe I haven't been a good guy. Maybe I don't have enough empathy. I can't help it. I'm a science guy, you know? I forget that no matter how fascinating these ghosts are, how much I want to show them to you, Mom, and to everyone, that they still have feelings. Maybe I forgot that.

Anyway. My life is essentially destroyed by this lie I've been forced to live for the last few weeks, and I'm pissed, and sad, and lost. It's hard to admit that, but now you know. I guess...

Ahem. Sorry. Something in my eye, right? Anyway. I guess this is a good time to tell you that when, in the far distant future, hopefully, I die...if I am one of the ghosts that remain, I will tell you. Look for me, I will be around.

Film me. If I can't show the proof, I will be the proof.

Gotta go.

Chapter 24

"Poppy!" Addie's eyes are wide as she peeks at me from around the banister. "I almost forgot you." She steps out and places a tiny hand on each tiny hip. "Where have you been?"

I try to look sufficiently admonished, but I'm grinning so wide she can probably see my tonsils. I stretch my arms toward her and let her crash into me for the best hug ever. "I'm sorry, Addie, I didn't mean to be away this long. How are you?"

The walls of the entryway are covered with scribbles, as high as someone about Addie's height might be able to reach with a chair and crayon to help. There are pictures of houses, of people, of cats with triangle ears and long whiskers, but mostly, there is a name.

Addie Addie ADELINE Addie

"Have you been practicing your name?" I inquire, casually.

"Yeah, some. They see my drawings sometimes but kinda forget about them, so I do new ones." She pulls on her sweatshirt, looks at the floor.

Buddy has already made his way downstairs, I assume he's using a bedroom and bathroom down there now that he's moved back in. "Are you glad your dad moved home?"

"Yes."

I frown. She's being shy, quiet. Have I really been gone that long? I move up the stairs toward her, cautiously. "Hey, is everything alright? You want to talk to me? Where's your grandma?"

"She's at the store." The other questions go unanswered, but she brightens. "Hey! Want to see my room?"

I smile. "Sure."

She grabs me by the hand and tugs me toward the hallway. I've only ever been in her grandmother's room, but there are two other doors I assume must belong to small bedrooms. "Daddy put a bunch of junk in the attic and downstairs and set it up for me." She opens the door. It's been painted orange and still has that latex paint smell, and there's a futon, a writing desk, a small television with a pile of DVD cases strewn in front of it. There are plenty of toys.

"Wow, this is really nice. Do you like it?" I run my hand along her desk, scattered with drawings and practiced letters.

"Mmm-hmm." She hops across the floor and jumps on the futon.

I come and sit beside her.

"I'm bored," she says dramatically, and throws herself backward as though fainting.

I pause. Does she mean 'bored' as in, right this second? Should I ask her to play a game, go for a walk? Or does she mean in general? "Oh, yeah? Tell me why you're bored."

"Well..." She can't continue her pretend fainting, and is already up again, wiggling around like an electron. "I don't know. I've already watched my movies and played with my toys."

"Yeah," I admit. "There's a lot of time in the day when you don't get sleepy, I know."

"Can you teach me letters?" The questions bursts out of her like she'd been holding it in since before I arrived, maybe since before I left last time. "I want to write letters."

"Ooh." I smile. "I think I could do that. It would be fun! How about you clean up your room and your desk and we'll have lessons. It'll be like school!"

"But there's no other kids."

I nod slowly. "It'll be like home school."

Addie's eyes light up. "Bethany from church does home school! She used to bring snacks to Sunday school because she had…" Addie shrugs. "She had a little phone on her belt that would tell her to have snacks. Nobody else was allowed, but sometimes she'd sneak me jellybeans."

I frown, trying to figure out what phone would dole out snacks. "Oh, diabetes?"

"Maybe. She was nice, for an older kid."

I laugh. "All right. We'll do home school like Bethany. Starting today!"

I clap once, and Addie starts running around her room, gathering toys into piles at top speed, all giggles and flashing limbs, making more of a mess than there was in her enthusiasm.

"Poppy?" Buddy calls. "If you're around, come see this downstairs."

"I'll be back soon, better hurry!" I say to the giggling girl, and wander downstairs like I'm in a dream.

Buddy is standing in front of our big whiteboard, which he's placed on a folding table in front of the washer and dryer. I assume from the pile of neatly folded clothes beside it that the table is usually for sorting laundry. There are two folding chairs next to it. "This'll work okay, right?" He rubs the back of his neck. "I'm doing my best here, you know. This is all…a lot. It's weird. I kind of feel like *I'm* the one left out."

That proclamation sets me on edge. I guess I didn't consider how having two ghosts in the house might make Buddy and Sharleen feel. As soon as I'm able, I'll have to tell Buddy that being dead is no picnic. He sits down at the table and picks up a marker.

The letters I make with his hand are so slow, so awkward. I hate it. It's frustrating when I have so many paragraphs to say, a whole book to tell him. But the four words I manage take so long that I leave my thought unfinished, as always.

We'll make it work
We'll make it work.

"Well," Buddy sits back, looking at the one word I've written.

It's been a few weeks of this strange new life. I go with Buddy when he works, I come home and teach Addie how to read and write. She's a fast learner, and very anxious. Buddy and I "talk" every night, sometimes into the morning. I feel bad about those nights, he needs his rest. He's not like me, and I need to remember not to be so selfish with his time.

"How much do you know about what happened with him?" he asks.

He doesn't wait for a response. He asks a lot of questions that don't get answers, in the interest of time. I asked him about the ghost hunter. Addie mentioned him briefly today while telling me a story. I'd forgotten all about him again, and the reminder felt like I'd left home with the curling iron plugged in. *Oh, shit, I forgot about August.* Forgot about that guy who threw me out a window, so I ruined his budding career. I left him to heat up, to melt the particle board bathroom counter he was set on, to slowly start to smoke and fizzle.

"I saw his confession. I don't know how you got him to agree to that. I didn't see it live, Ma had some friend send it to her, and she told me about it. But once she said he had a 'ghost' on there, I knew I'd have to watch it myself. I knew it was going to be you." Buddy pauses. He wants to ask something or say something, but delicately. He's choosing his words. It's only fair, I get to choose all my words so, so, slowly. "I saw you. I...well, it's embarrassing. But. First, I want to say, you're really beautiful, I'm sure. I might be biased." He gives an awkward laugh. "It's honestly impossible to tell what you look like, I'll show you the video if you want. But also..." The silence is thick with apprehension. "What happened to you? Do you hurt?"

I frown. I don't know what he's talking about. He's still holding the marker and resumes his position facing the board. I drag his hand into a single "?"

"Well, you're...here, let me just show you." He retrieves his phone from his pocket and fiddles around with it for a minute. While he finds what he's looking for, he says, "I can't help but wonder about Addie. Does she..."

I'm completely lost, but he finds the video. Not the video. It's a screen shot, cropped to show only me, with August's hand on my shoulder. Oh, right. I forgot about the blood from my trip over the balcony.

I'm not exactly there, in the photo. I mean, I *am*, it's obvious August has his arm around a person, and the person isn't transparent or vaporous or anything like that. It's almost like there's a camera glare, or even just poor lighting, making me just a little blurry. It's like I'm caught in mid motion. None of that hides the fact that my clothes are ruined with blood. It's spattered and pooled on the fabric, and even in my hair. There's two fingers worth of streaks of it down one side of my face. For having been thrown from a building, I think I look pretty remarkable, but yeah. It's ghastly. Poor Buddy probably thinks the visage is from my original death. He probably thinks Addie looks as bad, or worse.

That's recent don't worry

Each line takes forever, and Buddy's hand is sweating in mine. He's terrified, thinking his little girl is suffering the moment of her death for eternity, and it has taken me over a minute to reassure him with four words. And it's not enough, nowhere near enough info. I move his hand down, begin another painstakingly slow line.

Addie is fine I am fine no blood no hurt

Buddy's shoulders lose their tension, and he leans back and gives a relieved groan. "That's good. I was really upset, but I can't really talk to Addie, you know, and how would I ask? Would I even want to ask?"

I pat his shoulder. He doesn't know that Addie and I have developed a plan for tonight after dinner, to celebrate how far she's come with her writing. She's been practicing moving my hand to write, "I love you, Daddy," and "I love you, Gramma." I'll save the surprise. She and I are also planning on painting over all of her scribbles on the walls when Buddy and I come back again in two weeks.

"What happened, though? Was it just for the video? Is it fake?"

I sigh. I'm going to have to tell him, but I don't want him to go starting things with August, who even now might be sending licks of flames toward the towel rack.

We can *get hurt. He hurt me.*

Buddy shakes his head. "That son of a bitch. I knew he was no good. I *knew* it."

I'm okay now!

"Not the point," he says. "But it makes me feel a little better. He posted his video and Ma got real upset, thinking that he tricked her and Addie wasn't really here and all that. It's a lot for a woman her age to go through, you know? Almost like she lost Addie twice. When she called me, she was crying, saying she'd been foolish." He scratches his temple with the edge of the marker. "I almost wanted to believe it, you know. But I didn't. I knew you were here, and I knew Addie was here, and I knew, seeing you on camera, that you'd done something to make him get the attention off us. It worked. People lost interest in our house overnight. We stopped getting phone calls from the media, everything. It was all just over for us."

I breathe a sigh of relief. I wasn't sure it would work.

"Ma got used to the idea of Addie being around again, even though Addie never went anywhere, and it's been okay. Sometimes I think Addie's frustrated, lonely. Maybe I'm projecting that on to her, I don't know. I just wanted her to have someone to talk to. I'm glad you're here."

I'm glad I'm here, too, and I'm glad he shares my concerns with Addie. I think her reading and writing will assuage the "boredom", as she calls it, but for how long? What we have here can work for a while, but I have to be pragmatic. Sharleen won't be here forever.

Buddy won't be here forever. My heart clenches at the thought. Will Addie and I be enough for each other?

"Anyway," Buddy pulls me back from those wretched thoughts. "The news on Mr. Waters petered out, too. He hasn't been doing his show. Netflix pulled out, I think I saw. I have no idea what he's up to, if anything."

I bite my lip. Maybe it's not really fair what I did to him. He was only showing people what he could see, after all.

"You want some dinner?" Buddy asks. "I think Ma bought some salmon I should probably use."

I follow him upstairs, pensive and uncomfortable.

Addie's laying on her stomach in the hallway, a picture book open in front of her. Her head snaps up as soon as she hears me. "Ms. Poppy, what's this word?"

She insists on calling me, "Ms." Poppy while I teach her, because *all* teachers' first names are "Ms." Or "Mrs." according to her.

I squat down beside her. "Let's see, which word?"

She covers the offending word almost completely with her finger.

"Okay, let's sound it out. That first letter is..."

"A like apple!"

"Excellent." I beam down at her. She's really a smart kid, "And then..."

"L like love. Ah-Luh." She moves her finger between the A and L, repeating the sound s they make a few times. "But this one is hard."

"That's a hard one to remember. W, like..."

"Water!" *Like Waters.* I shiver. " Ah-luh-wuh. Alw-ah. Al-way. Always!"

"You are doing *so* well!" I pat her shoulder and start to stand.

Three knocks come from the front door. My stomach drops. *Not so soon,* I think. *Don't ruin this so soon.* I know, in my heart of hearts, that I spoke those knocks into existence by writing the ghost hunter's name a few minutes ago. I don't know how I know this, but it's clear as crystal. August Waters will be standing on the other side of that door, and he's going to have a crew, a camera. He's going to get first eye witnesses and new evidence, and he's going to get his life back.

"Addie," I say as calmly as I can. "Do you have a very secret hiding spot in this house?"

"Sure," she says.

"I'd like you to go in there now, please," I cut her off before she can expound. "And don't come out, okay? You stay in there until I call for you."

The knocks come again.

"Just a sec!" Buddy calls from the kitchen.

"Hurry now." I give her a little push. "Before your daddy gets to the door. It's very important, okay?"

"Okay...am I in trouble?" Her eyes are wide with curiosity, but a small frown creases her face.

"Of course, not. Scoot!"

I fall in step beside Buddy as he clambers down the stairs. "Buddy, don't open that." I say, "Buddy! Buddy." I grab his hand and pull him towards me, but I can't exert any force.

Sharleen pops her head out from the hall, her hair half done. "Who is it?"

"Not sure." Buddy says and opens the door as August Waters raises a hand to knock again.

Shit. I step out in front of Buddy as he asks what the hell August is doing here. August does not have a camera crew with him. We are not live on stream. He is by himself, and he looks like he hasn't slept in a week. His clothes are dirty, his blond hair sticks out in oily clumps. He's having a bad time.

He brought a gun. I woefully underestimated him.

Chapter 25

"August," I say as slowly and as calmly as I can, raising my hands up placatingly and taking a small step forward.

"Of course, you're fucking here," he says to me, completely ignoring Buddy. "Playing house? Real cute." He swings the gun off his shoulder and points it directly at Buddy's chest, right here in the late afternoon daylight. *Please, somebody be watching.* "Get inside."

Buddy doesn't move, puffs out his chest. "You wouldn't dare."

"Ask your girlfriend what I would and wouldn't dare." August says with that disgusting little scoff of a laugh. Then he leans forward conspiratorially. "Most people don't turn into ghosts, man. They just die. Don't get your hopes up." He pushes the barrel into Buddy's chest until he takes two steps back into the house.

"Hey, August." I grab onto his arm. "Look, I don't know what exactly you want, but they really don't need to be involved, okay? Let's just go. Come on."

"Up, up, up," August says, ignoring me, as he herds Buddy, and now Sharleen who had been making her way down the stairs, up into the kitchen.

Sharleen is screaming. Not in fear, necessarily, more in shock and rage. The names she's calling August are insults I have never heard in my many years on earth, let alone from an older lady who doesn't usually allow the word "damn" under her roof.

I don't know if it's the insults or what, but August's demeanor changes significantly during his walk up the stairs. Maybe he just didn't think he'd get this far. Maybe he's getting cold feet about whatever he'd planned to do next. I think about him planning to drive me here, buying me a cell phone, and then randomly leaving me in a ditch, instead. Maybe if I just say exactly the right things, I can talk him down. I try desperately to hear my own thoughts over the cacophony of my heart.

"Okay," I say. "Let's just talk for a second. What's your goal, here? We can—"

"Can you even grasp what it's been like?" August cuts me off. His words are high pitched and boyish, whining. The gun trembles in his hands. "I'd *finally* done it. Finally proved to everyone and myself that I'm not crazy. That this thing happens to me, that I didn't imagine it or make it up."

"August," I say. I'm proud at how calm my voice is. I don't feel calm. I'm terrified. I know I can't stop anything bad from happening here, and I would do *anything* to stop it. I'm useless. "August, think about what you're doing for a second. Remember how you felt last time you did something like this? It doesn't feel good."

"It doesn't have to feel good!" he screams. It's almost a sob. "It doesn't matter how I feel! It doesn't matter what I think or what I see or who I talk to!" He waves the gun around wildly. I press back against Buddy and Sharleen, like I could protect them. "Nobody believes me! You don't understand how awful that feels! And it's *your* fault."

I scoff. He pisses me off so badly. I'm losing the cool that I *need* to keep to protect Buddy and Sharleen, but his voice wriggles right under my skin. "*I* don't understand? August. You're the only person who has heard my voice in sixty god-damned years. And you know what? You suck to talk to."

I move as I'm saying the last words, drawing him away from Buddy. It works, kind of. He follows me and fires off two short bursts in my direction. The rifle discharging is *so* loud in the confines of the small kitchen. My ears ringing plunges everything into a strange unreality. I truly didn't believe he'd actually fire the weapon, despite our past confrontations. Something clips my calf, maybe a bullet or maybe a chunk of the countertop behind me as it took most of the impacts. I go down to a knee. But, Buddy calls out.

"Hey! You leave her alone." He stands up from his protective crouch over an *irate* Sharleen.

Damn it, Buddy.

August whirls the gun around and trains it on Buddy again. "It's *her* fault, I guess. But it's *your* fault, too. Why couldn't you play along, man?" He jerks his body like he wants to start pacing and waving his arms in frustration, then remembers he needs to keep the weapon trained on Buddy. "Why didn't you call me when I was looking for you? You and Addie could have been the biggest sensation the world has ever known. We would have been like kings." He's pleading, his left hand outstretched to Buddy. Sweat and tears mingle on his dirty cheeks. "Famous. Rich. Why didn't you just talk to your daughter for me?"

I hope beyond hope that Buddy comes up with something so heart breaking, so profound, that August drops the gun and falls to his knees in tears. It's really the only hope I've got at this point. The kitchen is deathly silent. There are bullet holes all along the cabinets behind me. Nothing will ever be the same in this house, I realize with a slight pang of sadness. It's irreparably damaged. I wonder where Addie is hiding. I hope she stays tucked away and silent, and I hope she can't hear what's going on out here.

Buddy finally speaks, having held August's gaze until the taller man looked away. "I don't like you. You're a pretentious asshole, and I don't want you speaking to my mother, *or* my daughter."

I watch thunderclouds gather in August's face. He aims the gun again as I move toward him and sends a spray of bullets wide of Buddy and Sharleen. Sharleen switches gears, obviously also seeing the change on the man's face and in his intent, and moans in terror and prayer on the floor. The windows behind her shatter like a tornado has touched down outside, but the storm is right here, looking down at his hands.

It's clear by the way August stares down that he wasn't fooling around and is actually just a terrible shot. He meant to kill Buddy there. He meant to kill *my* Buddy. I clutch my chest. "What in the actual *fuck* is wrong with you?!" I rush toward him and try to yank the gun out of his grip. I'm surprised to see that I am actually putting up a fairly significant fight for it, and yank hard, pulling him close to me.

"If you hurt a hair on either of their heads, I will make you regret every single day of your life *and* death," I growl at him, giving the gun another yank. "I've got nothing but time."

He's putting in too much effort on retaining control of the weapon to respond, and then I see his face clear. He smiles a little "did *I* do that?" smirk at me and pulls the trigger.

Stinging hot pain flashes in a wave across my entire midsection. The automatic sends bullets from my right flank to my left in a shining arc. A rainbow of hot, wet agony. I gasp and collapse into a tangle of limbs and blood.

"*What did you do*?!?!"

I slap my hands over my ears against the sound. The words are barely coherent through the sheer volume and horrible, shrieking pitch. The glass pane pieces still hanging on in the broken windows all fall from the frames in a sheet. Sharleen screams. Buddy covers his ears.

"*You hurt Ms. Poppy. You hurt her!*"

I'm all the way on the ground now. I look at the linoleum my cheek is resting on and see blood pooling around my face. From my ears. My ears are bleeding. I won't be able to drag myself to the threshold of the front door to undo this damage.

I try to turn my face to see more of the room. I need to get my eyes back on August and his gun, where did he go?

When I finally crane my head on my prone body far enough to see him, I also see her.

There is a jittering, girl shaped hole in the room, suspended about two feet off the ground. Inside that hole is madness. Her outline shudders and jerks and blinks in and out of existence completely, so fast that I worry about the live people in the room having seizures. A buzzing, tv static noise emanates from her, loud and horrible and grating, I feel like it's pulling the skin from my bones. What happened to Addie?

She speaks again, and the hole expands, changes shape, turns inside out. At one point I swear I'm looking out from her vantage point at the whole room. *"I thought you were nice. You're scaring my gramma!"*

The room goes pitch dark. Well, that's not exactly right. The room and all of its contents suck into the black hole that used to be a little girl named Addie. There is nothing. We are nowhere. I'm being crushed, being pulled apart. My body is on fire, or frozen solid, or maybe I don't exist at all. I can't breathe. I have no eyes. Finally, after seconds, or years, there is a whisper within the all consuming, absolute silence, a whisper in the terrible voice of the dead.

Get out.

The room reassembles with a concussive blast of energy that sends me flying about three feet into the air and back down against the cabinets. I give a tiny groan, but nobody hears me over August. August is screaming a scream so horrific and so childish that I thought, at first, the noise belonged to Addie. He is curled on the floor in a fetal position, the gun forgotten some feet away from him. I have a feeling that whatever I just felt of Addie's power, it was only a taste compared to what August has received. Buddy scrambles to his feet and lurches towards the gun. He snatches it up, flicks what I presume is the safety, and flips it by the strap over his shoulder like a backpack. He spins in a full circle, taking in every nook and cranny of the room.

"Addie? Adeline! Adeline Frances! Come here, baby. Where are you?"

I manage to push myself up into almost a sitting position, but I honestly wish I would hurry up and die because this is just horrendous. I can't breathe in properly, my lungs must be punctured. Blood keeps bubbling disgustingly out of my mouth when I try. But, sitting, I can see the room a little better. Buddy is crouched by his mother, who seems of course distraught, but unhurt. I say a silent prayer of thanks since I can't let out a sigh of relief. They're both okay. But, where is—

"Poppy?"

Addie is herself again, small and fragile, with a button nose and dimples. She's still wearing the pajamas I got her from Limited, Too, and her hair is in the puffy pigtails we did earlier today, laughing in the mirror together. "Hey, Addie." I try to say and smile. The words barely come out, they're more burble and groan than anything else. I must look like a horror show. The poor kid shouldn't have to see this.

"Addie?!"

Addie and I both jump. Well, Addie jumps, I blink as much as I'm able.

"I just heard Addie." Buddy is saying to Sharleen. "I heard her. She's here."

"Daddy!" Addie runs to Buddy and throws her arms around him. I smile and close my eyes, remembering Christmas Day, her being dragged around the house on his ankle.

"Addie, oh, my God. Oh, my God."

My eyes pop open. Buddy is hugging Addie. He *sees* her. He. Sees. Her.

I literally die from shock, probably.

I don't lose consciousness, of course, but by the time I've untangled my limbs, and scrambled to my feet, no worse for wear than a few ragged and dripping holes in my cute new dress, the whole family is before me. Buddy has Addie in his arms, and his mother is clutching his elbow.

"Hi," Buddy says to me. He's staring right into my eyes as though to look away would be to lose sight forever.

"Hi," I say back and can't help but stare back with the same desperation.

He grins. He can hear me. He can *see* me. "You look just like I imagined," he says, and I hope that's a good thing. He says it like it's a good thing.

"What did you do, Addie?" I whisper, but I can't take my eyes off of Buddy. What if I lose him?

"I took away that man's ghost glasses," Addie says simply. "I took them away and gave them to Daddy."

"His...ghost glasses." I repeat. "Of course."

The writhing form formerly known as August Waters moans.

Sharleen whispers, "Is she really here, Buddy?"

I decide to check on the would-be murderer...or is he an actual murderer? He's killed me twice now, after all. I'm afraid to approach him. I'm worried that I'll look down into his face and see gaping holes where his eyes might have been, or something even worse.

"You okay down there, August?" I ask cautiously.

He's whimpering. His arms are wrapped around his whole head, like he's trying to keep it attached to his body.

"August," I try again. I try to gently pull his arms away to look at them, but I can't break his grip.

"He can't hear us anymore, Poppy." Addie calls, and it sounds like she's much further away than just across the kitchen.

Oh, right.

"I'm going to call the police." Sharleen says conversationally. She brushes her hands on her pants and moves into the living room.

"Buddy, can you check on him?" I ask. I'm anxious.

"He'll be fine for a minute. Come here, will you?" Buddy sounds anxious, too. I look over. He's cradling Addie in his arms like she's a much smaller child, and he sinks to the floor. "Is she okay?"

August and his whining are immediately forgotten. "Addie? What's wrong?"

Addie rubs her eye with a knuckle. "I'm *sleepy*."

"Okay, baby, sure. You want to sleep in gramma's bed?" Buddy asks. He's grinning down at her, tears falling constantly off the tip of his nose and onto her pajamas.

"Wait..." I say.

Addie cuts me off. "Yeah, that would be good. You'll stay with me, right, Daddy? And Gramma? And Poppy?"

"I'll be with you the whole time." Buddy murmurs. I don't think he realizes what he's agreeing to. In fact, I *know* he doesn't. But I think I do. We don't sleep. We don't get tired. What will happen if Addie falls asleep?

There's already a murmur growing at the base of my skull, whispering, *this isn't fair, it's too soon it's too soon, just let them have a little time...*

"Addie," I manage. I feel like I'm shouting over the murmur that only I can hear. "Are you sure you're sleepy? What if we just all sit down and watch a movie or..."

Addie gives a big yawn. "It's time for me to sleep, Poppy."

She sounds so grown up.

"Get Sharleen," I say to Buddy. I put a hand on his shoulder, and he clambers back up from the floor. "She needs to be here." My eyes meet his, and it's clear to me that he still doesn't realize what's happening. He's just so happy to have his little girl in his arms.

Maybe I'm wrong. Maybe she'll wake up. Maybe it's different for her and she sleeps sometimes. *It's time for me to sleep, Poppy.*

I don't think I'm wrong.

We leave August without a second glance and move into the living room. Sharleen is placing her cell phone on the coffee table. "They'll be here in ten minutes," she says. "Should we tie him up or something? This is all so strange. I'll need you to explain to me, was that *Addie* I saw in there? She was so *loud*."

Addie giggles, then yawns. "I was just real mad. But I'm better now."

Buddy says to his mother, "She wore herself out with all that yelling. She's tired. She wants to sleep in your bed."

Sharleen smiles. "Well, of course, she can. Any time she wants to. She's not scary at all, she's my little angel."

We've been walking toward Sharleen's bedroom, and with every step my feet grow heavier. I need to tell them. I need to warn them. The room is cozy and warmly lit, and Sharleen rushes to the bed and turns the cover down, fluffs one of the pillows up. She pats it and grins toward Buddy. He slides Addie under the covers and tucks them under her chin, and she gives another little giggle.

Sharleen gasps. "Oh, sweet little Addie." She rushes forward and places a hand on the girl's cheek. "There you are. There you are."

"Hi, Gramma!"

I hang back by the door, the most awkward intruder on this family's reunion. I almost wish I were invisible to all of them again. But Buddy spares me a glance and reaches an arm back, beckoning me close. I feel like I'm being pulled forward by an invisible rope, I don't want to go, but suddenly, I'm there and Buddy puts the outstretched arm around my middle, like I belong.

"Buddy," I whisper. My lips are right next to his ear, so I'll take the opportunity while I can. I don't want to frighten Addie. "She might not wake up."

I feel his arm tighten around me as he freezes up. He starts to turn to look at me, but Addie reaches up from the bed and touches his cheek. "It's okay, Daddy."

It's not okay, I want to yell. It's not okay. Why does she get to go, but I'm still here? Why aren't I sleepy? I don't have anybody wishing every day that I was alive. I don't have anybody that needs their ghost glasses. Why is she leaving us when her family is still here?

"Sometimes," Addie says suddenly, and I break away from my thoughts with effort. "I'd start to forget what you look like, Daddy. And then I'd start to forget everything. I'd forget my name, and my face, and I'd just be this sad, scary thing. You saw her. I had to be her, when that August man hurt Poppy. I had to be her because she is strong, and scary, and loud."

We're all hanging on every word, even Sharleen. I guess Buddy's focus being so strongly on Addie helped her finally see, just like August's videos.

"But, I don't want to be strong and scary. I just want to be me. It was getting harder every day to remember. I'd have to look in the mirror and say, 'Adeline. That's me,' to keep the sad thing away. Gramma helped, she'd say my name. And Poppy, when you brought me clothes and brushed my hair. But, I just wanted Daddy to look at me and say my name. I just wanted Daddy to remember me." She gives another huge yawn.

"I'll never forget you, Addie. Not ever, ever. I never forgot you even when I couldn't see you," Buddy whispers.

"I know, Daddy. I love you. Good night."

Adeline Frances, aged five, closes her eyes for the last time and is gone.

The recent viral phenomenon, August Waters, has been arrested on two counts of attempted murder, among other charges.

Waters took the internet by storm earlier this year when he released video footage he claimed was proof of life after death. Waters had several videos involving different "ghosts" at several locations, and secured deals with major television networks to film ongoing projects.

That all came to an end three weeks ago when Waters released a video admitting his videos were fakes, citing his guilty conscience as the reason for exposing himself.

Apparently, he couldn't cope as easily with his fans' obviously disappointed reactions, and lack of interest in further trickery. Waters showed up at the residence that made him most well known, that of the now famous five-year-old, Adeline Frances. Fans and critics alike had been disgusted with Waters' treatment of the family, claiming he gave them false hope for their lost child and used their pain to further his career. Waters threatened the deceased girl's grandmother, Sharleen Frances, 58, and father, Sean Frances, 29, with an automatic rifle. He did significant damage to the home with the weapon, but thankfully, both the Frances family members escaped harm.

Waters is set for a hearing next week.

Chapter 26

H onestly, I'm glad the police are here. The last five minutes or so were the most awful and awkward I've ever had the misfortune to be around for. There was a lot of wailing from Sharleen, and dramatic patting of the bedclothes as though Addie might just be hiding in there somewhere. I wasn't able to comfort her, whisper to her, help her at all.

And my sweet Buddy. He just stared at that empty spot on the pillow where Addie's head had so briefly lain. He said nothing. His hand was still reached out where it had rested against that little head.

"Is she gone?" Sharleen had cried. "Buddy, where is she, where is she?"

"She's gone," I tell Buddy.

"She's gone," Buddy tells Sharleen.

"Where?"

"I don't know," Buddy and I whispered at the same time.

And then, thankfully, the doorbell rang, immediately followed by a pounding, and a call of "Police!"

And now, August, unhurt physically but now crying, shaking, is being led out of the house in handcuffs. He can speak. He did very little speaking to the police, but when Sharleen and Buddy told the story of August arriving and threatening to shoot them, shooting out their windows, and terrorizing them, he agreed numbly.

"The little girl stopped me," he said dully.

I'm sure he's about to be famous all over again, but he might not enjoy it so much this time. He never noticed me. He didn't even look for me. I don't mean anything to him anymore.

Buddy has kept an arm around me since he pulled me close to Addie's bedside. I think he's making sure that I don't disappear without telling him. I'm not even a little sleepy. It feels like this should be the end of my story, too, but apparently, I'm not going anywhere anytime soon. I don't mind his touch, though. It's been a very, very long time since I've had someone touch me, on purpose, with no malice.

We're in the kitchen, and Buddy and his mother are giving one of the two remaining officers their official statements. Cold wind blows through the broken windows behind us, and the other officer is photographing every single bullet hole and shard of glass. It's like there's a silent party going on with the flashing light bouncing around. I move to stand, and Buddy looks at me quickly. His face is just concern and pain and exhaustion.

"Hey," I whisper. I don't know why I'm whispering. I could jump on this table and start kicking off the cloth placemats while singing the star spangled banner, nobody would bat an eye besides Buddy. "I'm not going anywhere. Except to make a pot of coffee. You relax." I squeeze his hand.

The coffee pot is only about six feet from the table where they sit, so I'm not missing any conversation. "Make sure not to mention her," I say. "We don't want to muddle the situation. They think August is a con man or maybe mentally unstable."

Buddy nods as though deep in thought. Another vicious gust of wind rips through the kitchen and flutters the officer's notebook. "If you don't mind, I'm going to step into the other room and call someone to take care of those windows," Buddy says. "She can't be sleeping in a house with the windows busted out."

The officer gives a dismissive wave. "Sure, sure. We're almost done here."

I follow Buddy down to a family room in the basement. He holds my gaze for a long moment. "What are you going to do now?"

I sigh. "I don't know. I don't understand any of this. I don't—"

"It feels good in here," Buddy says suddenly.

"What do you mean?"

He pulls at his earlobe, just like Addie did when she was talking, anxious, excited. I can't help but smile a little, but it hurts, too. "I mean," he continues. "I think it's good that she left. I think she was supposed to, and I think she'll be happier and so will Ma. Maybe so will I."

I nod slowly. "The longer we stick around, the more difficult it can be, I think."

"The monsters? The ones you told me you see sometimes?"

He's so intuitive. He knew I was thinking about them. All of them. The attic spider and the big bird and the fat man. The hitcher. All of them and more, so many more, but mostly, the fat man. August's ghost. August's abandoned friend.

"Yeah," I breathe. "They used to be people, just like me and Addie. I think they just keep forgetting and losing themselves until all that's left is a nightmare."

"Was that what we saw of Addie today?" His voice breaks a little on her name, and my heart breaks a little with it.

"I think so. I think...I *think* coming back to herself after that. Maybe..."

Buddy brightens and grabs my hand. "It let her go! Finding herself, and remembering. Hearing her...hearing her name." He's crying now.

I smile. "I think maybe so." It didn't work for me like that. I've crossed that boundary, maybe more than once, and come back to my same half-self. But Addie, she was *so* powerful, so intense. The energy she must have expended in those few terrifying seconds must have been an astronomical amount. She was nothing *but* energy.

I don't want to tell him what I'm thinking now, I don't want to take this spot of happiness away from him with my selfishness, but again, he takes my words and speaks them. "It'll happen to you, too, won't it?"

I sigh, and sink down onto the brown shag carpet. The walls down here still have wood paneling and popcorn ceilings. I get the feeling that Sharleen doesn't spend a lot of time down here. "It will. It *has*, almost. I've been fighting it for a long time. I keep notes..." I trail off for a second as he joins me on the floor. "I forget pretty quickly, though. You almost lost me to the governor's mansion in Des Moines, one time." I laugh, but it's forced and sad.

"I'm not going to lose you." He's so solemn. This is a promise.

"Well, one day..."

"One day, you can decide to go. We'll figure out your real name. Like Addie."

"That would be nice." I concede.

"Buddy?" Sharleen calls down the stairs. "They're leaving!"

"Just a sec, Ma." he calls back, but then he gives my hands a little tug toward him, pulling my gaze back to his face. The proclamations aren't over. "Hey, what if we can help them?"

"The police?"

He laughs. "No. The monsters? We could find them and figure out who they might be, try to help them come back to themselves. So they can go."

I bite my lip. I'd been thinking about it, too. I've been thinking about it since the grocery store. He used to be just like me. All alone. But, I think of what he has become. I watched him rip fixtures from the ground and demolish them. Decimate them. Eat them. I can't risk Buddy getting too close to something like that.

But I feel like we were *so* close to breaking through to Charlie, when I was with August. If August were a better person, a braver person, a kinder person...more like Buddy.

"I want to help them," Buddy says, earnestly. "We could help together."

"We could," I finally say, and he leans over and kisses my cheek.

I grin stupidly. I almost feel alive.

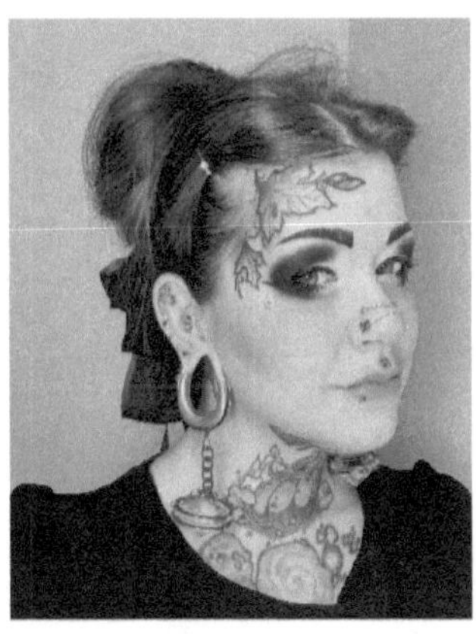

Rikki Goodwin is a professional body piercer by day and a horror/thriller author by night. She owns a successful piercing and tattoo studio. She resides in North Carolina.

www.ingramcontent.com/pod-product-compliance
Lightning Source LLC
Chambersburg PA
CBHW021140310726
48971CB00002B/411